P9-CQQ-670

Praise for *New York Times* Bestseller
Phillip Margolin

"It takes a really crafty storyteller to put people
on the edge of their seats and keep them there.
Phillip Margolin does just that."
Chicago Tribune

"Margolin writes with breakneck pacing and
just the right injection of lurid detail to make
chills race down readers' spines."
Publishers Weekly

And his previous sensational bestseller
Wild Justice

"*Wild Justice* is the scariest book I read since *Red
Dragon*. I couldn't put it down."
Michael Palmer, author of *The Patient*

"A terrific thriller. This page-turner kept me guessing
throughout."
Larry King, *USA Today*

"One scary book . . . A wild and terrifying ride . . .
perhaps the most satisfying ending in mystery fiction
this year."
Otto Penzler

Also by Phillip Margolin

HEARTSTONE
THE LAST INNOCENT MAN
GONE, BUT NOT FORGOTTEN
AFTER DARK
THE BURNING MAN
THE UNDERTAKER'S WIDOW
WILD JUSTICE

PHILLIP MARGOLIN

THE ASSOCIATE

HarperTorch
An Imprint of HarperCollins Publishers

This is a work of fiction. Names, characters, places, and incidents are products of the author's imagination or are used fictitiously and are not to be construed as real. Any resemblance to actual events, locales, organizations, or persons, living or dead, is entirely coincidental.

HARPERTORCH
An Imprint of HarperCollins*Publishers*
10 East 53rd Street
New York, New York 10022-5299

First HarperTorch paperback printing: August 2002
First HarperCollins hardcover printing: September 2001

HarperCollins ®, HarperTorch™, and ❦™ are trademarks of Harper-Collins Publishers Inc.

Printed in the United States of America

Visit HarperTorch on the World Wide Web at www.harpercollins.com

10 9 8 7 6 5 4 3 2 1

For Daniel and Chris

*My son and his new wife—two terrific people
on the threshold of a terrific life together*

Acknowledgments

I owe a debt of gratitude to the many people who volunteered their time and ideas to help me write this book. Since science has never been my strong point, I am tremendously grateful to Dr. Lynn Loriaux, who invented the fictional drug Insufort for me and answered many other science questions. Dr. John Lundy and Dr. Karen Gunson, the Oregon State Medical Examiner, taught me how human remains are identified. Ed Pritchard was my computer guru. I also want to thank Dr. James V. Parker and Dr. Susan Smith of the Oregon Regional Primate Research center.

I received invaluable information about the life of an associate at a major law firm from Alison Brody, an associate at Portland's Miller, Nash law firm, and Scott Crawford, Mike Jacobs, Melissa Robertson, Bryan Geon, Sharon Hill, Richard Vangelisti, Maria Gorecki, associates at the Stoel, Rives law Firm in Portland. I also want to thank Stoel, Rives partners, Randy Foster and Barnes Ellis. I want to make sure that my readers understand that the Reed, Briggs firm in *The Associate* is an invention and that the partners and associates in it are not based on any real person.

Mike Williams and Jonathan Hoffman are exceptional attorneys who are regularly involved in the high-stakes civil litigation that forms the backdrop for this book. I am very grateful to them for walking me through the steps the plaintiffs' and defendants' attorneys take in a product liability case.

I also received invaluable technical assistance from Mike Shinn, Dan Bronson, Mark Anderson, Chip Horner, Steve Millen of Riverview Cemetery, Dr. Nathan Selden, Detective Sergeant Jon F. Rhodes of the Portland Police Bureau, Sergeant Mary Lindstrand of the Multnomah County Sheriff's Office, and my good friend Vince Kohler.

Thanks also to my fantastic children, Ami and Daniel; Johnathan Hoffman and Richard Vangelisti; as well as Joe, Eleonore, Jerry and Judy Margolin, and Norman and Helen Stamm for their valuable comments on my first draft.

I have to thank Dan Conaway, my intrepid editor, for his insights. I am truly lucky to work with him. I am also very lucky to have Jean Naggar and everyone at her agency on my side.

People are always asking me where I get my ideas. In the case of *The Associate* there is an easy answer. Doreen, my incredible wife of more than thirty years, dreamed up the plot device that is at the heart of this book. I can't tell you what it is, because I don't want to ruin any surprises, but it's pretty clever, as is she.

THE ASSOCIATE

Prologue

An icy wind whipped down Mercer Street, rattling awnings, scattering paper scraps and raking Gene Arnold's cheeks raw. He turned up his coat collar and ducked his head to avoid the arctic chill. This wasn't the Arizona lawyer's first visit to New York City, but it was his first winter visit and he was unprepared for the biting cold.

Arnold was an unremarkable man, someone you could sit opposite for an hour and not remember five minutes later. He was of average height, tortoiseshell glasses magnified his brown eyes, and his small, bald head was partially ringed by a fringe of dull gray hair. Arnold's private life was as placid as his personality. He was unmarried, read a lot, and the most exciting thing he did was play golf. Nothing that had happened to him had even registered as a blip on the world's radar screen except for a tragedy he had endured seven years before.

Arnold's law practice was as tedious as his life, business transactions mostly. He was in New York to secure financing for Martin Alvarez, the king of the Arizona used car market, who wanted to expand into New Mexico. Arnold's successful meeting with a potential investor had ended sooner than expected, leaving him time to wander around SoHo in search of a painting he could add to his small collection of art.

Arnold's eyes teared and his nose started to run as he looked around desperately for shelter from the wind. An art gallery on the corner of Mercer and Spring streets was open and he ducked into it, sighing with relief when a blast of warm air greeted him. A thin young woman dressed in black was leaning on a counter near the front of the store. She looked up from the catalog she was reading.

"Can I help you?" she asked, flashing him a practiced smile.

"Just looking," Arnold answered self-consciously.

The art hanging on the white walls of the gallery did not fit into one category. Arnold glanced briefly at a series of collages with a feminist theme before stopping to admire some paintings that were more his style. Back home he owned several western scenes, brown and red mesas at sunset, cowboys on the trail, that sort of thing. These landscapes were of New England, seascapes really. Dories on a raging ocean, waves breaking on a deserted beach, a cottage scarred by the sea's salt spray. Very nice.

Arnold wandered over to a group of black-and-white photographs entitled *Couples*. The first grainy shot showed two teenagers holding hands in a park. They were viewed from behind, leaning into each other, their heads almost touching. The photographer had captured their intimate moment perfectly. The picture made Arnold sad. He would have given anything to be that boy with that girl. Being alone was the hardest thing.

The next photo showed a black couple sitting in a café. They were laughing, his head thrown back, mouth open, she smiling shyly, delighted that she was the source of such joy.

Arnold studied the photo. It wasn't the type of art that he usually purchased, but there was something about the photograph that drew him to it. He checked the information on the small, white rectangle next to the photo and learned that the photographer was Claude Bernier and the price was within his means.

Arnold moved to the third photograph in the series. It showed a man and a woman dressed for the rain striding across a square in the center of some city. They were angry, faces tight. The woman's eyes blazed, the man's mouth was a grim line.

"Oh, my God," Arnold said. He fell forward, bracing himself against the wall.

"Sir?" The young woman was staring at him, alarmed by his ashen pallor and his inability to stand upright. Arnold stared back, panicky, light-headed.

"Are you okay?"

Arnold nodded, but the woman was unconvinced. She hurried forward and slipped a hand under his elbow.

"Is there someplace I can sit down?" he asked weakly.

The woman led him up front to a chair behind the

counter. Arnold sagged onto it and put his hand to his forehead.

"Can I get you some water?" she asked anxiously.

Arnold saw that she was trying to hold it together. He imagined that she was thinking "heart attack" and wondering what it would be like to sit with a corpse while she waited for the police.

"Water would be good. I'm okay, really. Nothing to worry about," he said, trying to reassure her. "I'm just a little dizzy."

By the time the woman returned with the water Arnold had regained his composure. He took two sips and breathed deeply. When he looked up the woman was watching him and worrying her hands.

"I'm much better." He gave her a weak smile. "I'm just not used to this cold."

"Please, sit here as long as you want."

"Thanks." He paused, then pointed toward the exhibit. "The photographer, Bernier, does he live near here?"

"Claude? Sure. He's got a walk-up in Chelsea."

"I want to buy one of his pictures."

Arnold stood up slowly, steadier now, and led the woman to the photograph of the angry couple. As he crossed the room doubts assailed him, but they melted away as he drew closer to the scene that Bernier had captured.

"Do you think he'd see me today?" Arnold asked as he produced a credit card without moving his eyes from the photo.

The woman looked worried. "Do you feel up to it?"

Arnold nodded. She seemed on the verge of trying to change his mind. Then she carried the photograph to the front to ring up the purchase. As she waited for clearance from the credit-card company she used the phone. Arnold sat down again. His initial shock had abated and had been replaced by a sense of urgency and purpose.

"Claude can see you anytime," the woman told him as she handed Arnold his purchase and stationery from the gallery bearing the photographer's address and phone number. He memorized the address and placed the paper in his jacket pocket.

"Thank you. You've been very kind," he told the salesclerk before stepping into the street. A frigid wind greeted him, but Gene Arnold was too distracted to notice.

Part I

⬧

Monkey Etiquette

1

The headlight beams of Dr. Sergey Kaidanov's battered SAAB bounced off a stand of Douglas firs then came to rest on the unpainted wall of a one-story, cinderblock building buried in the woods several miles from downtown Portland. As soon as Kaidanov unlocked the front door of the building the rhesus monkeys started making that half-cooing, half-barking sound that set his nerves on edge. The volume of noise increased when Kaidanov flipped on the lights.

Most of the monkeys were housed in two rooms at the back of the building. Kaidanov walked down a narrow hall and stood in front of a thick metal door that sealed off one of the rooms. He slid back a metal sheet and studied the animals through the window it concealed. There were sixteen rhesus monkeys in each room. Each monkey was in its own steel mesh cage. The cages were stacked two high and two across on a flatcar with rollers. Kaidanov hated everything about the monkeys—their sour, unwashed smell, the noises they made, the unnerving way they followed his every move.

As soon as Kaidanov's face was framed in the window, the monkey two from the door in the top cage leaped toward him and stared him down. Its fur was brownish gray and it gripped the mesh with hands containing opposable thumbs on both arms and legs. This was the dominant monkey in the room and it had established its dominance within three weeks even though there was no way it could get at the others.

Rhesus monkeys were very aggressive, very nervous, and always alert. It was bad etiquette to look one in the eye, but Kaidanov did it just to show the little bastard who was the boss. The monkey didn't blink. It stretched its doglike muzzle through the mesh as far as it could, baring a set of vicious canines. At two feet tall and forty pounds, the monkey didn't look like it could do much damage to a one-hundred-and-ninety-pound, five-foot-eight male human, but it was much stronger than it looked.

Kaidanov checked his watch. It was three in the morning. He couldn't imagine what was so important that he had to meet here at this hour, but the person whose call had dragged him from a deep sleep paid Kaidanov to do as he was told, no questions asked.

Kaidanov needed caffeine. He was about to go to his office to brew a pot of coffee when he noticed that the padlock on the dominant monkey's cage was open. He must have forgotten to close it after the last feeding. The scientist started to open the door but stopped when he remembered that the key to the monkey rooms was in his office.

Kaidanov returned to the front of the building. His office was twelve by fifteen and stuffed with lab equipment. A small desk on casters stood just inside the door. It was covered by a phone book, articles from research journals, and printouts of contractions that the monkeys experienced during pregnancy. Behind the table was a cheap office chair. Along the walls were metal filing cabinets, a sink, and a paper towel dispenser.

Kaidanov walked around the desk. The coffeepot was sitting on a table alongside a centrifuge, scales, a rack of test tubes, and a Pokémon mug filled with Magic Markers, pens, and pencils. Above the table was a television screen attached to a security camera that showed the front of the building.

The pot of coffee was almost brewed when Kaidanov heard a car pull up and a door slam. On the television a figure in a hooded windbreaker ran toward the lab. Kaidanov left his office and opened the front door. The scientist peered at the hooded face and saw two cold eyes staring at him through the slits in a ski mask. Before he could speak, a gun butt struck his forehead, blinding him with pain. Kaidanov collapsed to the floor. The muzzle of a gun ground into his neck.

"Move," a muffled voice commanded. He scrambled to his knees and a booted foot shoved him forward. The pain in his face brought tears to his eyes as he crawled the short distance to his office.

"The keys to the monkey rooms."

Kaidanov pointed toward a hook on the wall. Seconds later a blow to the back of his head knocked him unconscious.

• • •

Kaidanov had no idea how long he had been out. The first thing he heard when he came to were the hysterical shrieks of terrified monkeys and the sound of cages crashing together. The scientist felt like a nail had been driven into his skull, but he managed to struggle into a sitting position. Around him filing cabinets had been opened and overturned. The floor was littered with gasoline-drenched paper, but that was not the only object doused in gasoline—his clothing, face, and hands reeked of it. Then the acrid smell of smoke assailed his nostrils and his stomach turned when he saw the shadow of flames dancing on the wall outside his office.

Fear dragged Kaidanov to his knees just as his assailant reentered the office holding the gun and a five-gallon can of gas. Kaidanov scurried back against the wall, much the way the more docile monkeys skittered to the back of their cages whenever he entered the monkey room. The gas can hit the desk with a metallic thud and Kaidanov' assailant pulled out a lighter. Kaidanov tried to speak, but terror made him mute. Just as the lid of the lighter flipped open, an insane shriek issued from the doorway. An apparition, engulfed in flame, eyes wide with panic and pain, filled the entrance to the office. The dominant monkey, Kaidanov thought. It had been able to force open its cage door because Kaidanov had forgotten to secure the padlock.

The term "monkey etiquette" flashed through Kaidanov's mind. He ducked his head and assumed a submissive position then watched out of the corner of his eye as his assailant turned and stared. The human and the primate locked eyes seconds before forty pounds of adrenaline-fueled, flame-tortured muscle launched itself through the air with a terrifying scream. Kaidanov saw the rhesus land on its prey and sink its fangs into his attacker's shoulder. As the pair toppled to the floor, Kaidanov staggered out the door and ran toward the woods. Moments later two shots rang out.

2

"Ready to rock-and-roll?" Joe Molinari asked as he ambled into Daniel Ames's tiny office.

"Not today," Daniel answered regretfully, pointing at the papers on his desk. "Briggs just laid this on me."

"We're talking happy hour, compadre," Molinari said as he slid his angular body onto one of Daniel's two client chairs.

The litigation associates at Reed, Briggs, Stephens, Stottlemeyer and Compton met for happy hour once a week at a popular steak house to bitch and moan about how hard they worked and how unappreciated they were—and to make fun of other lawyers who were not among those chosen to work at Portland, Oregon's largest and most prestigious law firm. Daniel enjoyed the camaraderie, but he knew that it would be impossible to drag himself back to the office after sharing a pitcher of margaritas with the gang.

"Briggs needs my memo tomorrow morning."

Molinari shook his head ruefully. "When are you going to learn to say no, Ames? I've got a picture of strikers outside an auto plant. I put it on my door when I'm full up. I can make you a copy."

Daniel smiled. "Thanks, Joe. I may take you up on that, but I've got to get this done."

"Hey, man, you've got to stand up for yourself. Lincoln freed the slaves."

"The Thirteenth Amendment doesn't apply to associates at Reed, Briggs."

"You're hopeless"—Molinari laughed as he levered himself out of the chair—"but you know where we are if you come to your senses."

Molinari disappeared down the corridor and Daniel sighed. He envied his friend. If the situation had been reversed Joe wouldn't have hesitated to go for a drink. He could afford to give the finger to people like Arthur Briggs and he would never understand that someone in Daniel's position could not.

Molinari's father was a high muck-a-muck in a Los Angeles ad agency. Joe had gone to an elite prep school, an Ivy League college, and had been *Law Review* at Georgetown. With his connections, he could have gotten a job anywhere, but he liked white-water rafting and mountain climbing, so he had condescended to offer his services to Reed, Briggs. Daniel, on the other hand, thanked God every day for his job.

On one wall of Daniel's narrow office were his diplomas and his certificate of membership in the Oregon State Bar. Joe and some of the other associates took their education and profession for granted, but Daniel had made it through Portland State and the U. of O. law school the hard way, earning every cent of his tuition and knowing that there was no safety net to catch him if he failed. He took pride in earning a spot in Oregon's best law firm without Ivy League credentials or family connections, but he could not shake the feeling that his hold on success was tenuous.

Daniel's office wasn't much, but no one in his family had ever even worked in an office. His mother waitressed when she was sober and serviced long-haul drivers when she was too drunk to hold a job. He phoned her on her birthday and Christmas when he knew where she was living. He'd had six "fathers" to the best of his recollection. The nice ones had ignored him, the bad ones had left him with night sweats and scars.

Uncle Jack, father number four, had been the best of the lot because he owned a house with a yard. It was the first time Daniel had lived in a house. Most of the time he and his mother stayed in trailers or dark, evil-smelling rooms in transient hotels. Daniel had been eight when they moved in with Uncle Jack. He'd had his own room and thought this was what heaven was like. Four months later he was standing half-asleep on the sidewalk at four in the morning listening to his mother's drunken screams as she pounded her hands bloody on Uncle Jack's bolted front door.

Daniel had run away from home several times, but he'd left for good at seventeen, living on the streets until he could not stand it, then joining the army. The army had saved Daniel's life. It was the first stable environment in which he had ever lived and it was the first time his intelligence had been recognized.

Daniel's dark jacket was hanging from a hook behind his door, his paycheck sticking out of the inside pocket. *Ninety thousand dollars!* The size of his salary still amazed him and he felt incredibly lucky to have been chosen by the powers at Reed, Briggs. Every day he half expected to be told that his hiring had been a cruel practical joke.

Daniel had talked with the recruiting partner who visited the law school only to practice his interviewing technique. His invitation to a second interview at the firm had come as a shock, as had the offer of employment. Reed, Briggs's hires were graduates of Andover and Exeter; they attended Yale and Berkeley as undergraduates and went to Harvard and NYU for law school. Daniel was no dummy—his undergraduate degree in biology was with honors and he had made the *Law Review*—but there were still times when he felt out of his league.

Daniel swiveled his chair toward the window and watched the darkness gather over the Willamette River. When was the last time he had left these offices when it was still light out? Molinari was right. He did have to learn to say no, to relax a little, but he worried that he would earn a reputation as a slacker if he turned down work. Just last night he had awakened, drenched in sweat, from a dream in which he cringed in the dark at the bottom of an elevator shaft as a car descended slowly, but inexorably, toward him. You didn't have to be Sigmund Freud to dope out the meaning of that one.

• • •

At 6:45, Daniel finished rereading a draft of his memo. He stretched and rubbed his eyes. When he pulled his hands away he saw Susan Webster smiling at him from the doorway. He couldn't decide what was more shocking—that she was smiling or that she'd deigned to pay him a visit.

"Hi," he said casually, consciously keeping his eyes off of her runway-model figure.

"Hi yourself," she answered as she perched gracefully on the arm of one of Daniel's chairs. She glanced at the papers spread across his desk.

"If you're not at happy hour you must be working on a case of monumental importance. Is that a brief for the United States Supreme Court or a letter to the president?"

Susan looked and dressed like a cover girl, but her degree from Harvard was in physics and she'd been in the top ten at Stanford Law. Because of their science backgrounds, Susan and Daniel had been chosen as part of a team that was defending Geller Pharmaceuticals against a claim that one of its products caused birth defects. During the six months that they had worked together she had never asked Daniel's opinion on anything and rarely addressed him, so he was surprised that she was talking to him now.

"This is a memo for Mr. Briggs," Daniel said finally.

"Oh? Anything interesting?"

"It's another one of Aaron Flynn's cases," Daniel replied.

"Flynn again, huh? He sure has his fingers in a lot of pies."

"I'll say."

"Which of our clients is he suing, this time?" Susan asked.

"Oregon Mutual. They insure Dr. April Fairweather for malpractice."

"The therapist?"

"Yeah. How did you know?"

"Arthur had me do some work on the case, too. It's really weird. Do you know the facts?" Susan asked.

"No," Daniel answered. "I'm just working on an evidence issue."

"This college student went to Fairweather because she was depressed and having trouble sleeping. She's alleging that Fairweather hypnotized her and caused her to develop false memories that her folks were in a satanic cult that did all sorts of stuff to her when she was a kid."

"What sorts of stuff?"

"Weird sex, torture."

"Sounds kinky. Is any of it true?"

"I doubt it."

"I met Dr. Fairweather once when she was with Mr. Briggs," Daniel said. "She seemed normal enough."

"Do you have a lot more work to do on the memo?"

"No. I just have to proof it once more."

"So you're almost done?" Susan asked.

"Pretty much."

Daniel didn't really imagine that Susan was going to suggest a drink or dinner—he pictured Susan's dates as rich, *GQ*-model types who drove exotic sports cars and owned homes in the West Hills with fabulous views of the mountains—but for just a second he fantasized that she'd been won over by his curly black hair, his blue eyes, and his engaging smile.

Susan leaned forward and spoke in an inviting whisper.

"Since you're finished with your work"—she paused dramatically—"could you do me a huge favor?"

Daniel had no idea where this was going, so he waited for Susan to continue.

"Coincidentally, it involves another one of Flynn's cases, Geller Pharmaceuticals," Susan said. "You know he made that request for production weeks ago?"

Daniel nodded.

"As usual, Geller took forever to get the documents to us. They're supposed to be delivered to Flynn by eight in the morning."

Susan paused.

"Renee has it in for me," she said. Renee Gilchrist was Arthur Briggs's secretary. "She knew I had important plans tonight, but she told Brock Newbauer that I could review the documents this evening. She claims that she forgot, but I know she did it on purpose." Susan leaned closer and spoke conspiratorially. "She is jealous of any woman Arthur works with. That is a fact. Anyway, since you're done, I was wondering if you could finish the document review?"

Daniel was exhausted and hungry. He'd been looking forward to going home.

"Gee, I don't know. I still have some more work on this memo and I'm pretty beat."

"I'll make it up to you, I promise. And there's not that much to do. Just a couple of boxes and you'd only have to give the papers a cursory review. You know, check for attorney work product or privileged stuff. It would mean a lot to me."

Susan looked desperate. He was almost done, and there wasn't anything he was going to do tonight. Maybe finish a book he'd been reading, if he wasn't too tired, or watch some TV. What the hell, it never hurt to do a good deed.

"Okay." He sighed. "I'll save you."

Susan reached across the desk and laid her hand on top of his.

"Thank you, Daniel. I owe you."

"Big time," he said, already feeling like a sucker. "Now go and have fun."

Susan stood up. "The boxes are in the small conference room near the copying machine. Make sure they get to Flynn's office by eight in the morning. And thanks again."

Susan was gone so quickly her disappearance seemed magical. Daniel stood and stretched. He was going to take a break anyway, so he decided to see what he'd let himself in for. He walked down the hall to the conference room and turned on the light. Five banker's boxes covered the table. He opened one. It was packed with paperwork. Daniel did a quick calculation and came up with a ballpark figure of three to five thousand pages per box. This would take all night, if he was lucky. This was impossible. He'd never get home.

Daniel hurried into the hall to see if he could catch Susan, but she was gone.

3

The Insufort case had started with the Moffitts. Lillian Moffitt worked as a dental hygienist and her husband, Alan, was an officer in the loan department of a bank. The day they found out that Lillian was pregnant was one of the happiest days of their lives. But Toby Moffitt was born with severe birth defects and their happiness turned to heartache. Alan and Lillian tried to convince themselves that Toby's bad fortune was part of God's mysterious plan, but they wondered what part of this plan could include heaping such misery on their little boy. All became clear to Lillian on the day she went to her neighborhood grocery store and saw a headline in a supermarket tabloid about Insufort, which called it the "Son of Thalidomide."

Thalidomide was one of the great horror stories of the mid-twentieth century. Women who used it during pregnancy bore babies with dolphinlike flippers instead of normal limbs. The article in the tabloid claimed that Insufort was as harmful as Thalidomide and that women who took the drug were giving birth to monsters. While she was pregnant Lillian had taken Insufort.

The night that the Moffitts read the article about Insufort they prayed for guidance. The next morning they called Aaron Flynn. The Moffitts had seen Aaron Flynn's television ads and they had read about the flamboyant Irishman's multimillion-dollar judgments against a major auto company and the manufacturer of a defective birth control device. "Could Mr. Flynn help Toby?" they asked. "You bet," he told them.

Soon after the Moffitts hired him, Flynn ran newspaper and television ads informing other mothers who had used Insufort that he was there to help them. Then he posted information about his case on corporate protest sites on the Internet. He also alerted friends in the media that Toby Moffitt's case was the tip of a product liability iceberg. This strategy brought in more clients.

One of the first things that Flynn did after filing *Moffitt* v. *Geller Pharmaceuticals* was to serve requests for discovery on Geller through its law firm, Reed, Briggs, Stephens, Stottlemeyer and Compton. Flynn asked for every document Geller had regarding the testing and analysis of Insufort, the warnings that had been provided to physicians dispensing the drug, copies of other lawsuits that had been filed, reports from physicians and others telling of problems with Insufort, data about the manufacturing process—and any other information that would help him discover the connection between Insufort and Toby Moffitt's terrible deformity. The boxes of paper that Susan Webster had conned Daniel into reviewing were only a few of the boxes of discovery that had flowed through the offices of Reed, Briggs to the law offices of Aaron Flynn since the Geller Pharmaceutical litigation had commenced.

Daniel was furious with Susan, but he took every task seriously, no matter how routine. At first he tried to read each page of each document, but his attention to detail waned after a few hours, as did his energy. By three in the morning he was barely aware of what was on each page. That's when he went to a small room on the twenty-eighth floor with a bed, an alarm clock, and a washroom with a narrow shower that was used by associates who were pulling all-nighters.

When the alarm went off at six, Daniel showered and shaved and, coffee in hand, attacked the remaining documents. There were still two boxes to go and an eight o'clock deadline to meet. Daniel remembered Susan saying that he only had to give the documents a cursory review. He hated doing anything halfway, but there wasn't much more he could do in the time remaining. At 7:30, Daniel began stuffing the remaining papers back in their boxes. He was almost through when Renee Gilchrist walked in, immediately noticing the boxes spread over the conference table and Daniel's obvious exhaustion.

Arthur Briggs's secretary was in her early thirties. At five nine, she was almost as tall as Daniel and she had the sleek, muscular build of an aerobics instructor. Renee's dark hair was cut short. It framed wide blue eyes, a straight nose, and full lips that were pursed in an angry frown.

"Is that the Geller discovery?" she asked.

"All one billion pages of it," Daniel answered groggily.

"Susan Webster was supposed to review that."

Daniel shrugged, a little embarrassed that Renee had found out that he'd been duped into doing Susan's work.

"She had plans for last night and I wasn't doing anything."

Renee started to leave, then she stopped.

"You shouldn't let her do that to you."

"It's no big thing. Like I said, she was busy and I wasn't."

Renee shook her head. "You're too nice a guy, Daniel."

        Wheeling a dolly loaded with cardboard boxes across the lobby of Aaron Flynn's law office gave Daniel the same queasy feeling he would have if he saw someone running keys along the side of a Rolls-Royce Silver Cloud. The exterior of Flynn's pre–World War I office building gave no hint of the grandeur Daniel encountered when he stepped out of the elevator on the seventh floor into a huge lobby that soared upward two stories. The lobby floor was made of shiny black marble and the space was decorated in rich dark woods and bronzed metals. Several columns of lapis-colored marble supported the ceiling. A balcony containing the library ran along three sides of the upper story. Carved into the middle of the lobby floor was a medallion displaying blind Justice holding her scales. Written around the rim in gold leaf were the words JUSTICE FOR ALL.

A young woman sat at the far side of the lobby on a high dais that looked more like a bench for a judge than a desk for a receptionist. Daniel was asking the woman where to leave his load when the man himself strode through a door that led to the inner sanctum. Aaron Flynn was talking quietly to another man with the shoulders and neck of a serious bodybuilder and the craggy, weather-beaten face of an outdoorsman.

"Let me know as soon as you find out where the card was used," Flynn said.

"I'll get on it," his companion answered. Then he walked past Daniel and out of the office.

On television, Aaron Flynn's deep voice asked viewers if they needed a champion to help them take on the mighty corporations that had wronged them. "You are not alone," he promised, his face at once sober and compassionate. "Together we will fight for justice, and we will prevail."

Flynn was equally impressive in person. He was tall and broad-shouldered with red hair and a face that radiated self-confidence and sincerity. His clients saw Flynn as a savior, but Daniel didn't trust him. Part of Daniel's duties on the team defending Geller Pharmaceuticals was to review the animal and human studies conducted on Insufort. They showed it to be a safe product. Daniel was convinced that Flynn's claim that the drug caused birth defects had no factual basis. It would not be the first time Flynn had tried to make millions by creating causes out of whole cloth.

Five years ago one of the networks had broadcast a horrifying story about a six-year-old boy who was killed in his driveway. His mother swore that her sports utility vehicle had surged forward suddenly when she stepped on the brake, driving her son through the garage door. Other victims of "sudden acceleration" surfaced. They claimed that their SUVs would surge forward when the brake was applied and could not be stopped.

Aaron Flynn had just opened his practice in Portland, but he had the good fortune to represent the plaintiff in the first "sudden acceleration" case. His million-dollar judgment against the manufacturer of the SUV made his reputation. In the end, the explanation for "sudden acceleration" proved simple. It was not caused by a mechanical malfunction but by human error: drivers were stepping on the gas instead of the brake. By the time the truth came out, the manufacturer had paid millions in damages and settlements, and attorneys like Flynn had made out like bandits.

Daniel had been introduced to Flynn when the lawyer visited the Reed, Briggs offices for a deposition, but the introduction was quick and Flynn had barely glanced his way during the proceedings. That was why Daniel was surprised when Flynn smiled and addressed him by name.

"Daniel Ames, isn't it?"

"Yes, Mr. Flynn."

"From the way you look, I'd guess you've not had much sleep."

"No, sir," Daniel answered cautiously.

Flynn nodded sympathetically. "Lisa can bring you to our coffee room for a mug of java and a muffin."

"Thanks, Mr. Flynn, but I've got to get back," Daniel answered, unwilling to accept gifts from the enemy even though the idea of coffee and a muffin sounded like heaven.

Flynn smiled to show he understood. Then he turned his attention to the stack of boxes on the dolly.

"So Arthur's got you slaving away doing document review. Not what you expected, I'll bet, when you were studying the opinions of Holmes and Cardozo at Yale."

"Actually, it was the U. of O."

Flynn grinned. "Then you must be one of the really bright lights if you were able to squeeze in between the lads and lassies of the Ivy League. I'm a graduate of the law school at the University of Arizona myself. Middle of the class."

He looked at the boxes of discovery again and sighed.

"You know, when I filed *Moffitt* v. *Geller Pharmaceuticals* this firm consisted of two partners and six associates. But since your client has been kind enough to answer my requests for discovery with such thoroughness, I've had to lease another floor and hire five new associates, ten paralegals, and eight support staff people to work on my little set-to with Geller."

"You're keeping me employed, too, Mr. Flynn," Daniel said, making a nervous joke to keep the conversation going. There was something about Flynn that made Daniel want to prolong their meeting. "It seems like you cross swords with Reed, Briggs pretty often."

"So I do," Flynn answered with a laugh. "If you ever grow tired of toiling away for evil corporate interests and decide you want to engage in some honest labor, give me a call. We public school boys should stick together. It was good seeing you again."

Flynn stuck out his hand. As they shook, the elevator door opened, attracting Flynn's attention.

"Before you go, I'd like you to meet someone."

Flynn released Daniel's hand and led him toward the office entrance. A haggard-looking woman in her late twenties was propping open the door with her shoulder and pushing a stroller into the lobby. In the stroller was a baby boy about six months old. His head was down and Daniel could not see his face. Flynn greeted them both.

"Alice, how are you? And how is Patrick doing?"

At the sound of his name, the little boy looked up. He had a mop of blond hair the color of new-mown hay and sky-blue eyes, but below his eyes something had gone terribly wrong. Where his lip should have been was a raw and gaping hole so wide that Daniel could see the saliva that moistened the back of the baby's throat. Patrick's left nostril was normal, but his deformed lip had pushed into the right side of the baby's nose, stretching it wide like Silly Putty. Patrick should have been adorable, but his cleft palate made him look like a horror-movie monster.

Flynn knelt next to the stroller and ruffled Patrick's

hair. The baby made a whistling, hissing sound that bore no relation to the cute cooing sounds made by normal babies. Daniel fought with every ounce of his energy to hide his revulsion, then felt guilty for being repelled by the child.

"Daniel, this is Patrick Cummings," Flynn said pleasantly as he watched the reaction of the young associate. "And this is Alice Cummings, Patrick's mother. She had the misfortune to take Insufort during her pregnancy."

"Nice meeting you, Mrs. Cummings," Daniel said, managing somehow to keep his tone light. Patrick's mother was not fooled. She could see that her son's looks repulsed Daniel and she could not hide her sadness.

Daniel felt awful. He wanted to get out of Flynn's office as fast as possible, but he forced himself to say good-bye and to walk to the elevator slowly so Patrick's mother would not think that he was fleeing from her son. When the elevator doors closed Daniel sagged against the wall. Up until now the children in the Geller case had only been names on a pleading, but Patrick Cummings was flesh and blood. As the car descended Daniel tried to imagine the life Patrick would lead. Would he ever have friends? Would he find a woman who would love him? Was his life over before it had started?

There was one other question that needed an answer: Was Insufort responsible for the fate of Patrick Cummings?

4

Irene Kendall had let the john pick her up in the bar at the Mirage a little before eight in the evening. He'd had a good run at the craps table and was high on his good fortune. She'd listened attentively while he bragged about his gambling prowess. When he started to feel his drinks Irene hinted that she might be amenable to a sexual adventure. It was only after she was sure the john was panting for it that she explained that she was a working girl and told him her rates. The john laughed and told her that the bell captain had pointed her out to him. He said he preferred sex with whores.

The john had paid up front and tipped her afterward, and he hadn't roughed her up or asked for anything exotic. The only downside to the evening was the motel, a by-the-hour fuck pad in a run-down part of town. A lot of Irene's clientele stayed in the classy rooms at the Mirage or the other upscale casinos on the Strip and the motel was definitely a comedown. Still, the room was clean and the john was satisfied with a quick in-and-out, so she didn't have to work hard for her money. When Irene got ready to go, the john surprised her by telling her that she could stay in the room because he had to catch an early flight. She accepted the offer and immediately fell into a deep sleep.

Irene never heard the door being jimmied and had no idea that there was someone else in the room until a gloved hand clamped across her mouth. Her eyes sprang open and she tried to sit up, but the muzzle of a gun pressed hard into the flesh of her forehead and forced her head deep into her pillow.

"Scream and die. Answer my questions and live. Nod slowly if you understand me."

The feeble light cast by the flashing neon sign on the bar next door revealed that the speaker wore a ski mask. Irene nodded slowly and the gloved hand withdrew, leaving the sour taste of leather in her mouth.

"Where is he?"

"Gone," she gasped in a voice hoarse with fear.

"Say good-bye, bitch," the intruder whispered. Irene heard the gun cock.

"Please," she begged. "I'm not his friend, I'm a pro. He was a pickup at the Mirage. He fucked me, he paid me, and he left. He said I could use the room for the night because he had an early flight. I swear that's all I know."

"How long ago did he leave?"

The prostitute's eyes shifted to the clock radio on the nightstand.

"Fifteen minutes. He just left."

Two cruel eyes studied Irene for what seemed an eternity. Then the gun withdrew.

"Stay."

The intruder vanished through the door. Irene did not move for five minutes. Then she raced into the bathroom and threw up.

Part II

The Smoking Gun

5

The main entrance to Reed, Briggs, Stephens, Stottlemeyer and Compton was on the thirtieth floor of a modern, thirty-story office building in the middle of downtown Portland, but Reed, Briggs leased several other floors. A week after delivering the boxes of discovery to Aaron Flynn's office, Daniel stepped out of the elevator on the twenty-seventh floor at 7:30 in the morning. This floor, where Daniel had his office, could only be entered by tapping in a code on a keypad that was attached to the wall next to one of two narrow glass panels that bracketed a locked door. Daniel started to reach for the keypad when he noticed what appeared to be some kind of microphone affixed to the wall above the keypad. Taped next to it was a sign that said:

REED, BRIGGS'S KEY ENTRY SYSTEM IS NOW VOICE-ACTIVATED. CLEARLY AND LOUDLY SAY YOUR NAME, THEN STATE "OPEN DOOR NOW."

On closer inspection Daniel could see that the "microphone" was really a round, metal cap from a juice bottle that had been taped to a small, plastic pencil sharpener. Both had been painted black. Daniel shook his head and tapped in his number. The lock clicked and he opened the door. As he expected, Joe Molinari was lurking behind a partition staring through the glass panel that gave him a view of the keypad.

"You're an asshole," Daniel said.

Molinari jerked him behind the partition just as Miranda Baker, a nineteen-year-old from the mailroom, approached the door.

"Watch this," Molinari said.

Baker started to tap in her code when she noticed the sign. She hesitated, then said, "Miranda Baker. Open door now." She tried the door, but it would not open. She looked puzzled. Molinari doubled over with laughter.

"That's not funny, Joe. She's a good kid."

"Wait," Molinari insisted, trying to stifle his laughter for fear that Baker would hear him. She repeated her name and the command. Molinari had tears in his eyes.

"I'm going to let her in," Daniel said just as Kate Ross, one of Reed, Briggs's in-house investigators, got out of the elevator. Kate walked up to Miranda as she was saying her name for the third time and yanking on the doorknob. Kate took one look at the sign and ripped it, the pencil sharpener, and the bottle cap off of the wall.

"Shit," Joe swore.

Kate said something to the young woman. They looked through the glass and stared coldly at Joe and Daniel. Miranda tapped in her code and opened the door. She flashed the two associates an angry look as she brushed past them.

Kate Ross was twenty-eight, five-foot-seven, and looked fit in tight jeans, an oxford blue shirt, and a navy-blue blazer. Kate stopped in front of the associates and held out the sign, bottle cap, and pencil sharpener. Her dark complexion, large brown eyes, and curly black, shoulder-length hair made Daniel think of those tough Israeli soldiers he'd seen on the evening news. The hard look she cast at Joe and Daniel made him glad that she wasn't carrying an Uzi.

"I believe these are yours."

Joe looked sheepish. Kate turned her attention to Daniel.

"Don't you have better things to do with your time?" she asked sternly.

"Hey, I had nothing to do with this," Daniel answered.

Kate looked skeptical. She dropped the bottle cap, pencil sharpener, and wadded-up sign into a garbage can and walked off.

"What a spoilsport," Molinari said when Kate was out of earshot.

Daniel hurried after Kate and caught up with her just as she was entering an office she shared with another investigator.

"I really didn't have anything to do with that," he said from the doorway.

Kate looked up from her mail. "Why should I care how you preppies amuse yourselves?" she asked angrily.

Daniel reddened. "Don't confuse me with Joe Molinari. I wasn't born with a silver spoon in my mouth. I'm a working stiff, just like you. I didn't like Joe's practical joke any more than you did. I was going to let Miranda in when you showed up."

"It didn't look that way to me," Kate answered defensively.

"Believe what you want to believe, but I don't lie," Daniel said angrily as he turned on his heel and walked down the hall to his office.

Reed, Briggs used a large wood-paneled room on the twenty-ninth floor for important depositions. As Daniel hurried toward it he narrowly missed running into Renee Gilchrist.

" 'Morning, Renee," Daniel said as he stepped aside to let her pass.

Renee took a few steps, then turned around.

"Daniel."

"Yeah?"

"Mr. Briggs thought you did a good job on the Fairweather memo."

"Oh? He didn't say anything to me about it."

"He wouldn't."

The partners never told Daniel what they thought about his work and the only way he could tell if they believed it was any good was by the volume of work they gave him. It dawned on Daniel that Briggs had been loading him up for the past month.

"Thanks for telling me."

Renee smiled. "You'd better get in there. They're about to start the deposition."

At one end of the conference room, a wide picture window offered a view of the Willamette River and, beyond it, Mount Hood and Mount St. Helens. On another wall, a large oil painting of the Columbia Gorge hung over an oak credenza. On the credenza, silver urns filled with coffee and hot water stood next to a matching platter loaded down with croissants and muffins and a bowl filled with fruit.

Dr. Kurt Schroeder, a Geller Pharmaceuticals executive who was about to be deposed, sat at the end of a huge, cherrywood conference table, with his back to the window. Schroeder's thin lips were set in a rigid line and it was obvious that he did not enjoy his position on the hot seat.

To Schroeder's right sat Aaron Flynn and three associates. To Schroeder's left sat Arthur Briggs, a reed-thin, chain-smoker who always seemed to be on edge. Briggs's jet-black hair was swept back revealing a sharp widow's peak and his eyes were always moving as if he expected an attack from behind. In addition to being one of the most feared attorneys in Oregon, Briggs was a mover and shaker of the first magnitude with a heavy hand in politics, civic affairs, and almost every conservative cause of note. Daniel thought that Briggs was probably a sociopath who had channeled his energy into law instead of serial murder.

To Briggs's left was Brock Newbauer, a junior partner with a sunny smile and whitish-blond hair. Brock would never have made the cut at Reed, Briggs if his father's construction company had not been one of the firm's biggest clients.

Daniel took the chair next to Susan Webster. Arthur Briggs shot him an annoyed glance, but said nothing. Susan scribbled, *You're late,* on her notepad and moved it slightly in Daniel's direction.

"Good morning, Dr. Schroeder," Aaron Flynn said with a welcoming smile. Daniel placed a legal pad on the table and started taking notes.

"Good morning," Schroeder answered without returning the smile.

"Why don't we start by having you tell everyone your occupation."

Schroeder cleared his throat. "I'm a board-certified pediatrician by training and am currently a senior vice-president and chief medical adviser to Geller Pharmaceuticals."

"Could you tell us a little bit about your educational background?"

"I graduated from Lehigh University with a chemistry major and biology minor. My medical degree is from Oregon Health Sciences University."

"What did you do after medical school?"

"I had an internship in pediatrics at the State University of New York, Kings County Hospital Center, in Brooklyn. Then I was assistant chief resident at the Children's Hospital of Philadelphia as a pediatric resident."

"What did you do after your residency?"

"I spent several years in private practice in Oregon before joining Geller Pharmaceuticals."

"When you joined Geller did it have any particular focus on pediatric drugs?"

"Yes, it did."

"Could you describe for us your job history after joining Geller?"

"I began in the clinical research and development division and rose through the ranks in various different positions of responsibility until I was appointed vice-president for medical affairs and later was promoted to senior vice-president. For the past eight years I've had responsibility for the development of, and gaining approval for, products we've discovered."

"And that would include Insufort?"

"Yes."

"Thank you. Now, Dr. Schroeder, I'd like to discuss with you the normal process for drug development and marketing and just sort of walk through the steps so that I'll have an understanding of what's involved in bringing a drug onto the market. And am I correct that the first step is identifying something that might have some pharmacological value?"

"Yes."

"And then you conduct preclinical studies, studies that are not done with humans."

"Yes."

"And the preclinical studies involve animals."

"Not necessarily. Prior to animal studies, you might conduct studies in tissues or cells. Maybe you would do a computer simulation."

"Okay, but at some point you get to the stage

where you do what are called preclinical studies to assess both safety and effectiveness?"

"Yes."

"And when you do preclinical studies, the results of those studies are submitted to the Federal Drug Administration, or FDA, for review in what's called an investigational new drug application or IND, is that correct?"

"Yes."

"What is an IND?"

"It's a request for an exemption from the regulations which preclude physicians or companies from giving a substance which has not been approved by the FDA to humans in a clinical situation. If the FDA approves the IND, you are permitted to conduct clinical studies of the drug with humans."

"Can I assume that you, as chief medical adviser to Geller Pharmaceuticals, were familiar with the results of the preclinical and clinical studies conducted to determine if Insufort was a safe and effective product?"

"Well, I certainly reviewed the studies."

Flynn smiled at Schroeder. "Can I take it that is a yes?"

"Objection," Briggs said, asserting himself for the first time. "Dr. Schroeder did not say that he read each and every study and all of the documents involved."

"That's true," Schroeder said.

"Well, Geller Pharmaceuticals conducted extensive preclinical rodent studies, did it not?"

"Yes."

"You were aware of the results?"

"Yes."

"And there were studies of primates, pregnant monkeys?"

"Yes."

"And you were aware of those results?"

"Yes, I was."

"And there were phase-one clinical studies of human beings?"

"Yes."

"And you know about those results?"

"Yes."

"Tell me, Dr. Schroeder, did any of the clinical or preclinical studies show that Insufort can cause birth defects?"

"No, sir. They did not."

Flynn looked surprised. "None of them?" he asked.

"None of them."

Flynn turned to the young woman on his right. She handed him a one-page document. He scanned it for a moment, then returned his attention to Dr. Schroeder.

"What about the study conducted by Dr. Sergey Kaidanov?" Flynn asked.

Schroeder looked puzzled.

"Do you have a scientist in your employ named Dr. Sergey Kaidanov?"

"Dr. Kaidanov? Yes, he works for the company."

"In research and development?"

"I believe so."

Flynn nodded and the associate to his right pushed copies of the document that Flynn was holding across the conference table as Flynn handed a copy to the witness.

"I'd like this marked Plaintiff's Exhibit 234. I've given copies to counsel and Dr. Schroeder."

"Where did you get this?" Briggs demanded as soon as he'd skimmed the page.

Flynn smiled and gestured toward Daniel.

"I received it as part of the discovery that young man over there delivered to my office a few days ago."

Every eye in the room focused on Daniel, but he did not notice because he was reading Plaintiff's Exhibit 234, which appeared to be a cover letter for a report that Dr. Sergey Kaidanov had sent to George Fournet, the in-house counsel for Geller Pharmaceuticals.

> *Dear Mr. Fournet,*
> *I have great concerns about thalglitazone (trade name, Insufort) based on the results emerging from our congenital anomaly study in pregnant primates. We have to date studied the effects of an oral dose of one hundred micrograms per kilogram, given for ten days beginning on the thirtieth day of conception, on the fetus in forty pregnant rhesus monkeys. The early results are striking—eighteen of the forty neonate primates (45 percent) were born with maxillofacial abnormalities, in some cases severe, the most severe being complete cleft lip and palate. It is unclear to me how this could have been missed in the rodent studies, but as we all know this does happen from time to time.*
> *The purpose of this letter and the enclosed preliminary results is to alert you to my findings, as I believe it will have important implications for our current phase II and III studies in human beings. I*

will forward a detailed anatomical and biochemical analysis when my study is completed.

Daniel was stunned. Kaidanov's letter was the smoking gun that could destroy Geller Pharmaceuticals' case, and Aaron Flynn had just told Arthur Briggs that Daniel had placed the lethal weapon in his hands.

6

While Daniel read the letter in shocked silence, Susan Webster's fingers flew across the keys of her laptop.

"I have a few questions about this document, Dr. Schroeder," Aaron Flynn said in a cordial tone.

Susan slipped beside Arthur Briggs and gestured at a case she had called up on her computer. She whispered hurriedly in his ear and Briggs shouted, "Objection! This is a confidential communication between Dr. Kaidanov and his attorney that has been inadvertently turned over to you. You had an ethical obligation to refrain from reading the letter once you saw that it was an attorney / client communication."

Flynn chuckled. "Arthur, this is a report of the results of a preclincal test on rhesus monkeys. Your client, probably at your suggestion, has been instructing its scientists to send all their test results to in-house counsel, so you can raise this silly objection to our discovery requests, but it's too transparent to take seriously."

"You'll take this damn seriously when I report you to the bar disciplinary committee."

Flynn smiled. "Take any steps you think you must, Arthur."

Flynn nodded and one of his associates sped several copies of a legal document across the polished wood table.

"I want the record to reflect that I have just served Dr. Schroeder and his counsel a request for production of Dr. Kaidanov's study and all supporting documentation, as well as a notice of deposition for Dr. Kaidanov and Mr. Fournet."

Flynn turned back to the witness. "Now, Dr. Schroeder, I'd like to ask you a few questions about the Kaidanov study."

"Don't you say a thing," Briggs shouted at the witness.

"Arthur, Dr. Schroeder is under oath and we're in the middle of his deposition."

Flynn's tone was calm and condescending, and it raised Briggs's blood pressure another notch.

"I want Judge Norris on the phone." A blood vessel in Briggs's temple looked like it was about to burst. "I want a ruling on this before I'll let Dr. Schroeder give you the time of day."

Flynn shrugged. "Call the judge."

Daniel barely heard what Briggs and Flynn said. All he could think about was the steps he'd taken when he reviewed the discovery. How could he have missed Kaidanov's letter? He had skim-read many of the documents, but he was specifically looking for privileged information. A letter to an attorney would have raised a red flag. It didn't seem possible that it could slip by, but it had. Daniel was devastated. No one was perfect, but to be responsible for an error of these proportions . . .

As soon as Judge Norris was connected to the conference room, Flynn and Briggs took turns explaining the legal arguments supporting their position in the Kaidanov matter. The judge was too busy to deal with a matter of this complexity over the phone. He told the attorneys to stop questioning Schroeder until he ruled and he ordered Briggs and Flynn to submit briefs on their positions by the end of the week.

As soon as Flynn and his minions cleared the conference room, Briggs waved Kaidanov's letter in Schroeder's face.

"What is this, Kurt?"

"I've got no idea, Arthur." The Geller executive looked as upset as his attorney. "I've never seen the damn thing in my life."

"But you know this guy Kaidanov?"

"I know who he is. He works in R and D. I don't know him personally."

"And he's working with these monkeys?"

"No. Not to my knowledge."

"What does 'not to my knowledge' mean? You're not holding out on me, are you? This letter could cost your company millions, if you're lucky, and it could sink Geller if you're not."

Schroeder was sweating. "I swear, Arthur, I've never heard of a single study that we've conducted that came back with results like these. What kind of company do you think we run? If I got wind of a study of Insufort with those results, do you think I'd okay human trials?"

"I want to speak to Kaidanov and Fournet immediately, this afternoon," Briggs said.

"I'll phone my office and set it up."

When Schroeder walked over to the credenza and punched in the number of his office, Briggs turned toward Daniel, who had tried to remain as inconspicuous as possible. Briggs held out his copy of the Kaidanov letter, which had sustained serious damage.

"Explain this, Ames," he demanded in a soft tone that was more frightening than the screams he'd expected.

"I . . . uh, Mr. Briggs . . . I've never seen it."

"Never seen it," Briggs repeated. "Was Flynn lying when he said that you gave it to him?"

Daniel glanced at Susan. She averted her eyes, but her body language revealed her anxiety. Daniel looked back at Briggs.

"Well?" Briggs asked, his voice slightly louder.

"He didn't mean that literally, Mr. Briggs. I was told to review five large boxes of documents that Geller produced in response to a demand for discovery." Daniel was the only one who saw Susan release her pent-up breath. "I was told to deliver the discovery first thing in the morning, eight A.M. I didn't see the boxes until eight the night before. There were roughly twenty thousand pages. I stayed at the office all evening. I even slept here. There were too many pages for me to review every one of them in that time."

"And that's your excuse?"

"It's not an excuse. Nobody could have gone through every page in those boxes in the time I had."

"You're not a 'nobody,' Ames. You're a Reed, Briggs associate. If we wanted nobodies we'd pay minimum wage and hire graduates of unaccredited, correspondence law schools."

"Mr. Briggs. I'm sorry, but—"

"My secretary will set up the meetings," Schroeder said as he hung up the phone. To Daniel's great relief, Schroeder's statement distracted Briggs.

Schroeder reread Kaidanov's letter. When he was done he held it up. He looked grim.

"I think this is a fraud. We never conducted a study with these results," he declared emphatically. "I'm certain of it."

"You'd better be right," Briggs said. "If Judge Norris rules that this letter is admissible in court, and we can't prove it's a fake, you, and everyone else at Geller Pharmaceuticals, will be selling pencils on street corners."

Briggs started to lead Newbauer and Schroeder out of the room. Daniel hung back, hoping to escape Briggs's notice, but the senior partner stopped at the door and cast a scathing look at him.

"I'll talk with you, later," Briggs said.

The door closed and Daniel was left alone in the conference room.

7

Daniel spent the afternoon waiting for the ax to fall. Around two, he dialed Susan's extension to find out what was going on, but her secretary told him that she was at Geller Pharmaceuticals with Arthur Briggs. An hour later, when he realized that he'd never get any work done, Daniel went home to his one-bedroom walk-up on the third floor of an old brick apartment house in northwest Portland. His place was small and sparsely furnished with things Daniel had transported from his law-school apartment in Eugene. Its most attractive feature was its location near Northwest Twenty-first and Twenty-third streets with their restaurants, shops, and crowds. But today the apartment could have been in the heart of Paris and Daniel would not have noticed. Arthur Briggs was going to fire him. He was sure of it. Everything he had worked for was going to be destroyed because of a single sheet of paper.

Something else troubled Daniel. He had been so worried about being fired that it was not until he was in bed, eyes closed, that the true importance of Dr. Sergey Kaidanov's letter dawned on him. Until he read the letter, Daniel had been convinced that there was no merit to the lawsuit Aaron Flynn had brought on behalf of Toby Moffitt, Patrick Cummings, and the other children allegedly affected by Insufort. What if he was wrong? What if Geller Pharmaceuticals knew that it was selling a product that could deform innocent babies? Daniel was part of a team representing Geller. If the company was knowingly responsible for the horror that had been visited upon Patrick Cummings and Daniel continued to defend Geller, he would be aiding and abetting a terrible enterprise.

Daniel tossed and turned all night and was exhausted when his alarm went off. By the time he arrived at Reed, Briggs the next morning, he was certain that everyone in the firm knew about his blunder. Daniel managed to get from the elevator to his office without meeting anyone, but he was barely settled behind his desk when Joe Molinari walked in and his day started to go downhill.

"What the fuck did you do?" Molinari asked in a hushed voice as soon as he shut the door.

"What do you mean?" Daniel asked nervously.

"The word is that Briggs has a hair up his ass the size of a redwood and you put it there."

"Shit."

"So it's true."

Daniel felt utterly defeated.

"What happened?"

"I don't want to talk about it."

"Look, compadre, I'm here for you."

"I appreciate the support. I'd just rather be alone now."

"Okay," Molinari said reluctantly. He stood up. "Just remember what I said. If there's something I can do, ask."

Molinari left. Daniel felt exhausted and the day had just started. It suddenly dawned on him that he had never gotten around to discussing with Susan her role in the discovery fiasco. If Susan went to Briggs and told him that she was partly to blame, it might help, and from what Molinari said, he could use all the help he could get. Daniel walked down the hall to Susan's office. She was wearing a cream-colored blouse and a gray pantsuit and looked as fresh and untroubled as a woman who had slept for twenty-four hours.

"Susan?"

"Oh, hi," she answered with a smile.

"Got a minute?"

Daniel started toward a chair.

"Actually, I don't." Daniel stopped in his tracks. "Arthur needs this yesterday."

"We really have to talk."

"Now is not a good time," she said firmly. Her smile was starting to look a little strained.

"I was hoping that you'd tell Arthur that you were supposed to review the discovery and that I helped you out."

Susan looked surprised, as if the idea had never occurred to her.

"Why would I do that?"

"So he'd know how big the job was and that I

didn't get started until the last minute," Daniel answered, trying to rein in his temper.

"Even if I was supposed to review the discovery, you're the one who did," Susan answered defensively. "If I tell Arthur, it won't help. All that will accomplish is getting me in trouble, too."

"If Briggs knew that we were both to blame it would take some of the pressure off of me."

Susan looked nervous. "*I* didn't go through the discovery. *You're* the one who missed that letter."

"You'd have missed it, too. Briggs would have missed it."

"You're right," Susan agreed quickly. "Look, you'll be okay. Arthur gets angry easily, but he'll be distracted by this mess and forget you delivered the letter."

"Fat chance."

"Or he'll see that you're right. That the letter was a needle in a haystack that no one could have found unless they were incredibly lucky. You don't have to worry."

"You're the one who doesn't have to worry," Daniel said with a trace of bitterness. "He'd never fire you."

Susan looked very uncomfortable. "I really do have to finish this assignment. It's research on the admissibility of Kaidanov's letter. Can we talk about this later?"

"When, after I'm unemployed?" Daniel shot back.

"I mean it, Daniel. I'll buzz you as soon as I get some free time."

• • •

Daniel could not concentrate on the pleading he was drafting because his thoughts kept drifting to the Insufort case. He could not believe that Geller Pharmaceuticals would intentionally sell a product that produced the horrible results he'd seen in Aaron Flynn's office. He had met many of the Geller executives. They weren't monsters. The results that Sergey Kaidanov wrote about had to be an anomaly.

Daniel set aside the pleading and opened a large folder that held all of the Insufort studies. He started with the earliest and worked his way through them looking for anything that would help. By the time he had finished his review it was almost one. Daniel suddenly remembered Susan's promise to call him when she was through with her work. He dialed Susan's extension and her secretary told him that she had left for the day. Daniel wasn't surprised. Deep down he knew that Susan was not going to help him. If he wanted to stay at Reed, Briggs, he was going to have to save himself, but how?

Suddenly he laughed. The answer was obvious. Sergey Kaidanov wrote the report that was about to torpedo Geller's defense. Kaidanov's study had to be flawed. If he could find out why Kaidanov had erred he would save the litigation and, maybe, his job.

Daniel dialed Geller Pharmaceuticals and was connected to the receptionist in research and development.

"Dr. Kaidanov isn't in," she told him.

"When will he be in?"

"I couldn't say."

"I'm an attorney at Reed, Briggs, Stephens, Stottlemeyer and Compton, the law firm that represents Geller Pharmaceuticals, and I need to speak with Dr. Kaidanov about a matter of importance to a suit that was brought against your company."

"I'm supposed to refer all inquiries about Dr. Kaidanov to Dr. Schroeder. May I transfer you to his office?"

"I don't want to bother Dr. Schroeder. I know how busy he is. I'd rather just speak to Dr. Kaidanov myself."

"Well, you can't. He's not in and he hasn't been in for more than a week."

"Is he on vacation?"

"I don't have that information. You'll have to talk to Dr. Schroeder. Do you want me to connect you?"

"Uh, no. That's okay. Thanks."

Daniel dialed information and discovered that Sergey Kaidanov had an unlisted phone number. He thought for a moment then phoned personnel at Geller Pharmaceuticals.

"I need an address and phone number for Dr. Sergey Kaidanov," he said to the clerk who answered. "He works in research and development."

"I can't give out that information over the phone."

Daniel was desperate. He had to get to Kaidanov.

"Listen," he said forcefully, "this is George Fournet in legal. We just received a subpoena for Kaidanov. He's out of the office and I've got to get in touch with him ASAP. If he doesn't show up for his deposition we're going to be held in contempt by the judge. I have a messenger waiting to hand-deliver the subpoena, but he's all dressed up with no place to go."

"I'm not sure . . ."

"What's your name?"

"Bea Twiley."

"Did you get mine, Ms. Twiley; George Fournet? I am the head of the legal department and I don't waste my time on frivolous calls. Do you want to go to court and explain to United States District Court Judge Ivan Norris why you're there instead of Dr. Kaidanov?"

8

It was a little after three when Daniel found Sergey Kaidanov's drab, gray bungalow in a run-down neighborhood on the east side of the Willamette. The paint was peeling and the front lawn had not been mowed in a while. It was not the type of home in which Daniel expected to find a research scientist who worked for a prosperous pharmaceutical company.

The weather had turned nasty and there was no one on the street. Daniel parked down the block and watched the house. The shades in the front windows were drawn and the old newspapers lying on the lawn told Daniel that no one was home. He hunched his shoulders to ward off the wind and shivered as he walked up the path to Kaidanov's front door. After ringing the bell three times, he gave up. Daniel raised the metal flap of the mail slot and peeked inside the house. Mail was scattered across the floor.

Daniel followed a slate path that ran along the side of the bungalow to the back of the house. A low chain-link fence ran around the edge of a small, unkempt yard. Daniel opened the gate and went to the back door. The shades on the kitchen window were drawn. He knocked a few times, then tried the knob. The door opened. Daniel was about to call out Kaidanov's name when he saw the chaos in the kitchen. Cabinets and drawers were open and their contents littered the floor. Daniel took a slow survey of the room. There was a layer of dust on the counters. The sink was full of dirty dishes. Daniel stepped gingerly over broken glass and shattered plates and opened the refrigerator. He was hit by the sour smell of decay. Greenish-gray mold covered a piece of cheese. Daniel uncapped a bottle of spoiled milk and wrinkled his nose.

A small living room opened off of the kitchen. Except for an expensive stereo that had been ripped out of its cabinet, most of the other furnishings looked secondhand. CDs were strewn around the floor. Daniel saw a lot of classical music and some jazz.

A bookshelf took up one wall, but the books it used to hold had been thrown around the room. Many of the books were about scientific subjects like chemistry and microbiology. Daniel spotted a few popular novels and several books on gambling and mathematics.

The contents of a liquor cabinet were lying among the books and CDs on the hardwood floor. Most of the bottles contained Scotch and many of them were empty. On top of the liquor cabinet was more dust and a framed photograph of a slightly overweight man in his early forties dressed in sports clothes.

Standing next to him was an attractive woman in a revealing sundress. They were smiling at the camera. The picture looked like it had been taken in front of a Las Vegas casino.

Daniel turned slowly, taking in the room again. This couldn't be a coincidence. Kaidanov's disappearance, the search of his home, and the primate study had to be connected.

A short hall led to the bedroom. Daniel edged into it, half expecting to find a mutilated corpse. Blankets and sheets were heaped on the floor, the mattress of a queen-size bed had been dislodged, drawers in a chest had been pulled out, and shirts, underwear, and socks had been strewn around the room. The doors to a clothes closet were open and it had obviously been searched.

Across the hall was a small office. More books had been pulled out of a bookshelf, but Daniel's attention was drawn to a monitor on Kaidanov's desktop. It looked odd sitting where it was supposed to be when everything else in the room had been tossed about. Daniel sat down and turned on the computer. As soon as it booted up, he tried to gain entry, but he needed a password. If Kaidanov had information about his study in the house it would be on his computer, but how could he access it?

Daniel turned off the computer and pulled the CPU tower out from under Kaidanov's desk. Using the screwdriver on his Swiss army knife, Daniel removed the sheet-metal cover of the computer's case, popped the cover, and pulled it off. He placed the computer on its side so he could see the motherboard, which held all of its electronics. Next to the motherboard was the hard-drive bay, a rack that held the hard drive in the computer. The hard drive was connected to the motherboard by a ribbon cable and a power cable. Daniel unplugged the cables from their connectors and unscrewed two more screws on the bay. He then flipped the CPU tower upright and took out two more screws on the other side. When all the screws were out Daniel gently slid the hard drive out of its bay. It consisted of a green circuit board encased in heavy black metal and was about the size of a paperback book. Daniel wrapped it in his handkerchief and placed it in his jacket pocket.

Daniel put the CPU tower back together and was sliding it under the desk when he froze at the distinctive sound of a bottle rolling across a wood floor. Daniel remembered that the liquor bottles were in the living room, which meant that he was trapped, because he would have to go through the living room to get out the front or back doors.

A shadow appeared on the corridor wall. Daniel could make out the bill of a baseball cap, but the shadow was too indistinct to tell him much more. He edged the door almost shut. The shadow flowed toward him along the wall. Daniel held his breath. If the intruder went into the bedroom he—Daniel—might be able to slip down the hall. If he went into the office first . . . Daniel opened the large blade on his knife.

Through the narrow gap in the door Daniel saw a figure in jeans and leather jacket stop between the two rooms, facing away from him. The intruder hesitated, then the office door slammed into Daniel with enough force to stun him. Before he could recover, his wrist was bent back and his feet were kicked out from under him. The knife flew from his grasp.

Daniel crashed to the floor and lashed out with a punch that brought a gasp from his attacker. The grip on his arm loosened and he broke it, then struggled to his knees. A knee smashed into his face. Daniel grabbed his attacker's leg, surged to his feet, and twisted. His assailant went down with Daniel on top, his head pressed against the leather jacket. A blow glanced off Daniel's ear. He worked himself into a position to punch back, then reared up. As soon as he saw his attacker's face he checked his punch and gaped in astonishment.

"Kate?"

Kate Ross stared at Daniel. If she was relieved to discover that her foe was not a psychopath, she didn't show it.

"What the hell are you doing here?" she demanded angrily.

"I could ask you the same question," Daniel snapped.

"I'm working on a case for Arthur Briggs."

"If you're looking for Kaidanov he's not here."

Kate hit Daniel in the shoulder, none too gently.

"Get off me."

Daniel stood up and Kate got to her feet.

"How did you know I was behind the door?" he asked.

"I saw you push it shut."

"Oh."

"Did you make this mess?" Kate asked as she surveyed the chaos in the office.

"It was like this when I got here."

Kate walked into the hall and stared into the bedroom. Then she said, "Let's get out of here before someone calls 911."

         Kate and Daniel agreed to meet downtown at the Starbucks on Pioneer Square, an open, brick-paved block in the center of the city. Daniel parked and found a table next to a window. When Kate walked in he was nursing a cup of coffee and watching a group of teenage boys, oblivious to the cold, playing hacky-sack in the square.

"I got this for you," Daniel said, pointing to a cup of coffee he'd put at Kate's place.

"You want to explain the B and E?" Kate asked without looking at Daniel's peace offering.

"Yeah, right after you explain the assault and battery," Daniel answered, peeved by Kate's offhand manner.

"When someone pulls a knife on you it's called self-defense, not assault."

Daniel flexed his still aching wrist. "Where did you learn that judo stuff?"

"I was a Portland cop before I went to work for Reed, Briggs." Daniel's eyebrows went up in surprise. "I still know the person who's in charge of burglary. Right now I'm undecided about whether to call him."

"Why, are you going to turn yourself in? I didn't hear anyone invite you into Kaidanov's house."

"Nice try, but Geller Pharmaceuticals is a Reed, Briggs client. Kurt Schroeder authorized the entry to look for Geller's property. So, let's start over. What were you doing at Kaidanov's house?"

"Did you hear what happened at the deposition in the Geller case?" Daniel asked with a mixture of nervousness and embarrassment.

"Dan, everyone in the firm knows about your screwup. It was the main topic of conversation yesterday."

"Do you know exactly what happened, why I'm in trouble?"

Kate shook her head. "I heard something about a document that you turned over to Aaron Flynn, but I don't know the details."

"Are you familiar with the Insufort litigation?"

"Only a little. I told Briggs that I wouldn't work on it."

"Why?"

Kate's tough demeanor cracked for a second. "My sister's kid was born with birth defects. She and her husband have gone through hell caring for her."

Kate took a sip of coffee. When she looked up she had regained her composure.

"Do you mind if I give you some background on the case?" Daniel asked.

"Go ahead."

"Insulin is a protein hormone secreted by the pancreas that helps the body use sugar in the form of glucose. Insulin becomes less effective in metabolizing glucose during pregnancy, which can cause some pregnant women to become diabetic. Insulin resistance during pregnancy must be treated because high sugar levels are toxic to a fetus and can cause birth defects. Geller Pharmaceuticals addressed the problem of insulin resistance during pregnancy by developing thalglitazone, which has the trade name Insufort. Insufort reverses the body's insulin resistance and prevents diabetes and its complications."

"But there are problems, right? Birth defects?" Kate said. "And isn't there a connection between Insufort and the Thalidomide scare from the late 1950s?"

"Yes and no. One tabloid called Insufort the 'Son of Thalidomide,' and there is a connection. A drug called troglitazone helped pregnant women solve the insulin resistance problem, but it also may have caused liver failure. Geller's scientists combined a glitazone with the thalido ring from Thalidomide and created a harmless product that helps pregnant women overcome diabetes during pregnancy."

"So why are women who take the pill giving birth to deformed babies?"

"It's either a compliance problem or coincidence."

Kate looked at him with disgust.

"No, it's true," Daniel insisted. "Many of the women who claim that Insufort caused their child's birth defect probably didn't take the pill as prescribed. Maybe they took it occasionally or irregularly or only a few times and their glucose rose to dangerous levels."

"So we're blaming the victim."

"Look, Kate, most women give birth to healthy babies, but some women give birth to babies who have problems. Sometimes we know why. Some anticonvulsant drugs cause cleft palate. Babies of older mothers are more prone to have birth defects. Maternal infections can also cause them. Then there's alcohol, tobacco, and drugs. But the causes of most birth defects are medical mysteries. The difficulty is that Americans have been taught that there is an answer to every problem." Daniel leaned forward and looked at Kate. "Americans can't accept the fact that shit happens. You get cancer, so you blame overhead power lines; you run someone over, so you blame your car. Are you familiar with the Bendictin cases?"

Kate shook her head.

" 'Morning sickness' is a problem for many pregnant women. For most it's unpleasant, but it can be deadly. You've heard of Charlotte Brontë?"

"The author of *Jane Eyre*."

Daniel nodded. "Hyperemesis gravida—'morning sickness'—killed her. In 1956, the FDA approved Bendictin, which was developed by Merrill Pharmaceuticals as a therapy for women with severe morning sickness. In 1979, the *National Enquirer* announced that Bendictin was the cause of thousands of defects in infants.

"The best way to determine if there is a cause-and-effect relationship between a drug and a problem is to conduct an epidemiological study. If a control group that hasn't taken the product has as many, or more, problems as the group that's taken the drug, you can conclude that there's probably not a casual connection between the drug and the problem. All of the epidemiological studies of Bendictin concluded that there was no statistical difference in the incidence of births of babies with defects in the two groups. That didn't stop lawyers from convincing women to sue.

"The plaintiffs' attorneys must have had some evidence of a causal connection between the drug and the defects.

"They used experts who altered the results of studies or conducted studies without proper controls or inaccurately reported doses. The plaintiffs lost almost every case because they couldn't show that Bendictin was to blame for any defects, but it cost Merrill Pharmaceuticals a hundred million dollars to defend all of the cases. In the end, a perfectly safe product was taken off the market because of all the bad publicity and other drug companies were scared to produce a drug that would help women counteract morning sickness. In 1990, the *Journal of the American Medical Association* reported a twofold increase in hospitalizations caused by severe nausea and vomiting in pregnancy since the disappearance of Bendictin. So who suffered? Only the innocent."

"Did all of the Insufort studies show that it's safe?" Kate asked.

"All but one," Daniel answered hesitantly.

Kate cocked her head to one side and watched Daniel carefully as she waited for him to continue.

"I'm in trouble because I missed a letter from Dr. Sergey Kaidanov when I reviewed some discovery that was turned over to Aaron Flynn. The letter discusses a primate study involving Insufort."

"And?"

A vision of Patrick Cummings flashed through Daniel's mind.

"The study showed a high incidence of birth defects in rhesus monkeys that had been given the drug during pregnancy," he answered quietly.

"Did Geller tell you about this study before the deposition?"

"No. Geller's chief medical adviser swears that he's never heard of it."

"I see." Kate sounded skeptical.

"The Kaidanov letter doesn't make sense, Kate. The percentage of defects was very high, in the forty-percent range. It's so out of line with the other study results that there's got to be something wrong."

"Maybe there's something wrong with Geller's other studies."

"No, I've never seen any evidence in any study of a link between Insufort and birth defects."

"Maybe you've never seen any evidence because Geller is hiding it. Remember the asbestos cases? The asbestos industry covered up studies that showed increased cancer in animals. It wasn't until a lawsuit was brought that it came out that they'd known about the problem for decades. The lead-paint industry continued to defend its product even though lead poisoning was one of the most common health problems in children under six and there was scientific documentation of the dangers of lead poisoning as early as 1897. And let's not forget the tobacco industry."

"Jesus, Kate, whose side are you on? Geller is our client."

"Our client is in the drug business to make a buck and it wouldn't surprise me if Geller covered up the Kaidanov study if the results are as devastating as you say they are. Do you think Geller markets Insufort to help women? Companies whose executives are men make a lot of these defective products that are used by women. There's Thalidomide, DES—the synthetic estrogen that was supposed to prevent miscarriages and caused vaginal cancer—and the Dalkon Shield."

"Plaintiffs' attorneys play on this sympathy for women to gouge money out of corporations with frivolous lawsuits so they can rake in millions," Daniel answered angrily. "They don't care about their clients or whether they really have a case. The Bendictin lawyers were hoping that jurors would be so appalled by the birth defects they saw that they'd forget that there was no evidence that Bendictin caused them. The breast implant cases used sympathy for women to sway public opinion even though there's no evidence of a connection between defects in silicone gel implants and connective tissue diseases like systemic lupus erythematosus and rheumatoid arthritis."

Kate looked fed up. "I have a good friend who's sterile because she used the Dalkon Shield. I worked on her lawsuit and I learned a lot about the way corporate America works. By the time the public discovers that a product is defective, the company has made so much money it can afford to buy off the victims. Tobacco is so flush it can make multibillion-dollar settlements and still keep trucking.

"And don't come down so hard on plaintiffs' attorneys. They can make millions when they win a case, but they don't make a penny if they lose."

"You think Aaron Flynn is a humanitarian?" Daniel asked, but his heart was not completely in tune with his words. As he spoke them he remembered Flynn ruffling Patrick Cummings's hair.

"Who else is going to represent the poor?" Kate asked. " 'Cause it sure ain't Reed, Briggs. If lawyers like Flynn didn't take cases for a contingent fee no one but the rich could afford to sue. And they risk their own money on expenses, which they don't recover if they don't win. A good, decent lawyer can lose everything if he doesn't prevail. The lawyer who sued when my friend became sterile did it to pressure the company into taking a dangerous device off of the market. He cared about Jill. If Insufort is disfiguring children the only way to make Geller stop marketing it is to expose the problem, and one of the best ways to do that is in the courts."

Daniel expelled the breath he'd been holding.

"You're right. Sorry. I'm just scared that I'm gonna lose my job because I missed that damn letter. And I'm certain there's something wrong with Kaidanov's study. It doesn't make sense that he could get those results with Insufort. That's why I was trying to find him. You know he hasn't been at work for a while?"

Kate nodded.

"When I went to Kaidanov's house I didn't plan on going in, but I saw that the house had been searched and I thought he might be hurt or worse. And I did find something that might help."

Daniel pulled his handkerchief out of his pocket and laid the hard drive on the table. Kate stared at it.

"If the study exists, and Kaidanov wrote up his results, it may be on here."

Kate laughed. "You stole Kaidanov's hard drive?"

"I didn't steal it. I was trying to protect Geller. Isn't that why you were there, to protect Geller's property?"

Kate hesitated and Daniel remembered something about her.

"Wait a minute. Aren't you the investigator who got into the hard drive in that wrongful termination case when we needed to recover E-mail that an employee erased?"

Kate smiled ever so slightly.

"Could you look at this? I tried at Kaidanov's house, but you need a password to log on."

"Why should I?"

"I told you before that I wasn't born with a silver spoon like Joe Molinari. Well, the truth is that I wasn't born with any kind of spoon. This job is all I've got. Briggs will need a scapegoat if Kaidanov's letter sinks the Insufort case, and I'm it. I know there's something wrong with Kaidanov's study. If I can prove it I can save the case, and I might save my job."

"What if the study is the real thing?"

Daniel sighed and shook his head. "Then I'm toast."

Kate made a decision. She held out her hand.

"Give me that," she said, flicking her fingers toward the hard drive. "We'll take it to my house and see what we can see."

9

Daniel followed Kate Ross into the West Hills along winding roads. At first, the streets were lined with houses, then forest began to predominate and the houses appeared farther apart. Kate lived at the end of a cul-de-sac separated from her neighbors on either side by a quarter acre of woods. Her modern glass-and-steel ranch perched on a hill overlooking downtown Portland.

Daniel followed Kate along a slate path through a small flower garden to the front door. A staircase next to the entryway led up to Kate's bedroom. She walked past it and through a living-room and dining-room area. The outer wall was all glass. Daniel glanced quickly at her expensive-looking furnishings. The abstract painting on the living-room wall was an original oil, and so was a smaller French country landscape. The chairs and sofa were covered in leather and the dining-room table was polished oak and looked antique.

Kate walked down another staircase across from

the kitchen to a workroom lit by fluorescent lights. Scattered around the basement room were several workbenches covered with monitors, wires, motherboards, and computer innards. A desk was affixed to one wall and ran its length. Over the desk was a bookshelf filled with computer manuals and books on computer science and other scientific subjects.

"Do you run a computer repair business in your spare time?" Daniel joked.

"Something like that," Kate replied as she removed Kaidanov's hard drive from her jacket pocket. She tossed the jacket over a chair, brushed her hair back, and seated herself at the wall-length desk. In front of her was a removable hard-drive rack into which Kate inserted Kaidanov's hard drive before snapping the rack into one of her computers.

"How are you going to get around the password?" Daniel asked nervously.

"No problem. I've written some software that has yet to meet a password it couldn't break."

"Where did you learn to do that?"

"Cal Tech."

Kate saw Daniel's eyes widen. She laughed.

"I was recruited into the computer crimes unit of the Portland Police Bureau out of college. It seemed a hell of a lot more exciting than sitting on my ass in some high-tech company. Now I do my own thing on the side. It pays well."

Kate turned back to the monitor and started tapping in commands on her keyboard. A minute later she smiled and shook her head.

"It's amazing. They all do this. I would have expected more from a scientist. His password's six numbers—probably his birthday."

"You're in?"

She nodded. "First thing I'm gonna do is make a magnetic copy of this little devil, just in case something goes wrong."

Kate's fingers flashed across the keyboard and lines of text began to appear on the screen.

"This should be finished in a minute."

"How come you quit the cops to go to work for Reed, Briggs?" Daniel asked to make conversation.

"That's none of your business, Ames," Kate snapped before swiveling her chair so her back was to him. Daniel was so surprised by her outburst that he was speechless.

"The copy is complete," she said a minute later, all business now. "Let's bring up Kaidanov's files."

Kate tapped in some commands. "The stuff that's still on here isn't about Insufort. If Kaidanov did have files about his monkeys, they've probably been erased."

"Shit."

"Not to worry. Unless special software was used, the files aren't really deleted. They'll still be on the hard drive. I just happen to have written a voodoo program that will raise the dead," Kate said as she tapped the keyboard. More text appeared on the screen. She stood up and waved Daniel in for a closer look.

"There appears to be a big block of files that was erased on March fourth. Sit down at the keyboard and hit 'page down' until you find what you want and we'll print it out."

Daniel took Kate's chair and stared at the monitor.

"There's a lot of stuff here."

"Give me some key words. I've got search software installed."

Daniel thought for a moment. "Try Insufort, rhesus monkeys, primates."

Kate leaned over his shoulder and tapped in some commands. Her hair brushed against his cheek. She smelled nice.

Suddenly the letter from Kaidanov to George Fournet appeared on the screen.

"That's it," Daniel said excitedly, but his excitement diminished as he scrolled through the files that followed the letter. When he stopped reading he looked grim.

"What's the matter?" Kate asked.

"Remember I didn't believe what I read in Kaidanov's letter?"

Kate nodded.

"Well, the deleted files are the supporting documents for Kaidanov's study. I've just skimmed them, but they appear to confirm his conclusions about the frequency of birth defects in the monkeys that were given Insufort."

"So the results of the study are real?"

Daniel nodded. "Which means I've just made my situation worse."

"But you may have helped get Insufort off the market."

"At the cost of my job."

"Do you really want to help Geller if it's marketing a product that destroys children's lives?"

Daniel didn't answer.

"Here's something else to think about," Kate said. "Who deleted Kaidanov's files and trashed Kaidanov's house? Who wouldn't want Kaidanov's research to be made public?"

Daniel still didn't answer.

"Geller Pharmaceuticals fits that profile."

"I don't know."

"Can you think of anyone else with a motive, Dan?"

"No, you're right. It has to be someone from Geller."

He remembered Patrick Cummings again.

"This is bad."

"And it may be worse. Where do you think Kaidanov is?"

"That's a stretch, Kate. Geller's people are businessmen, not killers." Daniel protested without much conviction.

"Wake up. We're talking about billions of dollars in losses if Geller has to take Insufort off of the market. And don't forget the lawsuit. How much do you think the plaintiffs will recover if Aaron Flynn proves that Geller intentionally marketed a dangerous product? After one successful lawsuit, every woman who's ever had a problem with Insufort will line up at Flynn's door and Geller will be swept away in a tidal wave of litigation."

Kate turned back to the computer and used the search program again while Daniel tried to figure out what he would do next.

"Yes!" Kate exclaimed a moment later as she pointed at the screen.

"Monkeys have to eat. That's an order for a crate of Purina monkey chow and there's an address. That must be the location of the lab."

Kate walked over to another computer. "I can get directions and a map on the Internet."

While she worked Daniel took a closer look at Kaidanov's study. The more he looked the more depressed he felt. Five minutes later Kate showed Daniel a map with directions to the lab from her town house.

"I dug up something else," Kate said. "After I got the map I found the assessment and taxation information on the property. The land is owned by Geller Pharmaceuticals."

10

Twenty minutes later Daniel was driving in the country on a narrow road with Kate beside him. The sun was setting and they had been quiet since leaving the highway. Kate was staring ahead and Daniel chanced an occasional glance at the investigator. Daniel had consulted with Kate at work a few times and she'd impressed him with her intelligence, but he had not been attracted to her. Now he noticed that she was good-looking in a rugged sort of way. Not model beautiful like Susan Webster, but interesting to look at. And she was certainly intriguing. He didn't know any other woman who wrote voodoo software programs and had been a cop.

"This is it," Kate said.

Daniel turned onto a logging road ignoring a "No Trespassing" sign. The shock absorbers on his secondhand Ford were not in the best of shape and Kate swore a lot after they left the pavement. She was registering another complaint when the road curved and a one-story building appeared. Just as they got out of the car the wind shifted and a strange odor made Kate's nostrils flare.

"What's that smell?" Daniel asked.

"It's a little like barbecue," Kate answered.

Pieces of glass covered the ground under a window that had blown out and the front door was charred and had buckled. Daniel peeked through the window cautiously, then jerked his head back. His face was drained of color.

"What is it?" Kate asked.

"There's a body on the floor. There's no skin. It's like a skeleton."

Kate extended a hand toward the door tentatively, worried that it might be hot. She touched her fingers to the metal. It was cold. Kate pushed and the door swung inward. She looked for a light switch and found one, but it didn't work.

"Do you have a flashlight?" Kate asked. Daniel got one from the car and Kate started inside. He tried to follow, but she stopped him.

"This is a crime scene. Just stay here and keep the door open so I can have a little more light."

Daniel propped open the door but did not go any farther. He was secretly grateful not to have to view the body.

Kate walked slowly toward the room she had seen through the window and stood in the doorway. Part of the roof had collapsed and a ray of fading sunlight illuminated a section of the room. Charred wooden beams had crushed a table and what had once been a video monitor. Near the monitor was a rack of plastic test tubes that had been melted by intense heat.

Kate edged around a burn-scarred desk that was tipped on its side. She noticed another roof beam resting on the top of two filing cabinets whose drawers had all been pulled out. The paint on the cabinets had blistered off. The metal was charred and scarred but intact. A breeze gusted through the broken window and drifted down through the gaps in the roof. It blew blackened scraps of paper around the room. The source of the paper was a pile of ashes in the center of the floor that Kate guessed had once been the contents of the filing cabinets.

Kate's eyes stayed on the pile for a moment more before being drawn, almost against her will, to the two bodies sprawled in the center of the room. One was human, its skull charred and its clothes seared to ash. Kate's stomach heaved, but she closed her eyes for a second and kept it together. When she opened her eyes they shifted to the second corpse. For a moment Kate was confused. The body was too small even for a child, unless it was an extremely young one. She braced herself and stepped closer. That's when she saw the tail. Kate backed out of the room.

"What's in there?" Daniel asked when she stepped outside.

"A human corpse and a dead monkey. I'm going to look down the hall."

"We should get out of here," Daniel said nervously.

"In a minute."

"No one's alive. We would have heard them."

"Just give me a second."

The light from the doorway barely reached the end of the hall, so Kate had to use the flashlight. She spot-

ted two open doors but had no idea what was inside.
The smell of burned flesh grew more intense as she
neared the rooms. Kate held her breath and cast the
beam inside. The first room was filled with cages,
each containing a monkey, and every monkey was
pressing against the wire mesh as if it had been trying
to claw through the wire when it died.

11

A uniformed officer was taking Kate and Daniel's statements when an unmarked car parked behind the van from the medical examiner's office. Homicide detective Billie Brewster, a slender black woman in a navy-blue windbreaker and jeans, got out of the car. Her partner, Zeke Forbus, a heavyset white man with thinning brown hair, spotted Kate at the same time she spotted him.

"What's Annie Oakley doing here?" Forbus asked Brewster.

"Shut the fuck up," the black woman snapped angrily at her partner. Then she walked up to Kate and gave her a hug.

"How you doing, Kate?" Brewster asked with genuine concern.

"I'm doing fine, Billie," Kate answered without conviction. "How about you?"

The black woman shot her thumb over her shoulder toward her partner.

"I was doing great until they partnered me up with this redneck."

"Zeke," Kate said with a nod.

"Long time, Kate," Zeke Forbus answered without warmth. Then he turned his back to her and addressed the uniformed officer.

"What have we got here, Ron?"

"Crispy critters," the officer answered with a sly smile. "If you ain't had dinner, I'll get you a bucket of KFM."

"KFM?"

"Kentucky Fried Monkey," the cop answered, cackling at his joke. "We've got a passel of 'em inside."

"Why am I investigating monkey murders?" Forbus asked. "Don't we have animal control for that?"

"One of the crispy critters ain't a monkey, that's why," the uniform answered.

"I understand you called this in," Billie said to Kate. "Why were you out here at night in the middle of nowhere?"

"This is Daniel Ames, an associate at Reed, Briggs, the firm I work for. One of our clients, Geller Pharmaceuticals, is in the middle of a lawsuit over one of its products. Up until last week all of the tests of the product came out favorable to Geller, but a scientist named Sergey Kaidanov reported negative results in a study of rhesus monkeys."

"The same type of monkeys we've got in there?" Billie asked with a nod toward the lab.

"Exactly. Everyone wants to talk to Kaidanov because the study could have a huge impact on the lawsuit, but he disappeared about a week ago."

"Anyone fixed the time of this fire?" Billie asked the uniform.

"Not yet, but it's not recent."

"Go on," Billie told Kate.

"Dan and I went to Kaidanov's house to interview him. He wasn't there, but someone had taken the house apart."

"What's that mean?" Forbus asked.

"Someone searched it and left a mess. We did a little investigating and found an address for the lab. We came out here hoping that we'd find Kaidanov and it looks like we have."

"You think the dead guy is your scientist?"

"I think there's a good chance he is."

"Let's take a look," Billie said to Forbus as she started inside. Kate took a step toward the door, but Forbus held out an arm and barred her way.

"No civilians allowed in the crime scene."

"Oh, for Christ's sake," Billie responded, glaring at her partner.

"Forget it. He's right. I'm not a cop anymore," Kate said, trying to sound unconcerned, but Daniel saw her shoulders slump.

"What was all that about?" Daniel asked as soon as the detectives were out of earshot.

"Old business."

"Thanks for covering for me."

Kate looked puzzled.

"You know, about my breaking into Kaidanov's house."

Kate shrugged. "You didn't think I'd burn you, did you?"

• • •

A deputy medical examiner was videotaping the office while a tech from the crime lab snapped 35mm photographs, then digital shots that could be fed into a computer and E-mailed if necessary. Billie took in the scene from the doorway. A corpse lay on its stomach near the center of the room. The flesh on its side and back had been burned off and the heat from the fire had turned the bones grayish blue in color.

"Any ID?" Billie asked the medical examiner.

"Can't even tell the sex," he answered.

"Is it a murder?"

"Best guess, yes. Deutsch says it's definitely arson," he replied, referring to the arson investigator. "And look at the skull."

The detective took a few steps into the room so she could get a better look at the corpse. The back of the skull had shattered. An exiting bullet or a blunt instrument could have caused the damage. She would leave that determination to the ME.

Billie moved nearer to the corpse and squatted. The floor was concrete, so they might get lucky. From other arson murders she had investigated, Billie knew that fragments of clothing and flesh on the front of the body might have escaped the blaze. Where the body pressed against the floor there would be less oxygen for the fire to feed on and some protection for flesh and fibers.

Billie turned her attention to a tiny corpse a few feet from the human. All of its hair and flesh was gone. Its skull had also been shattered. She stared dispassionately at the monkey for a few minutes then stood up.

"If you want to see more monkeys, there are two rooms filled with them down the hall," the medical examiner said.

"I'll pass," Forbus said, stifling a yawn.

Billie wasn't surprised that the bizarre crime scene bored her partner. He was a good old boy hanging on long enough to collect his pension so he could fish 365 days a year. The only time she'd seen him show any interest in a case was last week when they'd investigated a murder at a strip joint. Billie, on the other hand, was fascinated by anything out of the ordinary, and this crime scene was the most unusual she'd encountered in some time.

Billie wandered down the hall. The doors to the monkey rooms were open and Billie stood quietly, surveying the scene. The monkeys had died hard and she pitied the poor bastards. Death by fire was the worst way to go. She shivered and turned away.

12

The offices of the Oregon State Medical Examiner were on Knott Street in a two-story, red-brick building that had once been a Scandinavian funeral home. Arbor vitae, split-leaf maples, and a variety of other shrubs partially hid a front porch whose overhang was supported by white pillars. Kate parked in the adjacent lot and walked up the front steps to the porch. Billie Brewster was waiting for her in the reception area.

"Thanks for letting me come," Kate said.

"You're lucky Zeke is still in court. There's no way I could swing this if he was here."

"Like I said, thanks."

Kate followed Billie toward the back of the building. When they entered the autopsy room they found Dr. Sally Grace, an assistant ME, and Dr. Jack Forester, a forensic anthropologist, standing on either side of a gurney that had been wheeled between the two stainless-steel autopsy tables that stood on either side of the room. The body from the primate lab lay on top of the gurney. Just before Billie had left the crime scene, the deputy medical examiner and several firefighters wearing latex gloves had used the few scraps of clothing that had escaped destruction to lift up the corpse and place it in a body bag. The area around the body had been searched for skull fragments and they had been taken to the ME's office along with the body. The corpse of the monkey found in the room with the human remains had also been brought to the ME's office, along with skull fragments found near it. The monkey's corpse was lying on a second gurney.

"Hi, Billie," Dr. Grace said. "You're a little late. We're almost done."

"Sorry, I was tied up in court."

"Who's your friend?" the coroner asked.

Billie made the introductions. "Kate's ex-PPB and an investigator with the Reed, Briggs law firm. The dead man may have been an important witness in a civil case her firm is defending. She's been very helpful."

"Well, the more the merrier," Dr. Grace said cheerfully as she turned back to the corpse.

Forester and Grace were wearing blue, water-impermeable gowns, masks, goggles, and heavy, black rubber aprons. Kate and Brewster donned similar outfits before joining them at the gurney.

"We found out some interesting stuff," Forester said. "The monkey is a rhesus. Most research labs use them. We found some blood and flesh on its teeth and we're going to do a DNA match with the other corpse to see if that's where it came from. The surprise is the way the monkey died."

"Which was?"

"Gunshot," Dr. Grace answered. "We found a shell for a forty-five at the crime scene and the skull reconstruction shows an exit wound."

"Is that how this one got it?" Billie asked, motioning toward the remains on the gurney.

"That was my first thought, what with the skull blown out and all," Dr. Grace answered, "but we have a different cause of death with John Doe."

"Then it's a man?" Kate asked.

"We doped that out pretty easily," Dr. Grace said.

"Men's bones are larger because of the greater muscle attachment," Forester said, "so we either had an average- to below-average size male or a woman who pumped iron."

Forester pointed at the skeleton's crotch. All of the flesh had been burned from the bones in this area.

"The human pelvis provides the most reliable means of determining the sex of skeletal remains. The female pelvis is designed to offer optimal space for the birth canal and has a notch in it. A male pelvis is curved. This is definitely the pelvis of a male."

"And there were no ovaries and no uterus," Dr. Grace added with a smile. "That was a big clue."

Billie laughed. "So, how was John Doe killed?"

"First, you need to know that he was dead before he was set on fire," the ME said. "There was still some blood in his heart. It was deep purple instead of red or pink, so I guessed that carbon monoxide was not present. The test confirmed my guess. If he was alive when he burned I would have found carbon monoxide in his blood.

"His airways were also free of soot, which he would have breathed in if he was breathing when the fire started."

Dr. Grace bent over the corpse. "See these marks?" she asked, pointing to several notches that scarred one of the ribs. "They were made by a knife. The rib is in close proximity to the heart. Luckily, he was lying on a concrete floor, so his front was protected to a certain degree and the heart was preserved. It showed stab wounds and there was blood in the left chest and pericardial sac, which you'd expect with a stabbing."

"What about the skull? The monkey was shot. It looks like Doe's skull was blown out the same way," Billie said.

"Come over here," Dr. Grace said as she led the group over to a table covered by a white sheet that stood in front of a stainless-steel counter and sink. On the sheet were the fragments of Doe's skull that had been gathered at the crime scene. They had been painstakingly pieced together.

"Gunshots cause linear fractures that radiate out from the hole caused by the exit or entrance of the bullet. We didn't find linear fractures and you can see that there's no hole formed by the skull fragments.

"If the skull had been fractured by blunt force trauma from a club or baseball bat or something like that, we would have found sections of bone showing a depression from the blow."

"So what's the explanation?" Billie asked.

"The brain is blood-intensive. When the fire heated the blood it generated steam that blew out the back of John Doe's skull."

The detective grimaced.

"Was he stabbed to death at the lab?" Kate asked.

"I can't tell you that. We did find some fibers that were crushed into the fabric of his clothing and survived the fire. I'm having the lab test them. If they're the type of fibers you find in a car trunk, we can guess that he was transported to the lab, but that would only be a guess."

"What about time of death?" Billie asked. "Can you tell how many days he's been dead?"

"I can't do much for you there." Dr. Grace pointed to a sieve resting in a metal pot on one of the autopsy tables. "That's his last meal," she said, indicating pieces of steak, baked potato skin, lettuce, and tomato. "He was killed within an hour of eating, but how long ago I can't say."

Billie turned to Jack Forester. "Can you tell me enough about him for me to match him with a missing person report?"

"Well, we've got the teeth, of course. The guy has had dental work done. Brubaker's out of town," Forester said, referring to Dr. Harry Brubaker, the forensic dentist who was normally present at autopsies. "We'll get these over to him when he comes back from vacation. But he won't be much help until we have someone to whom he can match the dental work."

"Can you tell anything from the teeth?" asked Kate, who had read a few books in Forester's field.

"They do give us some idea of Doe's age," he answered. "We know a person is eighteen or younger if his wisdom teeth have not erupted, so this guy is definitely over eighteen. The degeneration of the skeleton also helps us with his age. Now this is very subjective, but the changes in this guy's spine tell me that he's probably older than thirty.

"The last thing I did was check out the configuration of the pelvis. Where the two halves of the pelvis meet in front is called the pubic symphysis and it wears with age. A guy named T. Wingate Todd made casts of the pelvis of a wide range of corpses whose ages were known. He found that the wear pattern on the pelvis is pretty consistent at different ages."

Forester pointed to a large Tupperware box that was sitting near the door. The lid was open and Billie could see several casts lying in foam.

"I matched the Todd casts to Doe. Taking all the other factors into account, I can give you a very subjective estimate of forty-five to fifty-five for our friend."

Forester pointed to the skeleton's nose.

"Now, I also know that we've got a Caucasian. An Asian's nasal aperture is oval, a black's is wide and short. This guy's is tall and narrow. Ergo, a Caucasian.

"You can also tell from the eye sockets. Whites' are the shape of aviator glasses, blacks' are squarer, and Asians' more rounded."

"Any way to tell eye color?" Billie asked.

Forester shook his head. "Not with a burn victim. The eyes burn out. But I can tell you the guy's height. He was between five eight and five ten. I got that from measuring his tibia and femur," Forester said, pointing to the corpse's shinbone and thighbone, "and comparing them to tables that were developed by measuring the lengths of the long bones of American casualties from the Second World War and the Korean War."

"So we've probably got a white male, five eight to five ten, of average build, and forty-five to fifty-five years of age," Billie summarized.

"Yup," Forester answered. "Get a possible and his dental records and Brubaker can give you a positive ID."

13

After dropping Kate at her house, Daniel drove home and fell into bed. Visions of a flaming laboratory jammed with screaming monkeys and deformed children haunted his dreams and he jerked awake more than once during the night. When he arrived at work the next morning, Daniel was pale and there were dark circles under his bloodshot eyes. He checked his voice mail and found a message from Renee Gilchrist telling him that he was expected in Arthur Briggs's office at eleven. This is it, Daniel thought. He slumped in his chair and looked around his office. A lump formed in his throat. He had worked so hard to get here and everything he'd earned was going to be snatched away because of a one-page letter.

At 10:54, Daniel pushed himself to his feet, checked his tie, and walked the last mile to Arthur Briggs's office. Renee announced Daniel's presence, then flashed him a sympathetic smile.

"Go on in. And good luck."

"Thanks, Renee."

Daniel straightened his shoulders and walked into the lion's den, an incredible corner office that was obviously the creation of an expensive interior decorator. With diplomas from Duke University and the University of Chicago law school, and framed tributes to its occupant, the room was a testament to the greatness of Arthur Briggs.

"Have a seat, Ames," he said without making eye contact.

The senior partner was reading a letter and he paid no attention to Daniel for a full minute. When Briggs finally signed his name and placed the letter in his outbox, he looked across his desk at the young associate with unforgiving eyes.

"Do you have any idea how much damage your incompetence has caused?"

Daniel knew that no answer was expected and he gave none.

"The partners met yesterday to discuss your situation," Briggs continued. "It has been decided that you should no longer work for this firm."

Though he had been expecting this, the words still stunned Daniel.

"You will be paid six months' salary and you can keep your health insurance for a year. That's very generous considering that your blunder could cost one of our best clients billions of dollars."

He'd been fired. At first Daniel felt shame, then his shame turned to anger and he stiffened.

"This is a crock and you know it, Mr. Briggs." His sharp words startled Daniel as much as they amazed

Briggs. "You're firing me because you need a scape-goat now that Aaron Flynn knows about the Kaidanov study. But finding out about that study might help Reed, Briggs avoid aiding and abetting a client this firm should stop representing."

Briggs leaned back in his chair and made a steeple of his fingers but said nothing. Daniel pushed on.

"I think Geller Pharmaceuticals is covering up Kaidanov's results. Did you know that the police are investigating an arson fire at a primate lab located on land owned by Geller? It's where Kaidanov conducted his study. All of his monkeys are dead. And it looks like Kaidanov is dead, too—murdered. Quite a coincidence, wouldn't you say?"

Daniel paused, but Briggs just continued to stare at him as if he were some mildly interesting insect. Briggs's lack of reaction at hearing Geller linked to murder and arson surprised Daniel. But Briggs had made a fortune by perfecting a poker face, so Daniel forged on.

"Kaidanov has been missing for over a week. His home has been searched." Daniel thought he saw Briggs twitch. "Mr. Briggs, I've examined Dr. Kaidanov's hard drive. Someone tried to delete the primate study, but I've seen it." Now he definitely had Briggs's attention. "The results support the conclusions in Kaidanov's letter. I think there's a good possibility that Insufort is very dangerous and that someone connected to Geller tried to cover up Kaidanov's report."

"How do you know that Dr. Kaidanov's home was searched?"

Daniel swallowed hard. "I went over there," he said, suddenly remembering that searching the house and taking the hard drive were felonies.

"Is that where you examined Dr. Kaidanov's hard drive?"

Daniel felt like a laser beam had pierced him and he appreciated the terror witnesses experienced during one of Briggs's infamous cross-examinations.

"I'd rather not say," he answered.

"Is that right."

Daniel did not answer.

"Taking the Fifth, are we, Ames?" A terrible smile creased Briggs's lips. Daniel felt trapped. "Obviously I can't force you to answer my questions, but the police can. What do you think will happen if they discover that someone has stolen the hard drive from Dr. Kaidanov's home computer and I tell them that you've confessed to me that you were at his house and examined the hard drive?"

"I . . . I was acting on behalf of our client."

Even as he said the words Daniel knew that the excuse sounded pathetic.

"It's good that you've remembered that there is an attorney / client relationship between you and Geller, even though you no longer work for this firm. If you know that, then you know that any information about Insufort on Dr. Kaidanov's hard drive is the property of our client."

Briggs's smile disappeared. "I want the hard drive by five o'clock today, Ames."

"Mr. Briggs . . ."

"If it's not here by five, you will lose your health

benefits, your severance pay, and you will be arrested.
Is that clear?"

"What are you planning to do about Insufort?"

"My plans are none of your business since you no
longer work for this firm."

"But Insufort is hurting babies. Someone at Geller
may have committed murder to cover up the truth.
The firm could be an accessory to—"

Briggs stood suddenly. "This meeting is over," he
said, pointing toward the door. "Get out!"

Daniel hesitated, then walked to the door. As he
crossed the room anger built in the pit of his stomach.
He opened the door halfway, then turned and faced
Briggs one more time.

"I've been scared and depressed about losing this
job ever since the deposition, because working for
Reed, Briggs really meant something to me. But
maybe this is for the best. I don't think I want to
work for a firm that would cover up the crimes
Geller is committing. We're talking about little children, Mr. Briggs. I don't know how you can look in
the mirror."

"You listen to me," Briggs shouted. "If you breathe
one word of what you've told me to anyone, you'll be
sued for slander and you will go to jail. How many
people are going to hire a destitute, disbarred lawyer
with a felony conviction? Now get the hell out!"

It wasn't until Daniel slammed the door to Briggs's
office that he saw that he'd had an audience. Renee
Gilchrist and a plain, middle-aged woman Daniel recognized as Dr. April Fairweather were both staring,
openmouthed. Daniel's anger turned to embarrass-

ment. He mumbled an apology and rushed toward his office.

Daniel was almost there when it dawned on him that Kate had the hard drive. He was about to go to her office when he saw a security guard standing in front of his door. He hurried the rest of the way. As soon as the guard spotted Daniel, he blocked the entrance.

"I work here," Daniel said. "What's going on?"

"I'm sorry, Mr. Ames," the guard said firmly but politely, "but you can't go in until we're through."

Daniel looked over the guard's shoulder. A second guard was emptying his files into a box.

"What about my things, my personal items like my diplomas?"

"You can have them as soon as we're through." The guard held out his hand. "I'll need your keys."

Daniel was thoroughly humiliated. He wanted to fight, to protest, to scream that he had rights, but he knew that there was nothing he could do, so he meekly handed over his office keys.

"How much longer will this take? I'd like to get out of here."

"We'll be done soon," the guard answered.

A crowd was starting to gather. Joe Molinari placed his hand on Daniel's shoulder.

"What's going on, Ames?"

"Briggs sacked me."

"Ah, shit."

"It wasn't a surprise. I've seen this coming since the deposition."

"Is there anything I can do?" Joe asked.

"Thanks, but it's over. Briggs needed a scapegoat and I'm it."

Molinari squeezed Daniel's shoulder supportively.

"Look, I know people. I'm going to ask around. Maybe I can line up something for you."

"I appreciate the offer, but who's going to hire me? What kind of letter of recommendation do you think Briggs is going to write?"

"Don't think like that. Briggs doesn't control every law firm in Portland. You're good, amigo. Any firm would be lucky to get you."

"I don't know if I want to keep practicing law, Joe."

"Don't be a defeatist asshole. This is like riding a polo pony. When you get thrown you don't just lie on the ground feeling sorry for yourself. You get your ass back in the saddle and play on. I'll give you a day to mope, then we're going to figure out how to get you back working horrible hours and taking abuse from intellectual inferiors."

Daniel couldn't help smiling. Then he remembered Kate.

"Can I use your phone? They won't let me into my office."

"Sure."

"Thanks, Joe. For everything."

"Aw shucks, you're making me blush."

Daniel shook his head. "You're still a jerk."

Joe laughed and they started walking toward Molinari's office. When they reached his door, Daniel turned toward his friend.

"This is a private call, okay?"

"Say no more."

Daniel closed the door and dialed Kate's extension. Joe stood guard outside.

"It's Daniel," he said as soon as she picked up. "Are you alone?"

"Yeah, why?"

"Briggs fired me."

"Oh, Daniel. I'm so sorry."

"I can't say I didn't expect it."

"You should fight this."

"I'm not sure I'd want my job back even if I could get it. Really, being fired might have been the best thing."

"How can you say that?"

"I told Briggs that Geller might be covering up the fact that Insufort causes birth defects in little children. He threatened to have me arrested, to sue me. He wasn't the least bit concerned that Geller is ruining the lives of all those kids and their parents. So I guess the question is, would I have accepted Reed, Briggs's job offer if I knew I'd be using my legal education to protect a company that destroys lives for profit?

"But that's not why I called. I wasn't thinking straight after Briggs told me I was fired and I told him that I had Kaidanov's hard drive. He wants it by five today or he's going after me."

"You didn't . . . ?"

"No. I didn't mention you. He has no idea that you have it and I want to make certain that he doesn't find out. Can you get it to me? Briggs says he'll have me arrested if I don't give it to him and I'm in enough trouble already. And we have a copy, anyway."

"What are you going to do with the information?"

"I don't know, Kate, and I'm too mixed up now to make decisions."

"I'll get you the hard drive before one."

"Thanks."

There was dead air for a moment. Then Kate said, "You're a good person, Dan, and good people land on their feet. You'll come out of this okay."

Daniel appreciated the sentiment, but he wasn't sure that was the way things happened in the real world.

14

As soon as she left the medical examiner's office, Billie Brewster drove west along the Sunset Highway. Twenty minutes later the detective took one of the Hillsboro exits and found herself in open country where rolling green hills and a sweeping blue sky formed a backdrop for the three interconnected, black-glass-and-polished-granite buildings in the Geller Pharmaceuticals complex.

The main attraction in Building A was an atrium with a three-story waterfall that started just under a tinted-glass roof and occupied one corner of the spacious lobby. Billie learned the location of Kurt Schroeder's office at reception and walked up a staircase near the atrium that led to the second floor. A glass-encased sky bridge connected the main building to Building B, which housed research and development.

Moments after Billie flashed her badge at Schroeder's secretary she found herself seated across from Geller's chief medical adviser.

"Dr. Schroeder, I'm Detective Brewster with Portland homicide."

"Homicide?" Schroeder said nervously.

"Yesterday evening I was at a building that was destroyed in an arson fire. There were approximately twenty dead rhesus monkeys inside. They were set on fire in their cages."

"That's terrible, but what does this have to do with me or Geller Pharmaceuticals?"

"The records show that Geller owns the property where the building is located. We think it's a primate lab."

Schroeder's brow furrowed. "All of our research is conducted in this building. We do own property apart from this campus for expansion, but it's undeveloped. If you found a lab, it wasn't Geller's."

"A body was discovered in the lab, Dr. Schroeder. The corpse was badly burned, but we can tell it's a forty-five- to fifty-five-year-old white male, and we think it might be Dr. Sergey Kaidanov."

"Kaidanov! My God! He disappeared more than a week ago. We've been looking for him. This is terrible."

"Was Dr. Kaidanov involved in primate research?"

"That's where the problem comes in. The plaintiffs in a lawsuit we're defending produced what purports to be a letter from Kaidanov in which he claims to be conducting a primate study for our company, but we have no record of his being assigned to conduct such a study."

"A lawyer from the Reed, Briggs firm told me

about that. That's where we got the idea that the victim might be Kaidanov."

Schroeder shivered. "God, I hope not."

"You can help with the identification by sending me Dr. Kaidanov's personnel file. His dental records would be very useful."

"I'll do what I can," he answered, apparently shaken by what he had learned.

Brewster handed Schroeder a paper with the location of the destroyed building.

"Can you check to see if your company has a lab on the property?"

"Certainly. I should have an answer for you in a day or so."

Brewster stood. "Thank you for your cooperation, Dr. Schroeder."

"Of course." He paused. "I hope you're wrong about Kaidanov."

"I hope so, too."

There were several phone messages waiting for Billie when she got back to the Justice Center. Halfway down the pile was a message from missing persons. Even though she was pretty certain of the identity of the body at the lab, Brewster had phoned them from the medical examiner's office and asked for a list of men who matched the description that Forester had given her. She dialed the extension for missing persons.

"Hey, Billie," Detective Aaron Davies said, "I got a

live one for you. A guy named Gene Arnold. He's a lawyer from Arizona. His partner, Benjamin Kellogg, reported him missing right around the time you're interested in. He disappeared while staying at the Benson Hotel. I'll give you Kellogg's number."

Billie dialed the Arizona number. The receptionist at the firm connected her with Benjamin Kellogg and she identified herself.

"Have you found Gene?" Kellogg asked anxiously.

"No, but I wanted to get some information from you so I can follow up on your report. Can you tell me why you think Mr. Arnold is missing?"

"I know he's missing and I'm certain that something is wrong. We're all very worried about him."

"Why is that?"

"He went to New York on business, Sunday, February twenty-seventh. He was supposed to come straight back. I had his flight number and everything, but he wasn't on the plane. Then he called from Portland on Wednesday, March first. He asked for me, but I was in court, so he spoke with Maria Suarez, our secretary."

"You weren't expecting him to go to Oregon?"

"No. I've worked with Gene for six years, Maria even longer. We can't remember him ever mentioning any contacts, business or social, in Oregon."

"Okay, what did he tell Ms. Suarez?"

"He wanted me to know that he would be away for a few days on personal business. Maria said he asked about his mail and messages, and then he gave her his room number at the Benson Hotel and said he'd keep in touch. The hotel called on Tuesday, March seventh

and said that Gene had reserved the room through
Monday but had not checked out. They wanted to
know if he still wanted it. I had no idea. The security
chief said that he was putting Gene's belongings in
storage. That's when I got scared that something was
wrong and I contacted your missing persons bureau."

"And no one's heard from him since?"

"Not a word."

"Is Mr. Arnold married?"

"He's a widower. His wife died about a year before
I started working here."

"Do you have a photograph of Mr. Arnold that
you could send me?"

"I can find one."

"Good. I also need the name and phone number of
Mr. Arnold's dentist."

Billie heard an intake of breath.

"You think he's dead?"

"I have no reason to believe that."

"You're homicide, right?"

Billie did not want to alarm Arnold's partner, but it
was obvious that he was already upset.

"Yes."

"I'm not naive, Detective. I've handled some criminal cases. I know why a homicide detective needs dental records. You've got an unidentified body that
might be Gene."

"I do have a body, but I'm pretty certain I know
who it is."

"Then why call me?"

"I've been known to make mistakes. But I don't
think I have in this case."

There was dead air for a moment. Finally Kellogg spoke.

"Gene's dentist is Ralph Hughes. If you give me your address I'll have him send you Gene's dental records."

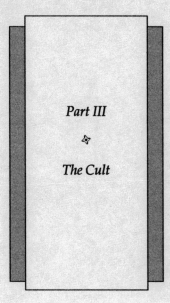

Part III

The Cult

15

After Daniel traded the hard drive from Kaidanov's computer for a cardboard box with his personal belongings, he left his former employer's domain with hunched shoulders and a crimson face. Even though he had no reason to be ashamed, he was grateful that no one he knew had been in the waiting room or the elevator.

That evening, Daniel's phone rang several times. A few happy-hour companions had made condolence calls and promised to keep in touch. Joe Molinari invited him out to a bar. When Daniel said he was not in the mood to party Joe urged him to keep the faith. Daniel would not have minded talking to Kate Ross, but she did not call.

Daniel slept late on Saturday then treated himself to an extravagant lunch at Wildwood. He knew it was foolish to spend so much money when he was heavily in debt with no prospects for employment and almost no savings, but the gesture felt important: he'd been fired, but not defeated. After lunch, Daniel wandered around the neighborhood, but it was hard being in a crowd of happy people. He envied them too much. The army had given him his first taste of self-confidence and the inkling of an idea that he could have a future. His college diploma was more than a piece of paper. It was proof that he could be somebody. The job with Reed, Briggs was beyond his wildest dreams. Now the job was gone, and with it his reputation. Daniel believed that he would always be known as the associate whose incompetence destroyed Geller Pharmaceuticals.

Sunday was hard to take. Since Reed, Briggs had hired him Daniel had spent most of his time, even weekends, in the office or thinking about things that he had to do at the office. Now there was nothing to dwell on except his failure. He killed the day by going for a long run and watching football. Shortly after six, he was preparing dinner when the telephone rang. The news was on but Daniel was not paying much attention to it.

"Dan, it's Kate."

"Oh, hi," Daniel answered, involuntarily breaking into a smile.

"Sorry I didn't call yesterday. I was in Astoria investigating an oil spill the coast guard claims is from a ship one of our clients insures. Did everything go okay after I saw you?"

"I gave the hard drive back and the cops didn't break in my door, so I guess so."

"Well, cheer up. I may have something for you. Natalie Tasman, one of the paralegals at Jaffe, Katz,

Lehane and Brindisi, is a friend. She told me that they're going to be looking for an associate soon, so I talked to Amanda Jaffe about you. You should give them a call tomorrow."

"Isn't Amanda Jaffe the lawyer who represented that doctor who was charged with those serial murders?"

"The same. The firm is small—there are only seven or eight lawyers—but everyone is top-notch. They practice criminal defense and plaintiff's litigation. I think you'll fit in over there a hell of a lot better than you fit in at Reed, Briggs."

"Thanks, Kate. You're a good friend."

"You're a good lawyer."

Daniel was about to reply when something on the television caught his eye.

"Hold on, Kate. There's something on TV about the fire."

On the screen, a reporter from one of the local television stations was standing in front of the burned-out shell of the primate lab.

"There is a bizarre twist in the multimillion-dollar litigation against Geller Pharmaceuticals, manufacturer of the pregnancy drug Insufort," the reporter said.

"Kate, turn on Channel Four, quick."

"Late yesterday," the reporter continued, "this station received copies of a study alleged to have been made on rhesus monkeys that were burned to death in the building behind me. According to the study, a significant percentage of the monkeys that were given Insufort during pregnancy gave birth to babies with birth defects.

"Eyewitness News has learned that Dr. Sergey Kaidanov, the scientist alleged to have authored the study and an employee of Geller Pharmaceuticals, has disappeared. We have also learned that the remains of an unidentified male were found in this building, which was destroyed by arson. According to the police, the man was murdered."

The picture changed and Aaron Flynn's face appeared on the screen.

"Earlier today, reporter Angela Graham talked with Aaron Flynn, the lead counsel for the plaintiffs in the Insufort litigation."

"Mr. Flynn, what is your reaction to this new information about Insufort?"

"Angela, I haven't had time to digest it all. I did learn recently that Dr. Kaidanov conducted this study, but I have not seen the study, so I can't comment. But the news that Dr. Kaidanov may have been murdered is shocking and raises the possibility of a cover-up.

"I must say that I am stunned by the possibility that evidence of the horrible effects of Insufort may have been intentionally destroyed."

The reporters moved to another story.

"Did you see that?" Daniel asked Kate.

"Yeah, and I just switched channels. The story was on the national news on Channel Six, too. Dan, I've got to ask: Did you leak the story?"

"Of course not. Briggs said he'd have me arrested if I told anyone what was on the hard drive." Daniel paused as what he'd just said sank in. "Oh, man. If Briggs thinks I leaked the study I'm screwed."

Kate and Daniel were silent for a moment. Then Kate asked the question they both wanted to ask.

"If you didn't tell the media and I didn't, who did?"

16

Billie Brewster sneaked a peek at the clock over the guard's station at the end of the visitors' room at the state penitentiary. Her brother noticed and he flashed her a tolerant smile.

"You got to go, sis?"

Billie was embarrassed at being caught. She'd never been able to put one over on Sherman.

"Duty calls, little brother."

"That's okay. Ain't no one wants to stay here longer than they have to."

"You remember that," Billie said as she squeezed his hand.

"You don't have to worry about me. I'm bein' good."

They stood and he hugged her tight. Billie hugged him back. She hated visiting her brother in this place, but she hated leaving him more. Every time the iron doors clanged shut behind her, she left a piece of her heart in the prison.

"Go on now," Sherman told her, flashing an innocent, toothy smile that almost made her forget that he was kept here by a trap of his own design.

Outside, a sleeting rain was falling, cold and unpleasant, like Billie's mood. As she walked along the sidewalk toward the prison parking lot, the detective hunched her shoulders. Her visits to her brother were always hard on her. After their father walked out, their mother had been forced to work two jobs. Billie was the only one around to raise Sherman. She was sixteen—still a child herself—but she'd tried the best she could to keep her brother straight. Her mother had told her repeatedly that it was not her fault that Sherman was at the penitentiary. She never really believed it.

This was Sherman's third fall, but his first since she'd joined the police force. He used to get nervous when she visited, afraid that someone would find out his sister was a cop. A high-school friend who was a guard at the penitentiary kept her up-to-date on Sherman. She knew he was in a gang. Since he'd joined and made a rep he'd loosened up. Billie hated what he was doing, but she wanted him safe. Life was loaded with trade-offs.

Billie kept herself from thinking about her brother on the trip back to Portland by listening to loud music and reviewing her cases. When she passed the Wilsonville exit, she phoned in for messages and was glad there was one from Dr. Brubaker, the forensic dentist. The murder at the lab was her most interesting case.

She got Brubaker on her cell phone. "Hi, Harry, what have you got for me?"

"An identification on the body at the primate lab."

"Don't keep me in suspense."

"It's the lawyer from Arizona."

"You're kidding."

"There's no question about it. The dental records of Gene Arnold match perfectly."

Completed in 1912, the thirteen-story Benson Hotel was listed in the National Register of Historic Places and was the hotel where presidents stayed when they visited Portland. Billie entered a luxurious lobby paneled in rich walnut, floored with Italian marble and lit by several crystal chandeliers, and found Kate waiting for her.

"Thanks for letting me tag along," Kate said as they headed for the reception desk.

"You've been straight with me about your information. It's the least I can do."

"I can't believe the body wasn't Kaidanov."

"I'd have lost a bundle myself if I was a betting woman."

Billie flashed her badge at a bright-eyed, Japanese woman and asked for Antonio Sedgwick, the hotel's chief of security. The woman went through a door behind the desk and returned a few minutes later with a muscular African-American in a conservative business suit. When the ex-Seattle cop spotted the homicide detective he flashed a big grin.

"Hey, Billie, haven't seen you in a while. You over here to scam a free lunch?"

"No such luck," Billie answered with a smile.

"Who's your friend?" Sedgwick asked.

"Kate Ross. She's an investigator with the Reed, Briggs firm."

Billie turned to Kate and pointed at the security chief. "You have my permission to shoot this man if he comes on to you. He's a notorious womanizer."

Sedgwick laughed.

"I ain't lyin'," Billie said with mock seriousness. "Shoot to kill."

"Besides ruining my love life, what brings you to the Benson?"

"One of your guests checked in on February twenty-ninth and disappeared by March seventh. Now he's turned up dead and I'd like to see his belongings."

Sedgwick snapped his fingers. "The guy from Arizona."

Billie nodded. "His name was Gene Arnold. What do you remember about him?"

"I never met him. He didn't check out on time, so we sent a bellman up to his room. There was a 'Do Not Disturb' sign on the door. We usually wait when we see that. At the end of the day I let myself in. It looked like he planned on coming back. All his stuff was there: toiletries on the sink, clothes hung up in the closet and neatly placed in the drawers. If I remember, there was even a book open on the end table, American history or something.

"We called his contact number to see if he was going to stay another day. They didn't know anything about it. We didn't need the room right away, so I left everything there for one more day. Then I had his stuff packed up and put it in the checkroom. If you want to take it I'll need a court order, but I can let you see it."

"That'll be fine for now."

The checkroom was to the right of the concierge desk. It was a narrow room with a high vaulted ceiling decorated with ornate molding that had been the hotel's original entrance. Its glory had faded over the years. Half the floor was marble but the other half was plywood and there were exposed pipes to the right of the door. Two bare sixty-watt bulbs produced the light that had once been provided by a crystal chandelier.

Arnold's valise was on a shelf to the left of the door. Sedgwick carried it to a small, unobstructed area near the front of the checkroom and opened it. Billie took out each item, inspected it, then placed it in a neat pile while Kate watched. When she was done she replaced the items carefully.

"Suits are over here," Sedgwick said, pointing at two suits on a pole that spanned the room.

Billie's inspection of the first suit revealed nothing, but she found a slip of paper written on the stationery of a SoHo art gallery in the inside pocket of the second suit jacket. It contained a name, Claude Bernier, a street address, and a Manhattan phone number. Billie and Kate wrote the information in their notebooks and Billie replaced the paper in the suit pocket.

"Mr. Bernier?"

"Yes."

"My name is Billie Brewster," the detective said as Kate listened on an extension in Sedgwick's office. "I'm with the Portland Police Bureau."

"Maine?"

"Oregon."

"I haven't been there for a while. What's this about?"

"I'm investigating a homicide and your name came up."

"You're kidding?"

"Do you know Gene Arnold, an attorney from Arizona? He was in New York in late February."

"Late February?" Bernier sounded puzzled. "Wait a minute. Is this guy bald, maybe forty-five? Glasses?"

"That's him," Billie answered after consulting the photograph that Benjamin Kellogg had sent her.

"Okay, now I've got him. Arnold, yeah. He was at my apartment. You say he was murdered?"

"Yes, sir. What can you tell me about the meeting?"

"Arnold bought one of my photographs from the Pitzer-Kraft Gallery. Fran works there. She called and told me that Arnold almost fainted while he was looking at it. She thought he was having a heart attack. Then he insisted on seeing me."

"What did he want?"

"He wanted to know everything about the couple in the photograph. That was the subject of the show, couples. This one was from Portland."

"What did you tell him?"

"Nothing much. They're all candid shots. I'd see a couple and snap them without them knowing I'd done it. I never got any names."

"Can you describe the couple in the shot that Arnold purchased?"

"It was a man and woman walking across that big open square you've got in the middle of the city."

"Pioneer Square?"

"That's it."

"Anything else you can tell me about them?"

"Arnold was pretty upset about that picture. He got more upset when I couldn't help him."

"Can you send me a print?"

"I think so. I'll have to look for the negative. I moved recently and everything's still a mess."

"Try hard, Mr. Bernier. That picture may show the person who murdered Gene Arnold."

17

"Brock wanted you to know that everyone is in the conference room," Renee Gilchrist said.

Arthur Briggs's mouth was set in a grim line and Renee noticed dark circles under his eyes. "Tell Brock I'll be right down," he said.

One of the lines on his phone rang. Renee headed for the phone, but Briggs waved her away.

"Briggs," the senior partner answered absently. Then he straightened up. "Put him through."

Briggs turned to Renee. "I want my calls held. Tell Newbauer and the others to go ahead without me. Shut the door on your way out."

Renee crossed the room as Briggs turned back to the phone.

"Dr. Kaidanov, there are a lot of people who are very anxious to speak with you," she heard Briggs say as she pulled the door shut.

● ● ●

Thirty minutes later Arthur Briggs entered a small conference room. Brock Newbauer and Susan Webster were seated on one side of a polished oak table. Facing them were Isaac Geller, the chairman of the board of Geller Pharmaceuticals, and Byron McFall, the company's president.

Geller was a medical-school dropout in his late forties who had made a fortune in commercial real estate when he met McFall, a powerfully built man ten years his junior, at a golf resort. The men hit it off immediately. By the time Geller was ready to return to Chicago and McFall to his investment firm in Seattle, they had agreed to talk about a possible investment by Geller in a financially troubled Oregon pharmaceutical company that was doing some interesting research. Both men had made millions as the result of their chance meeting.

"How bad is this thing, Arthur?" Geller asked as Briggs took his place at the head of the table.

"What's your take, Brock?" Briggs asked, addressing his junior partner.

Newbauer was surprised to be called on since Briggs was rarely interested in his opinion.

"Well, we've all heard the news. They're saying that man was set on fire and the monkeys, too," Newbauer said, stumbling. "It's terrible publicity. *The Oregonian* had an editorial this morning." Newbauer glanced across the table at Geller and McFall, then looked away quickly. "They're implying that the company had something to do with the murder."

"Which is utter hogwash," McFall said. "I want you to look into suing that rag for libel. And I want to find out who leaked that report to the press."

"I'm already on top of it, Byron," Briggs assured the irate executive. "What should we advise Geller Pharmaceuticals to do about the lawsuit, Brock?"

"I don't think we have a choice. Susan tells me there's a good chance that Judge Norris will let the Kaidanov letter in, and now it looks like Flynn has a copy of the study, too. If a jury hears evidence about the murder and the dead monkeys . . ." He shook his head despondently. "I think we have to seriously consider making a settlement offer."

Briggs nodded in a manner that made it appear that he valued Newbauer's advice before focusing his attention on Susan Webster.

"What do you think we should do?" he asked.

"I agree with Brock," Susan said firmly. "My research leads me to believe that Judge Norris will let Flynn use the Kaidanov documents at trial. If he convinces a jury that Geller Pharmaceuticals covered up Kaidanov's study, we'll lose the case and the damages will be astronomical. If Flynn convinces the jury that someone connected with Geller murdered Kaidanov and set fire to those monkeys, we'll need the world's biggest computer to figure the damages."

"This is bullshit, Arthur," McFall exploded. "I've talked with all our top people. No one knows anything about that damn lab or those fucking monkeys."

"Susan isn't suggesting you do. She's talking about a hypothetical situation so we can try to decide our best course of action."

"Which is?" Geller asked.

"I'd rather not say just yet," Briggs replied.

"Well, I insist that you do," McFall ordered angrily. "I'm the president of a company that pays your firm several million dollars a year. This is the biggest challenge Geller Pharmaceuticals has ever faced and we need your advice."

During McFall's tirade, Isaac Geller had been coolly appraising his corporate counsel. Briggs was calm and composed, completely unruffled by a verbal assault under which Geller had seen many strong men and women wilt.

"You're onto something, aren't you, Arthur?"

Briggs smiled noncommittally.

Geller turned to McFall. "Maybe we shouldn't press Arthur," Geller suggested quietly. "His representation has always been top-notch. I'm certain that there must be something very important afoot if he is playing his cards so close to the vest."

"I still don't appreciate our attorney keeping secrets from us, Isaac," McFall insisted to save face.

"I respect Arthur's judgment."

"Very well," McFall grumbled, "but this better be good."

Briggs stood. "Thank you, gentlemen. I'll be in contact shortly, and I don't think you'll be disappointed."

18

As soon as he got up, Daniel called Amanda Jaffe's office, but Amanda was in Washington County for three days handling pretrial motions in a murder case. After breakfast, Daniel went downtown and spent the day job hunting. He returned to his apartment, tired and discouraged, to find the light on his answering machine blinking. He pressed the play button, hoping that the caller was Kate or Amanda Jaffe.

"Ames, this is Arthur Briggs. I was wrong about you and I need your help. There's been a development in the Insufort case and you are the only one I can trust. Meet me tonight at eight."

The rest of the message told him how to get to a country cottage near the Columbia Gorge. Daniel's first reaction was that the message was a hoax engineered by Joe Molinari, but Daniel had heard Briggs's voice enough to know that it was his ex-boss on the phone. Only the message did not make sense. Briggs hated him, and even if he didn't, why would he need his help? He had partners, associates, and investigators galore. Daniel was a disgraced, disgruntled ex-employee—not exactly the person Briggs would be expected to call in an emergency. And why would Briggs want to meet miles out of town instead of in his office?

Daniel decided that there was only one way to discover if the call was genuine. He dialed Briggs's office.

"Renee, it's Daniel Ames."

"Oh, Daniel, I am so sorry. Are you okay?"

"I'm fine, thanks. Is Mr. Briggs in?"

"No. He's gone for the day. He'll be here in the morning."

Daniel thought for a moment.

"Mr. Briggs left a message on my answering machine. He said there was a new development in the Insufort case. He wanted to talk to me about it tonight. I'm supposed to meet him at a cottage off I-84 on the Columbia Gorge. Do you have any idea why he wants to see me or why he wants me to meet him at this cottage instead of his office?"

"No, but Arthur was excited about something today. This is a good sign, isn't it? Maybe he's going to rehire you."

"Yeah, maybe," Daniel answered thoughtfully. "Look, if Mr. Briggs phones in would you ask him to call me?"

"Sure."

"Thanks."

Daniel hung up and called Kate, but she was not in. He leaned back and stared at the wall. What would he do if Briggs offered him his job back? He'd convinced himself that he didn't want to work at the firm anymore, but did he really mean it? Working for Reed, Briggs had been his dream job.

Daniel made a decision. He wasn't certain that he wanted his job back, but he did want to hear what Arthur Briggs had to say. And he was very curious about the new development in the Insufort case that Briggs had mentioned. Maybe he had convinced Briggs that there was something wrong with the drug and Briggs was now on his side. The only way to find out was to meet with the man who had just fired him.

19

Dr. Sergey Kaidanov huddled like a hunted animal in a copse of cottonwoods and watched the cottage as daylight faded. Kaidanov had not had a decent sleep since fleeing from the lab. A damp, uncombed beard covered the lower half of his face and his clothes looked a size too big on his emaciated frame. The woods were damp and the cruel wind blowing off the Gorge chilled the fugitive, but running for his life had inured Kaidanov to hardship and made him cunning and cautious. He was also desperate.

The newspapers said that someone had died in the lab. If it hadn't been for the monkey, the police would have found two bodies. Then there was his escape in Las Vegas. His car had been parked in the shadows of the motel lot. He had been about to start it when another car driven by the same person who'd attacked him in the lab pulled into the space in front of his motel room. Kaidanov had watched until his pursuer was inside. He had only been a few blocks from the motel when he figured out that he must have been

traced through his credit card. It took another moment to remember that he'd told the whore that he
was taking an early flight. Kaidanov had skipped his
flight and used his credit cards sparingly since Vegas,
living on fast food and sleeping in his car. He smelled
and he was unshaven, but he was still alive. After
tonight, he might even be safe.

Headlights lit up the cottage. Moments later a
Mercedes parked out front. Kaidanov checked his
watch. It was 7:29. Arthur Briggs had arranged to
meet him at 7:30 so they would have time to talk before Briggs's associate arrived.

The lights went on in the cottage. Kaidanov scurried across the road. He'd checked out the cottage
earlier and he knew that there was a back door. He
made a wide circle around the house. There was a
farm next to the cottage, but the land directly behind
the house was heavily wooded. Kaidanov raced from
the cover of a stand of trees and knocked on the back
door. A moment later Arthur Briggs let him into a
small kitchen.

"Dr. Kaidanov?" he asked.

The scientist nodded. "Do you have something to
eat?" he asked. "I haven't had any food since breakfast."

"Certainly. There's not much, but I can make you a
sandwich."

"Anything. A drink would help."

Briggs motioned toward a kitchen table and started
toward the refrigerator. As he passed the kitchen door
Briggs saw someone enter the front room. He
stopped, puzzled, then walked out of the kitchen.

Kaidanov stood, tense as a startled deer. He heard Briggs say, "What are you doing here?" He was out of the back door before Briggs screamed, "Run!" and shots rang out.

Kaidanov plunged into the woods as the kitchen door slammed open. He had planned his escape route earlier and he never slowed. He could hear branches snap and the underbrush crackle behind him. He made a sharp turn and circled back toward his car, pausing briefly before racing on to make sure his pursuer kept going straight ahead. Through a gap in the trees, Kaidanov saw someone of average height dressed in a black windbreaker. A hood concealed the killer's face, but there was no doubt in the Russian's mind that this was the same person who tried to kill him at the lab.

Kaidanov had parked his car half a mile up a side road where it could not be seen from the street that ran in front of the cottage and could not be discovered without a thorough search. The engine started right away. Kaidanov left the headlights off until he was on the highway headed east. He had no idea where he was going. All he cared about was that he was still breathing.

20

I-84 runs along the Columbia Gorge and is one of the most scenic highways in the United States, but Daniel could barely see the magnificent vista created by the Columbia River and the high cliffs on either side of it because the sun had nearly set. Twenty minutes after leaving the city, he took an off-ramp and found himself on a two-lane road in sparsely populated countryside. After he had traveled two miles, he began to look for Starlight Road. The high beams of a speeding car blinded Daniel for a moment and he almost missed the street sign. Three-quarters of a mile later he spotted a modest cottage that was set back from the road.

A Mercedes, similar to one that Daniel had seen Arthur Briggs drive, was parked on the gravel driveway near the front door, but the house was dark. Daniel wondered why. He remembered the speeding car. Had it come from Starlight Road? He couldn't remember. Daniel parked his car facing the road in case he had to get away in a hurry. He left the motor running and walked toward the cottage.

Daniel paused on the doorstep and listened, but he heard no sounds inside. The night air was cool and a wind whipped through the trees. Daniel hunched his shoulders against the chill and rapped on the front door. It swung open slightly.

"Mr. Briggs," Daniel called into the dark interior. All he heard was the sigh of the wind. Daniel pushed the door open and was about to call out again when he saw someone stretched out on the floor. He knelt beside the body. It was Arthur Briggs. Blood had pooled around his ex-boss and Daniel was careful to avoid getting any of it on him. There was a bullet hole in Briggs's forehead and two more entry wounds in his torso.

Daniel started to reach out for Briggs to check for a pulse when he heard a car driving toward the house and headlights lit up the front room. Daniel leaped to his feet and raced out of the house. The headlights swung in his direction, illuminating his face. Daniel flung up his arm to block the driver's view and dove into his car, then he floored the accelerator and drove away like a madman.

21

Arthur Briggs was not the first murdered man Daniel had seen, but it had been years since his first encounter with violent death. Daniel was fifteen when he ran away from home for the second time. After two evenings of sleeping in doorways, he had spent his third night with two other runaways under the Broadway Bridge in an encampment created by the homeless. The sounds made by traffic passing overhead and the voices of the river were impossible to shut out, but most disturbing were the unfamiliar noises of the camp. Drunks wept softly and the insane raged at things others could not see. Daniel feared being beaten and robbed or worse, so he tried to stay awake. When he did nod off, the slightest noise near his bedroll would jerk him into full consciousness, knife in hand.

Around two in the morning Daniel had passed out from exhaustion only to be awakened by the sounds of two men fighting over a bottle of screw-top wine. He had looked on wide-eyed as the men struck each other with insane energy. When the fight was over the winner was covered in blood and the loser lay curled in a ball, moaning in pain. The wine bottle had been destroyed early in the struggle and the liquid victory prize had seeped into the dirt of the battlefield.

Daniel lay in his sleeping bag, stunned by the violence and paralyzed with fright. By the time he was able to move, the prostrate man had ceased to moan. Daniel had not slept for the rest of the night. In the morning, after he packed his gear, he had walked over to the dead man. The image of his first corpse was still a vivid memory and Arthur Briggs resembled him in many ways. His eyes were sightless, his skin waxy, and his incredible energy had drained away.

Halfway back to Portland the adrenaline that had fueled his mad escape began to wear off and reality set in. Briggs was dead and a witness had seen him running from the cottage. Did the driver get a good enough look to identify him? It was dark, but the headlights had caught him before he could cover his face. Daniel felt sick. He had been jailed as a teenager and he had hated the experience. If he went to jail now it would be for murder.

As soon as Daniel was back in his apartment he ran into the bathroom and examined himself in the mirror. He could see no blood, but to be safe, he changed his clothes and put them in the washing machine in the basement. When he returned to his apartment, he tried to think of ways the police could connect him to the murder. He was pretty sure that he hadn't left fingerprints in the cottage, but the witness may have gotten a good look at him. Then there was Renee

Gilchrist. He'd told her that Briggs wanted to meet him that night at the cottage. If she told the cops he was dead.

Suddenly Daniel remembered the recording of Briggs's call on his answering machine. The message would place him at the Starlight Road cottage at the time of the murder. Daniel had just finished erasing the tape when his phone rang. He waited. It rang again. Daniel picked up the receiver.

"Mr. Ames?"

"Yes."

"This is Detective Brewster of the Portland Police Bureau." Daniel's gut did a back flip. "We met the other night."

"Oh, right."

"I'm downstairs with another detective and some uniformed police officers. We'd like to talk with you."

"About what?" Daniel asked as he went to the window. Brewster was talking on a cell phone. Zeke Forbus was standing next to her. A uniformed officer was looking up at his window. Daniel pulled back.

"I'd rather not discuss the matter over the phone," Billie said. "Would you be willing to come downstairs?"

Daniel went through his options. He could stay in the apartment and the police would kick in the door and drag him out or he could go downstairs voluntarily. Either way he was going to be arrested; it was just a matter of how.

"Okay," Daniel said, "I'll be down in a minute."

Daniel looked around the apartment. His clothes were in the washing machine in the basement. The police would search his apartment, but they might not look downstairs. He started to leave when it dawned on him that he might be locked up. He needed to tell someone, but who? Daniel hesitated, then dialed Kate Ross. Her answering machine took the call.

"Kate, this is Daniel. The police are downstairs. I don't know what's going on," he said to protect both of them, "but check on me. If I'm not home I might be in jail."

Daniel hung up and locked the apartment. When he got to the ground floor he could see Brewster and Forbus waiting outside the door. He guessed that the uniforms would be on either side of it to grab him in case he had a gun. To avoid being roughed up, Daniel opened the door with one hand and held the other hand where it could be seen. As soon as he walked outside the two uniforms converged on him. One had his gun drawn. Daniel expected this, but it scared the hell out of him just the same.

"Please stand with your hands against the wall, Mr. Ames, and spread your legs," Zeke Forbus said.

"I'm not armed."

"Then there won't be a problem."

The frisk was fast and thorough. During the pat-down, the officer emptied Daniel's pockets and took his key ring.

"What is this about?" Daniel asked.

"We're investigating the murder of Arthur Briggs," Billie answered.

"Why are you talking to me?" Daniel asked. He immediately regretted saying anything when it occurred to him that most people would have expressed shock at the violent death of someone they knew.

"We have a witness who saw you driving away from the scene of the murder," Forbus said.

"We're here so you can explain why you were there," Billie told him. "If you have any information that can help us find Mr. Briggs's killer, we'd appreciate the help."

Daniel's mouth was dry. The only way the police could have found him this quickly was if the witness recognized him.

"I'd like to talk to an attorney before I say anything else."

"You seem like a nice enough person, Mr. Ames," Billie said. "If you have any explanation for what happened I'll try to help you."

Billie seemed so sincere that Daniel almost fell for her line, but he'd had run-ins with the police when he was on the street and he knew the game she was playing.

"Thank you, Detective, but I'd rather wait until I've talked to a lawyer."

Billie nodded. "We'll respect your wishes. Please turn around and put your hands behind you."

"Why?"

"I'm placing you under arrest for the murder of Arthur Briggs."

Daniel rode in the back of a patrol car with his hands cuffed behind him. He spent the first few minutes of the trip to the Justice Center trying to get comfortable and the rest of it with his thoughts, because no one spoke to him during the ride. By the time the car parked in the police garage, Daniel was sick with worry.

The Justice Center was a modern, sixteen-story building in downtown Portland that was home to the Multnomah County jail, two circuit and two district courts, state parole and probation, the state crime lab, and the Portland police central precinct. Brewster and Forbus drove behind the car transporting Daniel and escorted him up to the detective division. Neither detective spoke to him except to tell him what to do.

The detective division was a wide-open space that stretched along one side of the thirteenth floor. Each detective had his own cubicle separated from the others by a chest-high divider. As soon as he was brought into the office, Daniel's cuffs were taken off and he was placed in a small, cinderblock holding cell. Light was provided by a harsh fluorescent fixture that was recessed in the ceiling. The only place to sit in the tiny room was a hard wooden bench that ran along the back wall. There were no other furnishings.

Forbus sat with Daniel for a few minutes. He explained that Daniel would be held in the cell for a while and told him that he could knock on the door if he wanted to use the rest room or needed a glass of water. Then he closed the door and drew a metal sheet across a small, tinted-glass window in the door, cutting off all contact with the world outside the cell. Daniel stretched out on the bench, placed an arm across his eyes to shield them from the light, and tried to relax.

Twenty minutes later Forbus reentered the room

with a photographer who took several photographs of Daniel. As soon as the photographer left, Forbus gave the prisoner a flimsy, white, one-piece, disposable Tyvex jumpsuit made of paper that zipped up the front and felt slick and odd against his skin. The detective explained that Daniel would wear this suit until he was given a uniform in the jail.

When Daniel was dressed, Forbus led his prisoner across the hallway into a small interrogation room furnished with several, heavy wooden chairs and a table that was affixed to the wall. Daniel noticed a box of tissues on the table and wondered how many men had wept in this room.

Forbus made no attempt to question Daniel about the murder and Daniel had to fight an urge to open the subject. The detective asked Daniel's age, date of birth, and other statistical information for his custody report. He was tempted to refuse to answer the detective's questions, but he wanted to put off returning to the cell as long as possible. When Forbus had the information he needed he put Daniel back in the holding cell. His watch had been taken from him and he could only guess how long he stayed in the lockup, but it seemed like hours before he heard a key in the lock again and Billie Brewster came in.

"I'm going to take you over to the jail now," she said as she cuffed Daniel's hands behind his back. Brewster led him down a carpeted hall to an elevator that took them to the ground floor. After a short walk through Central Precinct and the garage, Daniel found himself standing on a red dot in front of a blue metal door in the reception area of the jail. The detec-

tive passed a custody report through a slot to a sheriff's deputy in a green uniform who was stationed behind a plate of thick glass.

"If you want to talk with me about what happened
at the cottage, tell one of the deputies," Brewster said
in a kind voice. Then she surprised Daniel by putting
a hand on his shoulder and saying, "Good luck,
Daniel."

As soon as Brewster left, the door behind Daniel
snapped open and he was ordered into a narrow concrete chute about six feet long and seven feet wide.
Another handcuffed prisoner was stretched out on a
bench that ran along the wall. Daniel was afraid to
ask him to move, so he stayed standing. A few minutes later a door at the other end of the room opened
and Daniel was taken out by a deputy who patted him
down before leading him over to a brightly illuminated area where his picture was taken again. After
that, Daniel was escorted to a window that opened
into a small medical facility. A woman on the other
side of the window asked Daniel for a medical history
then turned him over to another deputy for finger-
printing. Finally, he was led down a hall along a concrete floor and heard what sounded like a dog
howling. The guard prodded Daniel around a corner
and the howling turned to screams. They were coming from one of several single cells that lined the wall
of a large holding area. Blue metal doors fronted all
the cells. Toward the top third of the doors were narrow glass windows. A female deputy was talking
through a grille beneath one of the windows in a firm
voice. Daniel realized that the inhuman screams and

moans he had heard were coming from this cell.

"This isn't doing you any good, Mr. Packard," the woman deputy was saying, but Mr. Packard was unaffected by her attempts to calm him and continued to howl.

The guard unlocked Daniel's cuffs and placed him in a cell enclosed by chain-link fencing that stood in the center of the holding area. Another prisoner in street clothes was lying on a concrete bench. Daniel took a closer look at his cellmate, who was sleeping through Mr. Packard's insane lament. The man was stripped to the waist, revealing a torso covered with tattoos. It took an effort not to stare. To make it easier, Daniel turned away and looked at his surroundings through the grille. It dawned on him that no other prisoner was making any noise. He could see into some of the other holding cells through the slit windows and what he saw were men pacing, locked in with their own thoughts as Daniel was locked in with his.

At first Daniel tried to remember all he could about his other jail experiences so he could prepare himself to survive. He knew that being in jail was like being back in high school in a class made up of bullies, liars, and lunatics. Most criminals were irresponsible, angry men who were unable to succeed in the world and took out their frustrations on those who could. Daniel resolved to tell no one that he had graduated high school, let alone college and law school.

There was a second bench in the cell and Daniel stretched out on it. He had not slept and it had to be early morning by now. He closed his eyes, but the bright lights in the holding area, the hard surface, and the constant, unfamiliar noises made sleep impossible. Daniel tossed and turned for a while until his thoughts turned to the question he would have asked himself earlier if he had not been shell-shocked by the discovery of the dead man and the shame and terror of his arrest: "Who had killed Arthur Briggs and why?"

Daniel knew almost nothing about Briggs's private life, except that he was married and had two grown children. The only times he had been in Briggs's presence socially were at firm functions. From experience, Daniel knew that Briggs was a rude, abrasive man who was extremely aggressive in court, but he had no idea if Briggs had enemies—or friends, for that matter. It soon became obvious to Daniel that he lacked the information to make even a rudimentary guess about the identity of Briggs's killer, so he turned to motive.

In the message Briggs had left on Daniel's answering machine he had said that he needed to talk to Daniel about a new development in the Insufort case. He'd also said that he knew that he was wrong about Daniel and that Daniel was the only person he could trust. Suddenly it occurred to him: the Kaidanov report!

Daniel sat up. The new development in the Geller case must have involved the report, because that was the only aspect of the case of any importance that involved Daniel. It was the reason he was fired. What had Briggs talked about during their last meeting? He'd gotten furious when Daniel told him that Geller was covering up the results of Kaidanov's study. Of course! Briggs must have found out that Geller was involved in a cover-up. That would explain why he thought Daniel was the only person he could trust. The firm would lose Geller Pharmaceuticals as a client, and its hefty retainer, if Briggs exposed a plot to cover up Kaidanov's study, so he would not have been able to trust anyone at Geller or anyone in his own firm. But he could trust Daniel because Daniel had urged Briggs to expose the cover-up. The only problem with his theory was that he could more easily imagine Arthur Briggs involved in a conspiracy with Geller than exposing a cover-up by a client that brought millions to the firm.

But what if he was wrong about Briggs? He'd known so little about the senior partner. Maybe Briggs had spoken to the wrong people at Geller and they had silenced him. Daniel had to tell someone what he had figured out, but who? And what proof did he have? A wave of despair swept over him and all of his energy and excitement drained away. No one would believe him if he started talking about cover-ups and conspiracies. They would think he was a crazy, disgruntled employee. Just the type of maniac who would murder the person who had fired him.

An hour later a deputy brought Daniel and his comatose cellmate a brown-bag breakfast. The tattooed man continued to sleep. Daniel opened his bag and took out a baloney sandwich on pasty white bread, an orange, and a small carton of milk. He had no appetite and the sandwich looked repulsive, but

Daniel knew he had to eat to keep up his strength. He finished his meal shortly before a guard handcuffed him and led him out of the holding cell. The jail had a receipt for Daniel's possessions, which included his wallet. For a dollar fifty he was allowed to purchase a hygiene kit containing shampoo, toothpaste, and a toothbrush.

The guard took Daniel upstairs to the seventh floor. After a short walk from the elevator, Daniel was led through a sally port into a two-story-high, open area. At one end of the floor was a glassed-in rec room with a television. Along the walls were two tiers of cells. Daniel was told to strip. The guard took his Tyvex suit and gave him plastic shower slippers, a set of pink dyed underwear and socks, a pair of blue cotton pants with an elastic waist, and a blue, pullover, V-neck shirt. Then the guard told him to enter cell 7C.

The cell had a two-tiered bunk bed. A muscular Hispanic was stretched out on the lower bunk. He turned on his side and stared at Daniel with little interest. Along the wall was a concrete slab. Daniel saw that his cellmate's toiletries were at one end of the slab and he placed his on the other end. Behind the bunk was a narrow window that stretched the length of the cell and looked out at the new federal courthouse.

As soon as the guard closed the door, Daniel addressed his cellmate.

"How you doin'?"

"Okay," the man answered. Then he asked, "Whatchoo in for?" in a thick accent.

"Nothing much."

Daniel knew better than to talk about his case.

Every cellmate was a potential state's witness.

"Me, too," the man answered with a sly smile. "Name's Pedro."

"Daniel. I'm gonna sack out."

"Yeah sure."

Daniel remembered something he had learned the last time he was in jail. He grabbed his toothbrush before climbing into his upper bunk. He did not sleep, but he did spend several hours using the concrete wall to sharpen the end of the toothbrush into a sharp point in case his cellmate turned out to be less friendly than he seemed.

22

"Ames, your attorney's here."

Daniel was still groggy from a sleepless night and it took him a minute to process the fact that the guard was talking to him.

"What attorney?" he asked.

"How should I know? Get a move on."

As Daniel climbed down from his bunk he wondered if the court had already assigned him a public defender. The guard led him into the common area and through the sally port into a long corridor lined with noncontact visiting rooms where prisoners and visitors sat on either side of a thick glass window and conversed by telephone. A metal door at the end of the corridor led into a shorter hallway. On one side were two contact visiting rooms. Daniel could see into the closest room through a window that took up half the wall. It was furnished with a round table that was bolted to the floor and two molded plastic chairs. An attractive woman with shoulder-length black hair was seated in one of the chairs. When Daniel stepped into the room the guard closed the door and the woman stood up. Daniel was five eleven. The woman was almost as tall and had the broad shoulders and solid build of an athlete. She wore a conservative business suit.

"Hi, Daniel," she said, extending her hand. "I'm Amanda Jaffe."

Daniel colored. His jail-issue clothes were a size too big, his hair was uncombed, and he had a day's growth of beard. He also smelled.

Amanda smiled. "I bet this wasn't what you expected when you called for a job interview."

"What are you doing here?"

"Kate Ross phoned me after she tracked you to the jail. Why don't we sit down," Amanda said as she returned to her seat. Daniel remained standing.

"Look, Ms. Jaffe . . ."

"Amanda," she corrected.

"I can't afford to hire you. Kate must have told you that I just lost my job, my savings probably won't cover the cost of this consultation, and my job prospects have just plummeted to minus zero."

"Don't worry about the fee."

"I've got to worry about it. No matter what you charge, there's no way I can pay it."

"Daniel, please sit down. I'm getting a crick in my neck."

Daniel sat reluctantly on the other chair.

"Kate thinks very highly of you. She doesn't believe that you murdered Arthur Briggs."

"I didn't."

"Good. Then try to relax so I can get the information I need to get you out of here."

"But your money . . ."

"I'm taking the case pro bono and Kate is covering my expenses."

"I can't let you two do that."

Amanda's smile disappeared and she looked deadly serious.

"You're in big trouble, Daniel. You've been charged with murder. If you're convicted you're looking at life in prison or a death sentence. This is not the time to be proud. Accept our help. You need it."

Amanda's words had a sobering effect. Life in prison or execution. What was happening to him?

"Before coming here, I talked to Mike Greene, the prosecutor who's handling your case. He claims to have a witness who saw you running from the crime scene. She also says that she heard you have an angry argument with Arthur Briggs on Friday."

"Who's the witness?"

"Dr. April Fairweather."

"Fairweather! Are you kidding?"

"You know her?"

"She's a Reed, Briggs client, but she had nothing to do with the Insufort litigation."

"The lawsuit involving the pregnancy pill? What's that got to do with Arthur Briggs's murder?"

"That's why I was at the cottage. Briggs left a message on my answering machine telling me there was a new development in the case. He said he needed my help, which surprised the hell out of me since he'd just fired me for screwing up the case."

"I'm not following this. Maybe you should start at the beginning."

Daniel explained the Geller Pharmaceuticals case, the discovery of Dr. Sergey Kaidanov's letter, his search of Kaidanov's house, the discovery of the murdered man at the lab, and the leak of the study to the press. Then he told Amanda about being fired, his argument with Briggs, and what happened at the cottage.

"Now I know how the police figured out that I was there so fast," Daniel concluded. "Dr. Fairweather was in Mr. Briggs's waiting area when he fired me. She saw us argue. What I can't figure out is what she was doing at the cottage. Her case had nothing to do with the Geller case. It doesn't make sense that Briggs would have wanted her there if he was going to talk about Insufort."

Amanda was quiet for a moment. Daniel thought that she looked worried and he began to get nervous. Then she brightened and Daniel leaned forward expectantly.

"You have a motive to murder Briggs because Briggs fired you and threatened you, but the message on your answering machine shows that he changed his opinion about you for some reason. There's a chance I might be able to persuade Mike to hold off on an indictment if he hears the tape."

Daniel's face fell. "I erased it."

"What?"

"I panicked and I erased the answering machine tape just before the police came. It was proof that I was at Starlight Road when the murder occurred."

Amanda failed to conceal her disappointment and Daniel knew he'd screwed up.

"How long do I have to stay in jail?" he asked nervously.

"You're not going to get out quickly. Bail isn't automatic in a murder charge. I have to ask for a bail hearing and they're hard to win. If you had to stay in jail for a week or more, do you think you could handle it?"

Daniel felt sick, but he nodded.

"I've been in jail before."

Amanda tensed. "Tell me about that."

Daniel looked down at the tabletop. "My . . . my home life wasn't good. When I was a kid I ran away a lot." He shrugged. "When you're living on the streets there are a lot of opportunities to get in trouble."

"What kind of trouble were you in?"

"Burglary, assault. The cases never stuck, but I was arrested twice and I stayed in jail both times."

Daniel told her the approximate dates of his arrests and Amanda made some notes on her pad. Then she asked him several other background questions. When she was finished, she put her pad in her attaché case.

"I'm going back to my office to meet with my investigator. You'll make your first appearance in court at two this afternoon and I'll be there. This appearance will be over quickly. The judge will read the formal charges against you and make sure you have counsel. I'll ask him to set a date for a bail hearing and we'll request a preliminary hearing. Then we'll go from there. Do you have any questions?"

"No, not now. I'm too numb."

"I don't blame you. If I were in your position I'd be scared to death. But you have one thing going for you that gives me hope." Daniel looked up expectantly. "You've told me you're innocent and I do believe that the truth will come out."

Daniel should have found Amanda's words reassuring, but he remembered an editorial about the death penalty he had read recently. It had called for a moratorium on executions because of all the innocent people who were languishing on death row.

Kate Ross was waiting in the public reception area. She stood up the moment Amanda got out of the jail elevator.

"How is Daniel?" she asked anxiously.

"He's holding up okay. I get the impression that he's pretty tough. If I can't get him out on bail before the trial I don't think being in jail will break him."

"Will you be able to get him out?"

"I don't know, Kate. Mike Greene told me a little about the state's case. It's not airtight, but it's strong."

"What have they got?"

"Briggs fired Daniel and they argued in front of witnesses, so Daniel had a reason to shoot Briggs. They haven't recovered the murder weapon and they didn't find it when they searched Daniel's apartment, but Mike Greene will just argue that he threw the gun away. The really bad news is that an eyewitness saw Daniel running from the scene of the murder."

"Who is it? Give me the name. If there's evidence that the witness is lying, I'll find it."

"I appreciate the offer, but I'm afraid you're not going to be able to work on Daniel's case."

"Why not?"

"Conflict of interest. The eyewitness is Dr. April Fairweather, a Reed, Briggs client."

Kate's mouth dropped open. "You're kidding?"

"Daniel had the same reaction. She was supposed to meet with Briggs at eight-fifteen at the cottage where he was killed. She says she saw Daniel run out and drive away."

"You can't take Fairweather's word for anything, Amanda. She's—" Kate stopped suddenly. "Damn."

"What?"

"You're right. There is a conflict."

"Do you know something about Dr. Fairweather that I should know?"

Kate nodded. "But I can't talk about it. I learned it while working on her case. All I can tell you to do is dig deep."

"For what?"

"I'm sorry, Amanda. I'll have to talk to one of the partners before I can say anything. I suspect the partner is going to tell me that Fairweather will have to give her okay before I can talk to you, and I doubt she'll do it."

"Daniel will understand why you can't get involved. He knows you're helping him with expenses and he's very grateful."

"I wish there was something else I could do."

"Well, there isn't, for now, but don't worry. Herb Cross will conduct the investigation, and you know how good he is. If you want to show your support, be in court at two for Daniel's arraignment."

"I plan to be."

         The offices of Jaffe, Katz, Lehane and Brindisi, one of Oregon's premier law firms, took up the eighth floor of the Stockman Building in downtown Portland. Amanda's father, Frank Jaffe, and two law-school classmates had started their practice as soon as they passed the bar. Amanda had joined the firm six years ago after graduating with honors from New York University School of Law and serving a two-year clerkship at the Ninth Circuit Court of Appeals. As a reward for solving the Cardoni serial murder case, the firm's members had voted to make her a partner. Six months ago she had moved from one of the small offices used by the associates to a larger office with a view of the West Hills. Amanda had decorated her new office with two abstracts she'd purchased at a gallery near her condominium in the Pearl District and several photographs of Broadway that had been taken shortly after the First World War around the time that the Stockman Building had been constructed.

As soon as she returned from her meeting with Daniel, Amanda started making notes about her new client. She liked Daniel and she hoped that he was innocent, but she had been practicing criminal law long enough to know that you never took your client's word for anything, no matter how sincere they seemed. Daniel had a strong motive to murder his ex-boss, he had admitted being at the scene of the crime, and he had destroyed the answering-machine tape—the evidence that Daniel claimed would have proved his relationship with Arthur Briggs had changed.

Amanda leaned back and tapped her pen against her palm. What did Kate know that would help her cast doubt on the eyewitness identification made by April Fairweather? What difference would impeachment evidence make, anyway? Daniel was at the cottage. He'd told her so. That meant that Daniel could not testify, because he would have to admit that Fairweather had seen him. She sighed. This was not going to be easy. She was going to have to work very hard and be very lucky if she was going to keep Daniel Ames off of death row.

23

At Daniel's arraignment, Amanda Jaffe asked for a bail hearing and the judge set it for Friday. Daniel made a plan for getting through the week. It involved staying in his cell as much as possible and being as inconspicuous as possible when he was in the presence of other prisoners.

Every morning at ten o'clock the guards unlocked the bottom tier of cells and let the prisoners watch television, talk, and walk around in the glassed-in recreation area. This was the most frightening time for Daniel. He had found a corner of the room from which the television was not visible and he had stayed there until it was time to return to his cell. On Thursday morning Daniel made for his corner only to find a wiry white man with a shaved head and swastika tattoo on his muscled biceps headed the same way. Daniel tried to avoid him, but he did not move fast enough and they collided. Daniel's stomach clenched.

"Sorry," he mumbled.

The man glared. When Daniel did not look away fast enough, he moved close to him.

"What are you lookin' at, pussy?"

"Nothing," Daniel answered, praying that he could avoid a fight.

"You sayin' I'm nothing?"

Daniel had been a civilized human being for many years, but the next second he was back on the street, he was fifteen, and he was listening to George, an ex-con who had been kind to him until Daniel rebuffed his sexual advances with a broken bottle. George had tried to seduce Daniel with tales of life in the Joint that had been filled with survival tips. The tips had come in handy on the other occasions he'd spent time in jail and Daniel flashed on them now.

"I . . . I said I'm sorry," Daniel apologized again in a voice intentionally meek and subservient. The prisoner took a step forward.

"That ain't good enough," he was saying when Daniel stomped hard on his foot. When the inmate bent forward reflexively Daniel snapped a hard elbow into his face. Blood sprayed from the man's nose. Before he could get his bearings Daniel struck him again, this time in the throat. The inmate went down hard and his head made a hollow sound as it bounced off the concrete floor.

Daniel turned to see if anyone else was going to come for him. Most of the inmates gave the fallen man and his assailant a wide berth, but two prisoners with shaved heads started across the room. One man was slightly shorter than Daniel and had a weight lifter's build. His biceps expanded and contracted as he flexed his fists. The other man was tall and flabby, but he had pit bull eyes and huge hands.

Daniel knew there was no way he could take out two men, but he was poised to go at the weight lifter when the skinheads stopped abruptly. That's when Daniel noticed the four Hispanics who stood beside him. One was his cellmate.

"Whas up, bro?" Pedro asked the weight lifter.

"Get out of the way, monkey," he answered.

Pedro smiled, but he did not move. The weight lifter started forward.

"Break it up," a guard shouted from the door to the rec room. Three guards armed with truncheons backed him up.

"We ain't through with you, fucker," the fat skinhead said to Daniel, spitting on the floor between them. Then he touched the weight lifter on the arm and the two men backed into the crowd.

One of the guards knelt to check the unconscious man, who was covered with blood from his broken nose.

"Who did this?" he demanded. No one answered.

"All right, that's it. No more rec time. Get back in your cells."

The room cleared quickly.

"Thanks, man," Daniel said when he and Pedro were locked up. "I'd have been dead if you hadn't stepped in."

Pedro shrugged. "I don' like those skinhead motherfuckers."

"Well, it's appreciated."

Pedro smiled. "I didn' figure you for no fighter, but you clocked that Nazi good."

"Lucky punch."

Pedro's smile widened. "Sucker punch."

They both laughed. Then Pedro's smile fell away abruptly and he wagged a warning finger at Daniel.

"You watch your back. Those are bad people. They gonna hurt you if they get the chance."

Daniel nodded. Then he climbed onto his upper bunk. As soon as he was certain that Pedro could not see him, he let go of his self-control and started to shake.

24

Herb Cross, a slender African-American in his late thirties, led Amanda Jaffe up a narrow stairway to the second-floor office of Dr. April Fairweather. Fairweather worked over a hardware store in a low-rent building on Stark. The stairwell was dingy and poorly lit, as was the hall in front of the doctor's office.

Herb had briefed Amanda on what little he had discovered about the therapist during the ride from their law office. Fairweather did not have a criminal record. She had a single credit card and never let the charges get too high. Fairweather advertised herself as a consulting therapist and claimed to have a doctorate, but she was not licensed by any state agency. Then again she didn't have to be to practice her kind of New Age therapy. Fairweather lived in a cheap garden apartment in Beaverton, and Herb had talked to a few of her neighbors, but all he'd learned was that she never said more than an occasional hello.

The investigator opened a wooden door with a

frosted-glass window. On the other side was a small reception room. As Amanda closed the door, a short, mousy woman in a frayed gray business suit walked out of the interior office. Amanda noticed that Dr. Fairweather had not done much with her light brown hair. She didn't see any jewelry, either. The lawyer concluded that the psychologist was not someone who gave a lot of thought to her looks.

"Can I help you?" Fairweather asked as she eyed the investigator warily. She seemed frightened, so Amanda stepped forward and smiled.

"I'm Amanda Jaffe, the attorney representing Daniel Ames. This is my associate, Herb Cross. If you have a few minutes we'd like to talk to you."

Fairweather grew rigid. "No, I can't do that."

"I'm going to have a chance to talk to you in court, Dr. Fairweather," Amanda pressed. "I might be able to save some time if we clear up a few things here."

"I'm not supposed to talk to you," Fairweather answered. Her shoulders hunched and her gaze drifted toward the floor.

"Did the district attorney tell you that? Because you have the right to talk to anyone you want to. Talking to me would be the right thing to do."

"I don't want to do that and I'd like you to go."

"Okay." Amanda held out her card and Fairweather took it reluctantly. "If you change your mind please call me."

"That is one uptight lady," Herb Cross said as soon as the door closed behind them.

"Yes, she is," Amanda mused, "and I'd love to know why."

• • •

On the way back to the office, Amanda and Cross brainstormed about ways to get through Fairweather's armor. When they walked into the firm's waiting room, the receptionist handed Amanda a small box wrapped in brown paper. FOR AMES BAIL HEARING was written on the paper in block letters with a Magic Marker. There was no return address.

"This isn't how the DA's office sends discovery," Amanda said as she stripped away the wrapping paper. "Who brought it over?"

"A messenger," the receptionist answered.

"Did he say who sent it?"

"No."

The box was cardboard without any markings. Amanda lifted the lid. There was no note inside, but there was a videocassette. Moments later Herb Cross and Amanda Jaffe were sitting in the conference room in front of a VCR. A title informed the lawyer and the private investigator that they were going to see a speech that Dr. April Fairweather had given at a conference devoted to abuse survivors three years before. On the screen, a distinguished gentleman stepped behind a podium and introduced Dr. Fairweather in glowing terms. After the introduction Dr. Fairweather took the man's place at the podium and began to speak. A few minutes into the tape, the investigator and the attorney turned to each other.

"Is this for real?" Cross asked.

"I certainly hope so," Amanda answered.

25

Daniel barely slept Thursday evening worrying about what would happen the next day in the rec room. Fortunately, his bail hearing was set for Friday and early the next morning he was placed in chains and transported two blocks to the Multnomah County Courthouse, where he was lodged in a large open cell in the courthouse jail with other prisoners awaiting court appearances. At 9:45, two sheriff's deputies gave Daniel a suit that Amanda's investigator had brought to the jail for the hearing. As soon as he was dressed the deputies escorted him from the seventh-floor holding area to the courtroom where his case was to be heard.

The Multnomah County Courthouse is a blunt, functional building constructed of gray concrete whose exterior makes no pretensions to art. The interiors are another matter. The Honorable Gerald Opton's fifth-floor courtroom had grand, high ceilings, ornate molding, marble Corinthian columns, and a polished wood dais. The spectator section consisted of several rows of hard wooden benches set back behind a low wooden fence that separated the public from those having business before the court. The benches were packed because of the publicity Daniel's case had received, but Daniel spotted Kate Ross easily. She smiled at him. Daniel was embarrassed to have her see him in chains and all he could manage was a restrained nod.

Several partners from Reed, Briggs occupied the front row of the courtroom. Daniel wondered if the DA was going to use them as witnesses. Seated behind the partners with two other associates was Joe Molinari. He gave Daniel a thumbs-up, which made Daniel smile. The other associates nodded at him and he was relieved to see that some of his friends from the firm were still standing by him. Susan Webster was conspicuously absent.

Daniel scanned the crowd for other familiar faces and was surprised to see a young black man in a charcoal-gray business suit, armed with a pen and a legal pad, whom he recognized as one of the associates Aaron Flynn had brought to Kurt Schroeder's deposition.

When his guards brought Daniel into the courtroom Amanda Jaffe was talking to Deputy District Attorney Mike Greene, a large man who looked like a football or basketball player. Looks were deceiving. Greene was a gentle soul who played competitive chess and the saxophone instead of sports. The defense attorney and the DA had faced each other in court several times and they had started dating after the violent resolution of the Cardoni case.

Amanda heard one of the deputies unlock Daniel's handcuffs and hurried to her client. With his suit on, Daniel looked like any other young attorney, but three days in jail had taken their toll. As soon as his manacles were removed, Amanda led him to the defense table, where they conferred in whispers.

"Are you okay?" she asked.

Daniel shook his head. "You've got to get me out of jail. I've been in a fight and the guy has friends. They're going to come after me as soon as I'm back at the Justice Center. What are my chances of making bail?"

Amanda was about to answer when the bailiff rapped his gavel. She touched Daniel on the forearm.

"You're going to be okay."

The Honorable Gerald Opton entered the courtroom and everyone stood. Jerry Opton was one of three judges in the homicide rotation. These judges heard murder cases exclusively for one or two years so they could develop an expertise in this area of law. Assignment to the homicide rotation was usually reserved for experienced judges. Opton had only been on the bench for five years, but he had been a homicide specialist in the Multnomah County District Attorney's Office for ten years. He was a stocky, balding man whose features bore a faint resemblance to the actor Jack Nicholson. Despite being a career prosecutor before his elevation to the bench, Opton was a favorite of defense attorneys and prosecutors alike. He was scrupulously fair, well versed in the law, and ran his court with a firm hand that was softened by a wry sense of humor.

"Are we ready to go?" the judge asked the attorneys.

"Ready for Mr. Ames," Amanda said.

"Ready for the state," Greene intoned.

"Bailiff, please call the case."

The bailiff read the name and number of Daniel's case into the record. For purposes of the bail hearing, the parties had entered into a stipulation that Arthur Briggs had been shot with a .45-caliber bullet and a person other than Briggs had intentionally caused the death. This helped speed up the hearing because the prosecutor did not have to call the medical examiner as a witness. The parties had further stipulated that Daniel worked at Reed, Briggs until the week before the murder when Briggs had fired him. After reading the stipulation into the record, Mike Greene called his first witness.

In response to Greene's questions, Zeke Forbus told the judge that he had been summoned to the crime scene at Starlight Road and had interviewed Dr. April Fairweather. Dr. Fairweather had given him the name and description of a man she had seen leaving the crime scene and the car in which he had driven away. Forbus testified that he ran a check on the car owned by the man Dr. Fairweather named and he discovered that the car was the make and color that Dr. Fairweather had described. Finally, Forbus described Daniel's arrest.

"Good morning, Detective Forbus," Amanda said when the witness was turned over to her for cross-examination. Forbus did not answer. He distrusted defense attorneys and he especially disliked women lawyers.

"Were you present during the arrest of Mr. Ames and the search of his apartment?"

"Yes, ma'am."

"Did Mr. Ames make any incriminating statements to you or any other police officer or detective following his arrest?"

"He asked for an attorney, right away."

"Can I take it that means that Mr. Ames did not make any statement that incriminated himself in the murder of Mr. Briggs?"

"That is correct."

"Have Mr. Ames's fingerprints been found at the crime scene?"

"Not to my knowledge."

"When Mr. Briggs was found he was lying in a pool of blood, was he not?"

"Yes."

"Did you find any blood on Mr. Ames or his clothing?"

"Mr. Ames washed his clothes. We found them in a washing machine in the basement."

"Your Honor, would you please instruct Detective Forbus to answer my questions?"

Judge Opton smiled. "Come on, Detective. You're not going to score any points this way. Do everyone a favor. Listen to the question and answer it, okay?"

"Sorry, Judge," Forbus answered. "No blood was found on Mr. Ames or his clothing."

"Did you find the murder weapon on Mr. Ames or in his apartment?"

"No."

"You searched his car?"

"Yes."

"Find any blood or guns?"

"No."

"Would it be fair to say that the only evidence you have connecting Daniel Ames with the scene of the crime is the statement of Dr. Fairweather?"

"Yes."

"Thank you. No further questions."

"Mr. Greene?" Judge Opton said.

"We call Dr. April Fairweather to the stand."

Daniel turned sideways and watched Fairweather walk down the aisle toward the witness box. Whenever he saw her he got an impression of a person in hiding. Fairweather kept her eyes front and avoided looking at Daniel. When she took the oath she continued to look away from him.

"Dr. Fairweather," Mike Greene began as soon as the witness was sworn, "what is your profession?"

Fairweather sat erect with her hands folded in her lap and her eyes glued on the deputy district attorney. Her response was so soft that Daniel strained to hear her. The judge asked her to raise her voice and repeat her answer.

"I am a counselor."

"Is that what your doctorate is in?"

"Yes, and my master's degree."

"Is it as a result of your practice that you came to be a client of Arthur Briggs?"

"Yes, sir. A patient sued me. My insurance company employed Mr. Briggs to represent them in cases of this sort."

"Did you ever meet with Mr. Briggs at his office to discuss your case?"

"We met on several occasions."

"While at the office, did you ever meet the defendant, Daniel Ames?"

"Yes. Mr. Briggs introduced me to him. He told me his name and we shook hands."

Daniel remembered that Dr. Fairweather had also refused to meet his eye when Arthur Briggs had introduced them. When he'd shaken her hand it had been damp and cold, and she'd jerked it away as if she was afraid Daniel would trap it.

"Did you see Mr. Ames a second time at the Reed, Briggs offices?"

"Yes."

"When was that?"

"The Friday before Mr. Briggs was killed."

"Please describe that occasion for the judge."

"I was sitting in the waiting area in front of Mr. Briggs's office when the door opened. Mr. Ames stood in the doorway with his back to me speaking to Mr. Briggs."

"Can you remember anything he said?"

"No, but I could tell that he was angry."

"How do you know that he was angry with Mr. Briggs?"

"I could hear Mr. Briggs shouting at him, then Mr.

Ames slammed the door. When he turned around he looked furious. Then he saw me and Mr. Briggs's secretary and he rushed away."

"Did you have a third occasion to encounter Mr. Ames?"

"Yes, sir."

"When was that?"

"The night of the murder."

"Where were you?"

"At a cottage on Starlight Road."

"What time was it?"

"A little after eight."

"How do you know that?"

"Mr. Briggs's secretary called me earlier in the day and told me that there had been a development in my case and Mr. Briggs needed to meet with me at the Starlight Road address at eight-fifteen that evening. I'm always punctual and I checked the clock on my dashboard when I turned into Starlight Road."

"What did you see as you approached the cottage?"

"I saw Mr. Ames. He was running and he looked upset. When he saw my car, he threw his arm in front of his face. Then he dashed to his own car and drove away at a high rate of speed."

"How can you be sure that it was Mr. Ames you saw at the cottage?"

"As I said, I'd met him before and he ran right into my headlight beams. It was like watching someone on a stage standing in a spotlight."

"And there is no doubt in your mind that it was Daniel Ames, the defendant, whom you saw running from the cottage on Starlight Road?"

"None."

"For the record, do you see Mr. Ames in court today?"

"Yes."

"Please point him out for the judge."

Fairweather shifted in her seat and pointed her finger at Daniel, but she still would not look him in the eye.

"After Mr. Ames drove away, what did you do?"

Fairweather paused before answering the prosecutor's question in the same soft monotone in which she had spoken during all of Greene's direct examination.

"I parked my car and entered the house. The lights were off and it took a moment for my eyes to adjust. Then I saw Mr. Briggs lying on the floor. I walked over to him and I knew at once that he was dead."

"How did you know that?"

"He was lying in a pool of blood. I knelt down and felt for a pulse, but there was none."

"What did you do next?"

"I left the house and used my cell phone to call 911."

"Thank you, Dr. Fairweather. Your witness, Ms. Jaffe."

"What is your date of birth, Dr. Fairweather?" Amanda asked in a friendly tone.

"July twenty-ninth, 1957," Fairweather answered, averting her eyes.

"And where were you born?"

"Crawford, Idaho."

"What is your father's name?"

Daniel thought he saw Fairweather flinch.

"Herman Garlock," she answered, her voice dropping again.

"And your mother?"

"Linda Garlock."

"If your parents are both named Garlock, why are you named Fairweather?"

"I changed my name legally five years ago."

"What was your given name?"

"Florence Garlock."

"When is the last time you spoke to either of your parents?"

"I don't know the exact date. It would have been around 1978."

"You haven't had any contact with them for more than twenty years?"

"That's correct."

"Can you tell me why?"

"I did not wish to contact them."

"Wouldn't you agree it's rather unusual for a daughter to have no contact with her parents for twenty years?"

"Objection, relevance," Mike Greene said.

"Is the witness's relationship to her parents relevant to this case, Ms. Jaffe?" Judge Opton asked.

"It is, Your Honor, but I'll withdraw the question for now."

Amanda turned her attention back to the witness.

"Do you have any siblings?"

"I have a younger sister, Dorothy."

"Has your sister maintained a relationship with your parents?"

"Yes."

Amanda made a few notes, then switched to another subject.

"I'd like to talk to you about your educational background. What school or schools awarded you your master's and Ph.D.?"

"Templeton University."

"Where did you receive your undergraduate degree?"

"I don't have one."

Amanda looked surprised. "I'm a little confused," she said. "Before you can get a master's and a doctorate, don't you have to graduate from college?"

"That was not a requirement at Templeton."

"Is Templeton University a regular school with a campus and a football team?"

"Templeton is a correspondence university. I attended by mail."

"How long did it take you to get a master's degree and a Ph.D. by mail?"

"About three years."

"Each?"

"Total."

Amanda had Judge Opton's attention and Daniel noticed that Mike Greene was starting to look nervous.

"What major are your degrees in?"

"Theocentric counseling."

"I don't believe I've heard of that. Could you explain theocentric counseling to Judge Opton?"

"Theocentric is God-centered. There's no specific religious connection," Fairweather said without turning to the judge. Daniel had the impression that she was not speaking to anyone in particular, as if she was distancing herself from what was happening in the courtroom.

"Dr. Fairweather, is Templeton an accredited university like Oregon State?"

"I don't believe so."

"And you're not licensed by any state agency, are you?"

"No."

"Let's go back to your parents. Was your father abusive to you when you were a child?"

"Objection. This is totally irrelevant."

Amanda stood. "To the contrary, Your Honor. If you will give me a little leeway here, you will see that this line of questioning goes directly to the issue of this witness's credibility and competence."

Judge Opton took a moment to decide what to do. He did not look happy.

"I'm going to let you continue based solely on your assertion that you can prove relevance. If I'm not convinced pretty quickly, I'll uphold Mr. Greene's objection."

"Thank you, Your Honor. Dr. Fairweather, was your father abusive?"

"Yes."

"In what way?"

"Sexually, physically, and emotionally."

"Since what age?"

"I don't know exactly. My earliest memory would be somewhere around four or five."

"When you say 'physical abuse' what do you mean?"

"Hitting, choking, being locked in closets," she answered in a flat, emotionless tone that reminded Daniel of the way he might describe something he saw on the evening news.

"And 'sexual abuse'?"

"Touching, intercourse."

"He had intercourse with you at four?"

"Yes."

"Anything else?"

"Sodomy, oral sex. He . . . he used objects. Bottles, other things."

"How long did this go on?"

"Until I left the family."

"How old were you then?"

"Twenty-one."

"So this went on for 17 years?"

"Yes."

"Every year?"

"Every week."

"Did you report this physical and sexual abuse to anyone?"

"I . . . I may have tried to report it to my teachers. I can't remember."

"Would it surprise you to learn that my investigator has spoken to several of your teachers and they have no memory of your making any such complaint?"

"Like I said, I can't remember if I did or not."

"Did your mother know what was going on?"

"She participated."

"How?"

"She performed oral sex on me, inserted objects in my vagina, my rectal area."

"What kind of objects?"

"A broom handle, a gun."

"A gun?"

"Yes."

"What kind of gun?"

"I don't know."

"Was it a rifle or a pistol?"

"I can't remember."

"Was your sister also molested?"

"I think so."

"Did she ever complain about this abuse?"

"She has no memory of it."

"But you think she was abused sexually?"

"We shared a bedroom from six to seventeen or eighteen and I believe my father came into the bedroom and had sex with my sister."

"How often?"

"Two to three times a week."

"And she doesn't remember this?"

"She denies it."

"Ms. Jaffe," Judge Opton interrupted. He was obviously upset. "Where are you going with this?"

"A few more questions and it will all be clear, Your Honor. I promise."

"It better be, because I am this close to ending this examination."

Amanda turned her full attention to the witness and went for the kill.

"Other than your parents, were you ever sexually abused by anyone else?"

"Yes."

"How many people molested you?"

"I'm not exactly certain."

"Can you give the judge a ballpark figure?"

"Maybe fifteen. Maybe as many as thirty-five."

Judge Opton frowned.

"Can you identify any of the other people who sexually molested you, these fifteen to thirty-five people?"

"No."

"Were they men or women?"

"It's hard to say."

"Why is that?"

"They were wearing robes with hoods. They wore masks."

The judge leaned forward.

"Can you describe these costumes?"

"They were black-hooded robes, they reached the floor. When I was little it seemed to me that the people could fly, that they floated instead of walking. Now I realize that it just seemed that way because the robes covered their feet."

"Can you remember anything else about the costumes?"

"They had circular medallions."

"Did the medallions symbolize something?"

"They symbolized the fact that these people worshiped Satan."

"So you were molested by Satan worshipers?"

"Yes."

Amanda now had the judge's full attention. Mike Greene struggled to appear nonchalant, as if mass molestations by devil worshipers were a commonplace occurrence in his life.

"Where did these attacks take place?"

"Sometimes in a barn. I also remember the basement of a church."

"Can you give the judge some idea of what happened at these meetings? For instance, why don't you tell him the worst experience you can remember."

"One time I was taken to the barn and tied down to a table and an abortion was performed on me . . ."

"An abortion? You were pregnant?"

"Yes."

"How old were you?"

"Thirteen."

"And they aborted you?"

"Yes. And then I was forced to eat the fetus of my . . . my child."

Judge Opton struggled to maintain his judicial composure.

"How often were you taken to these satanic group meetings?"

"About once a month."

"And how old were you the last time you went?"

"I believe I was eighteen or nineteen."

"Was your sister also taken to these ceremonies?"

"Yes, but she denies it. She says she has no memory of them."

"Were other people's children at these meetings?"

"I remember two or three."

"Was anything done to these other children?"

"They were put in boxes with insects," Dr. Fairweather answered in the same monotone she'd used to answer all of Amanda's questions. "Snakes were made to crawl on them, electric shock was used, they were made to eat parts of animals, photographs were made of them having sex with adults."

"Were there animal sacrifices at these meetings?"

"Yes. I remember cats, dogs. Once there was a sheep."

"What did they do?"

"They cut the belly of the animal open. Sometimes they hung it from the ceiling, cut open the belly, the organs would fall on the people, or the children were forced to eat it."

"Were there human sacrifices?"

"Yes."

"Where were they?"

"In a barn."

"Do you know where the barn was?"

"It was in the country, way out. There were high trees all around and the only light was in the barn from lanterns. Inside, there were blackout curtains to keep out sunlight or to prevent people from seeing in."

"What happened in the barn on the first occasion when you saw a human sacrifice?"

"This man was tied up from the rafters with his hands above his head."

"Was he clothed?"

"No, he was naked."

"Was he screaming or fighting?"

"Yes."

"What happened to this man?"

"The people took knives and flayed his skin off."

"Was he alive when this happened?"

"Yes."

"How many people were involved?"

"I can't remember. More than fifteen."

"And they all were involved in skinning this man alive?"

"Some were chanting and playing drums and calling on demons."

"Do you know why the victims were selected for the ritual?"

"They were selected because they were Christians."

"What happened to the body after it was taken down?"

"There was a ceremony in which the blood was drunk from a chalice, people had sex, that kind of behavior."

"What did the blood represent?"

"Whoever drank the blood of a Christian got that person's power."

"What were these satanic cult members hoping to achieve by following Satan?"

"They wanted to live with Satan for eternity and have everything they wanted, and when Satan overcame the world, you would be a chosen one."

"How were the victims found?"

"The way I understand it, there were people in the cult who were programmed to capture Christians for these ceremonies."

"Were they captured at random off of the street?"

"That's how I understood it."

"Flaying someone alive is murder, isn't it, Dr. Fairweather?"

"Yes."

"And these people probably had families who would worry about them?"

"I suppose."

"Did you ever tell the police about these horrible things that happened to you and these other people?"

"No, I couldn't."

"Why is that?"

"I was terrified and scared for my life."

"Well, you left the cult at twenty-one and you're in your forties now. So you've been away from your parents and these people for twenty years. Didn't it ever occur to you to tell anyone about this after you broke away?"

"I wasn't able to tell anyone."

"Why is that?"

"I was led to believe from the time I was very young that there were members of the cult who could read my mind and that I was constantly being watched and . . ."

"Yes?"

"I believe there were some medical mind-control experiments performed on me by doctors who were members of the cult."

"What was the purpose of these experiments?"

"To make me behave and do what they wanted."

"What were these experiments?"

"I remember having electrical shock. I remember people giving me certain words or codes or phrases and then telling me what I needed to do when I heard them."

"Where did this happen?"

"In a place that was like an operating room. There

were bright lights over my head. I was naked and strapped down. They attached electrodes to my head. That's all I remember."

"How did these experiments work? What did they do to you?"

"There was a phrase said and they would say, 'When you hear this phrase you will do thus and such. Do you understand?' And no matter what I said, they would say, 'We don't believe you,' and I would get more shocks. And at some point they would stop. I guess when they thought I was under control."

"Were you ever given these codes or phrases?"

"Yes."

"How?"

"On the phone or someone in the street would give me a sign. They might say the phrase and I would have to do what I was told."

"What types of things were you told?"

"If I saw red I was supposed to try and kill myself, but not succeed."

"Fake a suicide?"

"Yes."

"Were you ever ordered to do this?"

"Yes, several times."

"How did you attempt suicide?"

"I cut my wrists."

"How many times?"

"I can't say for sure."

"Were you ever hospitalized for this?"

"Twice. I was sent for psychiatric treatment."

Amanda Jaffe was about to ask another question when Mike Greene stood and buttoned his suit jacket.

"Your Honor, I think this might be a good time for a recess."

"I agree, Mr. Greene. We'll recess for fifteen minutes. Dr. Fairweather, you can step down, but you'll have to be back in court when we reconvene. I'll see counsel in chambers."

The judge left the courtroom through a door behind the dais. Daniel turned to Amanda and looked at her wide-eyed.

"She's nuts," he said.

"Yes, she is," Amanda answered with a comforting smile. "And we are sitting in the catbird seat. You hang tight while I talk to the judge. Hopefully, I'll have good news when I come out."

"How did you know about that Satan stuff?"

"I'll tell you later."

Amanda and Mike Greene left the courtroom and Joe Molinari walked up to the bar of the court. One of the guards told Joe they could talk across the low fence but could not touch or exchange anything.

"Thanks for coming," Daniel said.

"Hey, dude, this is the best show in town, and your lawyer kicks ass. You and me are going to be at happy hour this afternoon."

Daniel knew better than to get his hopes up, so he just smiled.

• • •

"What is going on here?" Judge Opton asked Mike Greene as soon as the judge and the two attorneys were seated in his chambers.

"Believe me, I had no idea she was going to say that stuff."

Opton shook his head. "Just when you thought you've seen it all. Well, Mike, what are we going to do?"

Greene exhaled. "Fairweather and Forbus are my only witnesses. You've heard everything I've got."

"Are you going to argue that you've proved by clear and convincing evidence that Mr. Ames murdered Arthur Briggs? Because you've got to do that before I'll deny bail."

"She still saw what she saw, Judge," Greene answered halfheartedly.

"Your witness sees a lot of things. What's your position, Amanda?"

"The only evidence connecting Daniel to the murder is the testimony of Dr. Fairweather and I don't believe she's a credible witness."

"You don't have to be diplomatic. We're not on the record. The woman is a total fruitcake. Fucking electrodes. Jesus, Mike, where did you dig her up?"

Greene didn't answer.

"Okay, here's what we'll do when we go back outside," Opton said. "You'll end your cross, Amanda, and you'll rest, Mike. You can argue against bail, but I'm going to grant it, understood?"

Greene nodded. Opton turned to Amanda.

"What can your client afford?"

"Daniel's on his own and he's almost broke, Judge.

As you heard, Reed, Briggs just fired him. His mother doesn't have a dime and he doesn't know where his father is. He worked his way through college and law school, so he's up to his nose in debt and he doesn't have much in savings. I'm taking the case pro bono."

Opton's eyebrows raised. Amanda ignored his surprise and continued.

"I think you should release him on his own recognizance. Daniel swears he's innocent and there isn't any credible evidence that links him to the murder. Even if you believed Dr. Fairweather, the best you have is Daniel running from the scene, but no evidence that he had a murder weapon or shot Briggs."

"Mike?"

Greene looked defeated. "I'll go on the record against recog, but I can't make a great argument against it, right now."

"Okay. I'll let you protect your office. You can make an impassioned plea. Just don't go on too long." Opton stood up. "Let's get this over with."

Mike Greene looked grim when he emerged from the judge's chambers and Amanda Jaffe's face betrayed no emotion. As soon as Amanda sat down she turned to Daniel.

"Judge Opton decided that Fairweather is nuts. He can't take her word for the ID, so Mike has no evidence connecting you to the scene of the crime. You'll be out of jail by noon."

"It's over? I'm free?"

"Don't get too excited. You're still charged with murder, but the judge is going to release you on your own word. You're going to be recogged, so you won't have to post bail."

"Thank you," Daniel said. "You're amazing."

"I am good," Amanda replied, "but we wouldn't have won without your guardian angel."

"Did you have any idea this was going to happen?" Mike Greene asked Zeke Forbus. "Because I love to have a little advance notice whenever I'm going to make a total fool out of myself in court. It gives me time to buy a disguise so I can make a quick escape."

Greene rarely got upset and Forbus was rarely embarrassed, but today had not been a normal day.

"Believe me, Mike, I was as surprised as you are. Fairweather seemed a little uptight when I talked to her, but I had no idea she was crazy."

Greene turned his chair toward the window in his office so he would not have to look at the homicide detective. A chessboard on his credenza displayed a position in the Queen's Gambit Declined that the prosecutor was studying. He stared at it for a moment in hopes of distancing himself from his real-life problems, but it was no use. He swung his chair back so he was face-to-face with Forbus.

"Where do we go from here, Zeke?"

"I still think he did it, so I'm going to try and find a way to prove Ames was really at the cottage."

"Any idea how you're going to do that?"

Forbus shook his head.

"Well think, damn it. We've got to move. The preliminary hearing is set for next week. Normally, I'd bypass it by getting a secret indictment out of the grand jury, but I've got nothing to show them. I'm going to have to dismiss the charges against Ames if we don't come up with something fast."

26

Daniel was so stunned at the speed with which his bail hearing ended that he barely heard the legal arguments. As soon as the judge ruled, the guards took him back to jail, where he waited to be processed out. Daniel had spent the past week tamping down his emotions, but he finally let himself believe that he would soon be out of jail. When the numbness wore off he became euphoric and he stayed high until it dawned on him that he was still the defendant in a murder case. He had been freed because there was no corroboration for April Fairweather's testimony, but what would happen when the police talked to Renee Gilchrist? Would she tell them about his phone call on the afternoon of the murder? Was that enough evidence to change the judge's mind about bail? By the time Daniel's property was returned, depression had set in.

Amanda had arranged to have the jail release Daniel through the garage so he could avoid the press. She told him that someone would be waiting for him.

Daniel expected to see Amanda's investigator, but Kate Ross was standing in the shadows of the garage when he walked out of the jail. She flashed a big smile and Daniel's depression evaporated as soon as she hugged him.

"You don't smell too bad," Kate joked after she let him go.

Daniel's face split with a huge grin. "Neither do you."

"Come on. Let's get something to eat," Kate said. Daniel had not thought about food all day, but he was suddenly famished.

"You up for baloney on white or something a little more exotic?" Kate asked.

"I'm up for anything that is not baloney on white."

Kate's car was parked a block away. As they walked to it Daniel savored the heat of the sun, the brush of the breeze on his face, and the knowledge that he could walk to Kate's car or not, as he chose.

"How are you feeling?" Kate asked when they were on the road.

"Okay. I sort of shut down when I was in jail. It's going to take me a while to believe I'm really out."

"Amanda's good," Kate reassured him. "She'll keep you out."

"I'll say she's good." Then Daniel remembered Amanda's cryptic remark. "When I thanked her for winning the bail hearing Amanda said that I have a guardian angel. Do you know what she meant?"

Kate's smile disappeared. "Yeah, I do. We talked about it this morning. Amanda destroyed Fair-weather because she received a videotape of a speech

Fairweather gave a few years ago. She was talking to a group of so-called satanic ritual abuse survivors and she told them that she had been a victim of a satanic cult. Most of what Amanda used in her cross was in Fairweather's speech."

"Who gave Amanda the tape?"

"It was sent anonymously. She thought that I sent it."

"But you didn't?"

"I've seen the tape. It was in Fairweather's case file at the office," Kate said in obvious distress. "I wanted to tell Amanda about it, but I couldn't for the same reason I couldn't investigate Fairweather for Amanda."

"Hey, you've done more for me than anyone could," Daniel reassured her. "I'd still be in jail if you didn't ask Amanda to take my case."

"Then you understand? Fairweather is a client. There's a conflict."

"I would have thought less of you if you'd violated your trust."

Kate looked relieved.

"Does Amanda have any idea who sent the tape?" Daniel asked.

"No, but everyone at the conference knew about it. So did everyone at Reed, Briggs who was working on the case and anyone they told. Then there's Aaron Flynn and the people in his firm. I don't know if they were aware of the tape before the hearing, but Flynn's investigators are good."

"Boy, you've certainly narrowed the number of suspects."

Kate smiled, relieved that Daniel was not mad at her.

Daniel became quiet.

"What are you thinking?" Kate asked.

"That this isn't the first anonymous message someone has sent recently."

"You're talking about the Kaidanov study."

Daniel nodded.

"I thought about that," Kate said. "We don't know that the same person sent both packages. Is there a connection between the Insufort case and Fairweather's?"

"I can think of two. Briggs was the defense attorney in both cases. He told Fairweather to come to the cottage at eight-fifteen and he wanted me there at eight, which means he wanted us there at the same time."

"What's the other connection between Fairweather and the Insufort litigation?"

"Aaron Flynn. He represents the plaintiffs in both cases."

Daniel suddenly noticed that they were almost at Kate's house.

"I thought we were going to lunch."

"We are. Amanda didn't want you out in public, so we're eating at my place. You're staying with me, too. Your place is a mess. The cops trashed it when they searched. I didn't think you'd want to spend your first day of freedom with a mop and dustpan. I've got a nice guest room and Herb Cross brought over a valise with clothes and other things. You'll even be able to use your own toothbrush."

Kate pulled into her driveway and parked.

"You're a good friend," Daniel said warmly.

"That I am, and you'll need a few if we're going to get you out of this mess."

Daniel showered and changed into a clean pair of jeans and a baggy sweatshirt. When he opened the bathroom door he smelled brewing coffee. He followed the aroma into the kitchen and found Kate reading the afternoon edition of the newspaper. She looked up and smiled.

"Can I fix you some eggs and toast?"

"Yeah, thanks."

Kate walked to the stove. "How do you like your bacon?"

"On a plate," Daniel cracked. Kate's laugh brought Daniel an unexpected degree of pleasure.

Kate took three thick strips and laid them in a pan. Daniel sat at the kitchen table and read the story about his case in the late edition of the paper.

"I thought *The Oregonian* was fair," Kate said as she scrambled the eggs. "They wrote that Amanda cast serious doubts on Fairweather's identification and they pointed out that there wasn't any other evidence connecting you to the murder."

That should have made Daniel happy, but it didn't. He was waiting for the other shoe to drop when the police interviewed Renee.

Kate placed a plate piled high with eggs, bacon, and toast in front of Daniel, then brought him a cup of coffee.

"I'd never guess that you had this domestic streak," Daniel joked.

"Don't get used to it," Kate answered, tossing a set of keys next to Daniel's plate. "You're on your own after tonight."

"What are these?"

"A spare set of keys to my house. I'm going to be away for a few days and you'll need them."

"Where are you going?"

"To Arizona."

Daniel looked confused.

"While you were getting yourself arrested the cops found out the identity of the dead man at the lab. It wasn't Dr. Kaidanov."

"Who was it?"

"An Arizona lawyer named Gene Arnold."

"What was he doing at the lab?"

"No one knows. His partner doesn't even know what he was doing in Oregon. Arnold went to New York on business, saw a photograph in an art gallery of two people walking across Pioneer Square, and flew here. He checked into the Benson and disappeared. Now we know where he went, but not why. I'm betting the answer is in Arizona."

27

Kate rented a car at the airport and drove to Desert Grove under a vast blue sky along a desolate highway surrounded by desert and red-rock mesas. She appreciated the stark beauty of the scenery, but for someone who had spent her life in the Pacific Northwest there was too much sun and too little green. Shortly before one, Kate parked in front of a flat, modern, one-story building on the outskirts of town. ARNOLD & KELLOGG, ATTORNEYS-AT-LAW was stenciled in gold on a plate-glass window that fronted the street.

Benjamin Kellogg, a big-boned Scandinavian in his early thirties with wheat-colored hair, ushered her down the hall to his office.

"Thank you for meeting with me on a Saturday," Kate said when they were seated.

"Gene wasn't just my law partner, Ms. Ross. I'd appreciate hearing anything you can tell me that will help me understand what happened."

"Quite frankly, no one—the police, my firm, no one—has any clue to why your partner died where he did. That's why I'm here."

"I'll help if I can," Kellogg assured her.

"My firm is defending Geller Pharmaceuticals in a lawsuit that questions the safety of Insufort, one of its products. Information about a study allegedly conducted by our client surfaced during a deposition. The results of the study supported the plaintiff's claim that the drug is harmful. Soon after the existence of the report was discovered, the lab where the study was conducted was destroyed in an arson fire. Your partner's body was found in the ruins. Was Gene Arnold or your firm connected in any way with this litigation?"

"No."

"Can you think of any reason for Mr. Arnold to come to Oregon?"

Kellogg looked completely baffled. "I'm sorry, Ms. Ross, but I have no idea why Gene was in Oregon. We don't have any cases there."

"Has Mr. Arnold ever mentioned friends or business acquaintances who live in Oregon?"

"No, but Gene hired me six years ago, fresh out of law school. I only made partner last year. I don't know much about things that happened here before I moved from Phoenix, except for the murders, of course. They were news statewide."

"What murders?"

"Gene's wife and the wife of our biggest client were kidnapped and murdered. It probably wasn't a big deal out of state, but it was major news in Arizona." Kellogg shook his head. "It was really horrible. First, Martin's wife was killed, then Gene's. Neither one of them ever really got over it."

Kate leaned forward. "This is the first I've heard about these murders. Can you fill me in?"

"I don't know much more than what I read. Like I said, this was before I moved to Desert Grove, about seven years ago. I didn't know Gene then, or Martin Alvarez."

"Who is Martin Alvarez?"

"He's the wealthiest man in Laurel County. A year or so before I got here his wife was murdered during a bungled kidnapping attempt. Paul McCann, a local guy, was arrested. Then Gene's wife was kidnapped and murdered. For a while Gene was a suspect in his wife's murder, but they dropped the charges. It was a horrible time for Gene. He was still a mess during the first year I worked here."

"Did they ever catch Mrs. Arnold's killer?"

"No."

"Can you give me any more details?"

"Not really. It was all over by the time I started working for Gene and he never talked about it."

"Who would know more about the murders?"

Kellogg hesitated. "There's Martin, but I'm not certain he'll see you."

"Why is that?"

"Martin worshiped his wife. He was devastated by her death. From what I hear he was very gregarious before she was killed. Everyone says that he threw the best parties; he was very active in the community and a great contributor to local charities. That all changed after his wife died. He's very reclusive now. He rarely leaves his hacienda, even to conduct business."

28

The Alvarez ranch was several miles out of town. There was no marker on the highway and Kate would have missed the turn onto the dirt track that led to the hacienda if Benjamin Kellogg had not given her precise directions. Kate drove on through a swirl of dust, but there was no sign of civilization. On both sides of the road clumps of desert plants clung to the arid and rocky ground and giant cacti stretched their arms toward a blue sky marred only by occasional wisps of clean white cloud. Kate was beginning to wonder if she'd made the right turn when an expanse of brown adobe walls materialized in the distance.

A guard inspected Kate's identification before directing her to a parking area in front of a massive whitewashed Spanish-style house with a red tile roof. She noticed another armed guard as she walked up a flagstone path to a front door of carved oak, which opened before she could knock.

"Miss Ross?" asked a slender, light-boned woman

of middle age dressed in a plain dress and comfortable shoes.

"Yes, ma'am."

The woman smiled. "I'm Anna Cordova, Mr. Alvarez's assistant. He's out at the pool."

Cordova inquired politely about Kate's plane trip as she led the investigator across a tiled entryway, down four wide hardwood steps, and across a sunken living room. A blanket with an intricate American Indian design decorated one wall and an oil painting of a cattle drive decorated another; a glass case in a corner displayed pre-Columbian art. Kate walked by a stone fireplace and a painting that looked like a Georgia O'Keeffe.

Outside, into the heat again. But this time there was shade from a roof that overhung a wide patio of brownish-red Spanish tile. At the end of the patio was a pool wide enough for six lap lanes and deep enough at one end for a diving board. An armed guard stood in the shadows created by the high wall that surrounded the compound. His eyes followed Kate as she crossed the veranda, but Kate lost interest in him quickly. Her attention was drawn to a heavyset man in white cotton pants and a loose-fitting short-sleeve shirt who was seated under an umbrella at a circular glass table, staring toward the pool.

Martin Alvarez stood when he heard the women approach. Kate guessed that he was six two. A black eye patch covered his right eye and a scar ran across his temple, reddish white against his dark, pockmarked skin. There were streaks of gray in his jet-black hair. A bushy mustache covered his upper lip.

Alvarez's shoulders were thick and his forearms were heavily muscled. The investigator's immediate impression was that he was a hard, unforgiving man.

"Martin, Miss Ross is here," Anna Cordova said.

Alvarez crossed the pool deck with a determined stride.

"Gene is dead?" he asked without preliminaries.

Kate nodded.

"There is no mistake?" Alvarez asked. His face betrayed no emotions.

"No."

"The details, please. And do not spare my feelings. I am hardened to violence. Nothing you tell me will be worse than what I've already experienced."

"Mr. Arnold was killed with a sharp instrument, probably a knife. He didn't suffer. His death would have been quick."

"Why did it take you so long to identify him? Kellogg reported him missing weeks ago."

"His body was found in the ruins of a laboratory in the woods, several miles from downtown Portland. Mr. Arnold's body had to be identified through dental records because the body burned with the building."

There was a quick intake of breath.

"He was dead before the fire was set," Kate added quickly to put Alvarez's mind at ease.

"Why don't you continue your conversation by the pool." Cordova pointed to the glass-topped table. "I'll have Miguel bring you some refreshments. Would you like an iced tea?" she asked Kate.

"That would be fine, thank you."

Alvarez walked back to the table. Kate sat across from him under the shade of a large umbrella.

"Do you have any suspects?" Alvarez asked.

"No. The police don't even know what Mr. Arnold was doing in Oregon."

"I don't either. Gene was in New York to obtain financing for one of my business ventures. I expected him back as soon as he was finished."

"So he wasn't supposed to go to Portland after he was through in New York?"

"No."

"Have you ever had any dealings with the Geller Pharmaceutical Company?"

"No."

"Can you think of any reason why Mr. Arnold would be interested in primate research?"

"No. Why do you ask?"

Kate gave Alvarez a brief explanation of the Insufort case. Alvarez blanched when she mentioned Aaron Flynn's name.

"Is something wrong?" Kate asked.

"Seven years ago a man named Paul McCann murdered my wife. Aaron Flynn was his attorney."

"Was Flynn a big man with red hair?"

"Yes."

Kate told Alvarez about the Bernier photograph.

"My best guess is that Mr. Arnold came to Oregon to talk to one of the people in the picture. Maybe Flynn is in it. Do you know why that would have been such a shock?"

Alvarez's brow furrowed and Kate thought that he looked genuinely perplexed.

"I can only guess that seeing Flynn brought back memories of his wife's murder," Alvarez answered after some thought.

"Were the murders of your wife and Mr. Arnold's related?"

"Yes."

Kate let that rest for a moment.

"How did Mr. Arnold get along with Flynn when they were living in Desert Grove?"

"I don't think they saw much of each other outside of professional meetings," Alvarez answered stiffly. Then he paused, lost in thought, before shaking his head. "None of this makes sense."

"It might help me to make sense of it if I knew more about what happened here, seven years ago."

Alvarez hesitated. Kate could only guess at how painful his memories must be. After a moment he fingered his scar.

"If you think it would help . . . ?"

"I don't know if it will, but we have nothing to go on now."

"I've spent seven years thinking about the murder of my wife, trying to piece together what happened. I'll tell you what I know and what I learned from others if it will help you catch the person who murdered Gene." He pointed at his sightless eye. "He may be the same person who did this to me."

Part IV

✧

Death in the Desert

29

1

It was morning in the desert. As Patty Alvarez rode Conquistador toward the red-rock canyons to the east, a crimson tinge appeared along the horizon. Then the sun began to grow huge, displaying thick waves of red-hot gas and yellow flares so bright that she couldn't gaze directly at them.

Patty liked to ride first thing in the morning because it was still cool. In an hour rivulets of sweat would be running between her breasts and her blouse would stick to her hot skin. That's when she would turn for home.

Conquistador was a King-bred quarter horse, a reddish-brown bay with a black mane and tail who had once been a champion. Martin Alvarez had presented Conquistador to his wife on her thirty-second birthday and he was Patty's favorite. As they raced across the narrow valley, she felt the muscular bay moving between her legs, reminding her of the things

Martin had done to her that morning before she left the hacienda. There were two stallions in her life. Patty smiled at the thought.

One way to cut the heat was to race through the gaps between the stone monuments that spread out before her. In the canyons, the narrow rock walls shot up to the sky and cast cooling shadows over the trail. Conquistador knew the route of their morning run by heart, so Patty could concentrate on the view. Patty believed that the mesas had been painted by nature and sculpted by God. She never tired of looking at them. They were red or brown or yellow, depending on the light, and she imagined that she saw the faces of Indians or the bodies of muscular warriors in the rock.

The land in front of the canyon was flat and the huge boulders that marked both sides of the entrance were big enough for a man to hide behind. Conquistador was drawing alongside the massive stone pile on the right when two men appeared abruptly from behind the boulders to the left. They wore navy-blue ski masks, jeans, and jackets that were zipped to the neck, a bizarre outfit to wear in a land where the heat of the day was over one hundred degrees. As the man in front raised his hand toward Patty, palm outstretched, the other man leveled a rifle at her horse.

Patty knew instantly what was happening. Martin was rich, very rich, and he loved Patty past caring. Everyone knew this, and Patty was certain that these men knew it, too. They would use Martin's love to make him pay a fortune in ransom for her. And once he paid she was certain that she would die.

Patty dropped her body forward, hugging Conquistador as she kicked her heels into his flanks. The bay sprang forward. Wind like a freight train barreled past the quarter horse. Hooves beat against the parched ground, dust flew. The men jumped aside. Patty saw a swirl of light and shadow in the canyon, and freedom. Then a shot rang out in the still desert air.

2

There were seventy thousand people living in Laurel County, Arizona, but there was no debate over who among them was the richest and most powerful. Martin Alvarez was a bear of a man with a broad flat face the color of tanned leather. He wore his hair in a ponytail, had diamond studs in his ears, and wore buckskin jackets, hand-tooled cowboy boots, and bolo ties. Martin had started with one used-car lot on the outskirts of town and now owned car dealerships all over the state, as well as a statewide chain of retail stores and profitable land holdings. But Martin's proudest possession was his wife, the redheaded, green-eyed former Miss Laurel County.

Patty Alvarez was fifteen years Martin's junior. When the most powerful man in Laurel County started courting her she had been scared to death, but she knew that marrying Martin meant security. And there was the prestige of being Mrs. Martin Alvarez. She would go from being a name scratched into the stalls in the high-school boys' room to the top of Laurel County society. So she had said yes when Martin proposed and had been happily surprised to find that she had grown to love the husband who doted on her.

The Martin Alvarez seated behind the large oak desk in the hacienda's home office was a man on the verge of violence. The only thing keeping him civilized was the absence of a target. Seated on the other side of the desk were FBI Agent Thomas Chandler, Detective Norman Chisholm of the Laurel County Sheriff's Office, and Ramon Quiroz, the Laurel County district attorney. Several other law enforcement officers were also crowded into the room. Two FBI technicians were working on Martin's phone.

"I know you've told Mr. Quiroz and several others what happened today, but I'd like to hear it firsthand, if you don't mind," Chandler said.

Martin looked ready to explode. He was tired of talking, he wanted action, but he restrained himself and recounted the day's events to the FBI agent.

"Patty rides every morning. Sometimes we ride together, but I had a conference call at seven, so she rode alone. She usually takes the same route and she's usually back between eight and nine. When she didn't return by ten I grew worried. I brought one of the men and we went looking for her."

Martin paused. Chandler watched him control his anguish and anger.

"We found Conquistador near the entrance to a canyon roughly four miles east of here."

"Conquistador is her horse?"

"Was. He's dead," Martin replied bitterly.

"And your wife was missing?"

Martin nodded. "But there was blood on the rocks where Conquistador fell."

"I've got my forensic people out there now," Chandler said. "They'll analyze the blood to see if it's from the horse."

He did not mention the other, obvious possibility.

"What did you do after you found Conquistador?"

"I called Ramon from my cell phone. Then we waited by the horse."

"Tell me about the call from the kidnappers."

"As soon as Norm arrived he told me to go home. He was worried it was a kidnapping and they'd call while I was out. They did, about two hours ago. They said no cops, but Ramon and Norm insisted that I bring you in."

"That was a very smart move."

"Unless they kill Patty," Martin said, turning his steady eyes on Chandler.

"These people want money, Mr. Alvarez. That's what this is all about. There won't be any money if they kill your wife."

Chandler waited a beat, hoping that Martin would relax a little. He didn't.

"Please tell me, word for word, as best you remember, what was said during the call."

"It was a man but he disguised his voice. He said, 'We've got your wife. If you want her to live it will cost you one million dollars. We want it in unmarked bills. Nothing larger than hundreds.' I told him it would take a day to get the money. He said he would call back with instructions. I asked to speak to Patty. He hung up. That's everything. The call didn't take long."

"Okay," the FBI agent said.

"I want honesty, Chandler," Martin demanded.

"Total honesty. What are my wife's chances?"

Chandler looked grim. He shook his head.

"I have no idea what your wife's chances are. There are too many variables. So I'm not going to guess or give you a best-case scenario. The honest truth is that I don't know. All I can promise is that we will do everything in our power to get your wife back."

3

The kidnappers told Martin to leave the ransom money under a log that crossed over Rattlesnake Creek in the mountains several hours' drive from Desert Grove. Martin's banker had the money ready, but on Chandler's instructions, Martin told the kidnappers that it would take two more hours for the bank to put the ransom together. Martin drove to the bank to pick up a large duffel bag stuffed with money while Chandler used the darkness to infiltrate a heavily armed team into the woods near the stream.

Thomas Chandler had been raised in Philadelphia, educated in Boston, and trained for his job in Quantico, Virginia. Nothing in his childhood, his schooling, or his FBI training had prepared him for lying for hours in a cold, damp forest on sharp, stony ground. Chandler had only been able to remain motionless for a little while. Soon he was shifting his body every few minutes, doing the best a city boy could to move quietly.

Scanning the area around the creek only took his mind off his discomfort for a little while. The wide stream twisted through the woods, the water deep and clear as it boiled over several boulders that changed the course of the creek. Through night-vision glasses the area looked like a neon video game.

Chandler was turning his collar up as protection against the cold mountain air when a noise made him freeze. He checked his watch. It was after ten, just about the time Alvarez would be arriving. A twig cracked and the agent saw a flashlight beam light up a stretch of the trail that wound through the woods to Rattlesnake Creek. Chandler focused his night vision-glasses on the spot where a tree felled by lightning lay across the waterway. Moments later Martin Alvarez came into view carrying a large duffel bag across his broad shoulders. Chandler watched Alvarez wedge the bag under the log. When he stood up, Alvarez cast a quick look around before returning the way he had come.

As soon as Martin disappeared up the trail Chandler trained his glasses on the duffel bag, but nothing happened. The bag lay under the log, the stream ran swiftly between its banks, and the stillness of the forest lay over the agent like a blanket. Chandler found it impossible to watch the duffel bag continuously. Besides, he knew that the snipers hiding in blinds throughout the forest and the other agents in the capture team were on alert. He shifted for comfort and closed his eyes. He was starting to nod off when fear of falling asleep jerked him back to his duty. Chandler chided himself, slapped his face to stir his adrenaline, and refocused his glasses on the log just as a man dressed entirely in black rose out of the creek and grabbed the duffel.

Chandler unholstered his weapon. "FBI! Freeze!"

Automatic fire sprayed through the woods from somewhere on the other side of the creek. Chandler hit the ground. The man with the duffel fled down the stream using the burst as cover. Chandler heard the other agents return fire. He got to his feet and raced into the frigid water. The fleeing man suddenly darted out of the stream and into the forest with Chandler in pursuit. It was hard to move in the dense underbrush. The agent tripped over a root and stumbled forward just as another burst of automatic fire shredded the foliage above his head, showering him with leaves.

As soon as the gunfire stopped Chandler regained his footing. He heard ragged breathing and the sound of someone smashing through the bushes. Then a shot rang out, followed by a sharp grunt, and one of the snipers yelled, "He's hit."

Chandler raced ahead until he burst into a clearing, nearly running into a large man wearing a ski mask and bleeding badly from a leg wound. The man tried to pivot on his injured leg and stumbled. Chandler drove into him, taking him to the ground. Moments later a chokehold ended the brief fight. By that time several other agents assisted in subduing the captive.

"Where's the other one?" Chandler demanded as soon as he caught his breath.

"They're after him," one of the agents answered.

Chandler remembered the duffel bag. He turned in a circle, then asked for a flashlight. He shined the light over the area where he'd just fought. Then he asked the handcuffed prisoner, "Where's the ransom money?"

An agent pulled off the ski mask. The man he confronted was six feet tall. His face had the ruddy complexion of someone who worked outdoors and his red hair was plastered across his forehead.

"Where is Patty Alvarez?" Chandler demanded.

The man looked beat, but he did not look beaten.

"I want a lawyer," he answered. "I ain't sayin' nothin' before I talk to a lawyer."

Chandler knelt next to the man, gripped his chin, and forced his head up so they were eye to eye.

"If Patty Alvarez is dead, you're facing the death penalty," Chandler whispered so only the man could hear what he said. "If you cooperate right now we can deal. Keep asking for a lawyer and I'll be smiling at you when they pull the switch."

Chandler released the man's chin. The man broke eye contact. Two winded agents burst into the clearing. They started to speak, but Chandler held up his hand and led them out of earshot of the prisoner.

"There's a deer trail a half mile up the creek," one of the agents said. "We followed it for a mile. It crosses a deserted logging road that wasn't on any of our maps. There were fresh tire tracks in the dirt."

Chandler swore. The prisoner's accomplice must have grabbed the duffel bag while the two of them were out of his sight. Chandler pushed past the other agents and walked up to the prisoner.

"Your partner has the money and he's gone. That means you are going down for every charge I can think of unless you help us, right now. You have one minute to make up your mind."

4

Martin Alvarez focused intently on the testimony of Lester Dobbs, who had cut a deal shortly after his arrest near Rattlesnake Creek, then led the FBI agents to the shallow grave where Patty Alvarez was buried. However, someone other than Dobbs had captured the attention of Paul McCann, the man who was on trial for Patty's murder.

Melissa Arnold was the court reporter for the Laurel County Circuit Court during the trial of *State* v. *McCann*. Every day while court was in session, she sat in front of the dais from which Judge Melvin Schrieber presided typing every word that was spoken in court onto her stenograph machine with amazing accuracy. The ability to type with accuracy was not the only amazing thing about Melissa Arnold. She had long, honey-blond hair that hung to her shoulders, pale blue eyes, and full lips. The consensus around the courthouse was that she had the most beautiful legs anyone had ever seen. The rest of Melissa's body was also outstanding. So outstanding, in fact, that Paul McCann could not keep his eyes off her, even though Lester Dobbs was giving testimony that could send him to death row.

Paul McCann was addicted to women, so it was not surprising that his attention was riveted on the most stunning woman in the room. Women were also addicted to Paul. He was a big man who dressed in loud clothes and sported gaudy jewelry. He wore his styled hair a little long, left his mustache a trifle bushy, and exposed his curly black chest hair whenever possible. Most men thought he looked tacky, but a certain class of woman found him irresistible and he did nothing to discourage their advances.

"Mr. Dobbs, how are you employed?" Ramon Quiroz, the Laurel County district attorney, asked his star witness. Ramon wore an ill-fitting brown suit. He was short, fat, and laid-back. He was also extremely tough to beat in court.

The question about employment proved to be a stumper for Lester Dobbs, who stared at Ramon the way he might if the prosecutor had asked him to explain quantum mechanics. Dobbs fidgeted in the witness chair and looked uncomfortable in the cheap blue suit that Quiroz had purchased for him.

"I ain't employed right now," Dobbs answered after a lengthy pause.

"That's true, Mr. Dobbs," Ramon agreed with admirable patience, "but before your arrest you did work, did you not?"

"Sure."

"Well, then, why don't you tell the jury what kind of work you performed."

"I worked construction for Mr. McCann," Dobbs answered, nodding toward Aaron Flynn's client. At the mention of his name, the defendant reluctantly shifted his gaze from Melissa Arnold's breasts and focused his attention on his chief accuser.

"What exactly were you constructing?"

"Sunnyvale Farm."

"Which is?" Ramon prompted.

"A housing development. We was building forty-three homes, or was supposed to before the money run out."

"How did you learn that Mr. McCann's project was in trouble?"

"He told me. That's why we did it. For the money, so's he could pay off his creditors and keep the project going."

"Objection," Aaron Flynn said, rising to his feet.

"Yes, Mr. Dobbs," Judge Schrieber lectured, "please listen carefully to the question and only answer what you are asked."

"Jurors," Schrieber continued, "please ignore everything Mr. Dobbs said, except his statement that Mr. McCann told him that the Sunnyvale project was in trouble."

"Mr. Dobbs, you are an ex-convict, are you not?" Ramon continued.

"Yes, sir. Several times."

"Did Mr. McCann know this?"

"Oh, yeah. That's why he thought I'd help him, because I'd been in prison. He said he needed someone with criminal experience."

Flynn objected on the grounds that the answer was not responsive and the judge lectured Dobbs again. Dobbs didn't appear to be bright enough to understand what he was doing wrong. If the jurors suspected the same thing, they might also conclude that Dobbs was too dumb to make up his testimony.

"Mr. Dobbs, why don't you tell this jury how you

came to be involved in the kidnapping and murder of Patty Alvarez."

"Okay. Best I recollect, it was one evening in April," Dobbs said, turning toward the jurors. "I was sittin' at the bar in the Red Rooster Tavern, mindin' my own business and drinkin' a beer. Mr. McCann come in the tavern. Next thing I know, he's askin' me if I'd like to join him for a beer in a booth."

"Was it unusual for you and Mr. McCann to have a drink together?"

"Yes, sir, it was. In fact, this was the first time I'd ever talked to Mr. McCann, except on the job, and then it would be about problems on the site, stuff like that."

"What did you two talk about?" Ramon asked.

"Nothin' much, at first. Sports, the weather."

"Did the conversation turn to Sunnyvale at some point?"

Dobbs glanced over at McCann. He looked as if he was embarrassed that he was testifying for the state.

"Mr. McCann told me that Sunnyvale might not get built. There was money owed or some such. If he couldn't come up with it, the project was doomed. That's how he said it, 'doomed.' "

"What did you say to that?"

"Well, I was wonderin' if I'd lose my job, because it paid pretty good. Mr. McCann said everyone would lose his job if he couldn't pay off the loan. Then he asked me about the prison. Which one I'd been in, whether it was hard to be inside. It caught me by surprise, because he just jumped from one subject to another without no warning."

"Did you tell him about prison and what you did to be sent there?"

"Yes, sir. He seemed right interested. Especially when I told him that I've been in for aggravated assault and armed robbery."

"Now, just so the jury will know, those were two different convictions?"

"Yes, sir."

"And you've also been convicted of assault twice where you didn't go to prison."

"I got probation on that."

"Okay. Now, what happened after you told Mr. McCann all about prison?"

"Nothin' then. We just drunk some more beer, talked about some fight. Mike Tyson, I think. Then he looked at his watch and said he had to go. And he did."

"So, the defendant didn't mention anything about Mrs. Alvarez?"

"Not till the next time."

"And when was that?"

"About three days later. I was walkin' to my car after work when Mr. McCann stopped me. He asked me if I was interested in making some extra money. I said, 'Sure.' He said to meet him in the parking lot of the Red Rooster at ten. I thought I misheard him, so I asked him if he'd said the parking lot. He said this was a private matter and he didn't want no one to know we was talking."

"What happened in the parking lot of the Red Rooster?"

"Mr. McCann drove up and told me to get in this

car he was driving. It wasn't his normal one, which is this bright red sports car. This one was black, a plain old Ford. Anyway, I got in and he drove me out into the desert where it was only the two of us and he asked me what I would do for fifty thousand dollars."

Several jurors turned to look at each other and there was murmuring in the back of the courtroom.

"What did you answer?"

"I thought he was kidding, so I joked back that I'd do most anything. Then, just in case it wasn't a joke, I told him I wouldn't kill no one. That's when he asked if I would commit a crime short of murder and I asked him what he meant."

Dobbs took a sip of water before turning back to the jury.

"Mr. McCann told me that his company was in big trouble, but he had a foolproof way of fixing up his problems. He asked me if I'd heard of Martin Alvarez. I said, 'Sure.' Everyone in Desert Grove knows who he is. Mr. McCann said that Mrs. Alvarez— Patty, he called her—was the light of Mr. Alvarez's life and that he would do anything to protect her from harm, including paying over a large sum of money that could be used to keep the Sunnyvale project afloat. I asked how much money we was talking about and Mr. McCann said that Martin Alvarez could part with one million dollars without batting an eye."

"What did you tell the defendant when he said this?" Ramon asked.

"I said, in that case, I was gonna want more than fifty thousand to help."

5

Desert Grove was baking and the ancient air conditioner barely stirred the air in the courtroom. The judge called the morning recess and most of the observers filed out to get a cool drink or wash their faces in the rest room, but Martin Alvarez did not move. Soon he was alone in the front row staring hard, first at Dobbs, then at Paul McCann. Ramon Quiroz saw what was going on. He leaned across the low railing that separated the gallery from the judge and attorneys and whispered something to Alvarez. When Quiroz was through talking, Martin stood and left the courtroom.

When court resumed, Dobbs testified that Paul McCann knew that Patty Alvarez loved to ride in the desert and that she rode in the morning before the heat of the day. According to Dobbs, McCann planned to ambush her out of sight of the hacienda. Alvarez would be tied up, blindfolded, and taken in the back of a van to the basement of an abandoned house in the next county. The plan called for Dobbs to baby-sit Alvarez while McCann negotiated the ransom. Nothing went the way it was supposed to.

"Mr. McCann picked me up in his van real early. We drove out to this spot in the desert where there's this big outcropping of rock that Mrs. Alvarez always passed and we parked the van behind the rocks so Mrs. Alvarez wouldn't see it."

"What happened next?"

"We waited until Mr. McCann said he saw her coming. He had binoculars, but even I could see the dust. So we put on our ski masks and took out our guns. . . ."

"Who supplied the guns?"

"Mr. McCann."

"Go on."

"The plan was that Mr. McCann would jump out and wave his hands to stop the horse. Then I'd grab Mrs. Alvarez and tie her up. Only, it didn't work that way. Mr. McCann was standing out there waving and she did slow down. Then something spooked her and she spurred the horse and tried to ride past us. Once she took off, that would be that. And that's when Mr. McCann done it."

"Did what, Mr. Dobbs?"

"Shot the horse. BAM! It was like in the movies. The horse was up on its hind legs, pawing at the air. It was almost like slow motion that horse rearing up, the blood pouring out. It paused up in the air for a moment, then took two steps back and toppled over, right onto the rocks and right on top of Mrs. Alvarez.

"I just stood there watching. I couldn't believe it. The shot was real loud, like a thunderclap. Then there was a dull thunk when Mrs. Alvarez's head hit the rocks and a thud when the horse came down on top of her. When I heard the thunk I knew we were in big trouble. Right away I was thinking that she was dead, and I was right."

"What did Mr. McCann do after he shot the horse?"

"He just stood there like he was paralyzed. I did, too, but I recovered after a moment. The first thing I did was ask him why he did it, but he was just staring. I don't think he planned shooting the horse. I think he just did it on the spur of the moment."

"What happened next?"

"I ran over to Mrs. Alvarez. She was a mess. Her head was mashed between the horse and the rock. Mr. McCann staggered over. He could barely keep his feet. He tried to ask me if she was dead, but he couldn't say the word."

"What word is that?"

" 'Dead.' He just couldn't say it. So I said it for him. As soon as I did he just sat down in the dust and started talking to himself."

"What did he say?"

" 'Oh, God, oh, God.' He said that a few times and 'What are we gonna do now?' I told him we should get the fuck—uh, get outta there."

"Did he agree?"

"No. He put his hands over his ears and told me to shut up so he could think. I said, 'Fine,' but I was plannin' to take the van if he didn't move soon. Then, just as I was getting ready to go, he did something that surprised me."

"And what was that?"

"He took out his cell phone and made a call."

"Mr. Dobbs, until this point how many people did you think were involved in the kidnapping?"

"Two. Me and him."

"Did you discover that there was a third person in on the plot?"

"Yes, sir, but I don't know who it was, because I

only heard Mr. McCann's side of the conversation and he never mentioned a name."

"Please describe the phone conversation to the jury."

"It was short. First, he said everything had gotten . . ." Dobbs paused and looked up at the judge. "Uh, can I use the F-word, Your Honor?"

"Accuracy is very important, Mr. Dobbs," Judge Schrieber replied. "Please make sure that you use the exact words that you claim the defendant used."

"Okay," Dobbs said, turning back to the jurors. "He said everything had gotten fucked up and he explained about having to shoot the horse when Mrs. Alvarez tried to escape. Then he listened for a while. Mr. McCann had his mask off by then and I could see him turning red like he was being chewed out. After a minute I heard him ask what he should do. He nodded his head a few times, then hung up. I asked him who he was talking to, but he said it was none of my business. I said it damn well was because I was an accessory to this whole thing, including Mrs. Alvarez being dead. That's when he told me the plan."

"Which was?" Ramon prodded.

"To pretend she wasn't dead. To bury the body and demand the ransom anyway. He told me that was the only way any of us would get any money."

"What did you say to that?"

Dobbs shrugged. "I said, 'Okay.' I was in it for the money and Martin Alvarez wouldn't know his wife was dead. What difference would it make?"

6

Court broke at five when Lester Dobbs finished his testimony. Aaron Flynn said a few words to his client and packed up his papers while the guards took Dobbs back to the jail. After law school, Flynn had received no offers from the firms and government offices in Phoenix and Tucson. Desperate for work, he had applied to the Laurel County District Attorney's Office on the day a deputy DA resigned. Two years later Flynn left to set up a solo practice in a shabby storefront office a few blocks from the courthouse. He scraped by, paying the bills by taking anything that came in the door, until Paul McCann came along.

McCann planned to turn land on the outskirts of Desert Grove into a housing development called Sunnyvale Farm and he put Flynn on retainer to deal with his legal affairs. Flynn thought that McCann would be a constant source of easy money, but he was soon spending all his time on McCann's problems. First there were labor troubles, then Flynn had difficulties obtaining permits from the county supervisors. He was perplexed until someone let slip the fact that Martin Alvarez was interested in the land upon which McCann was building. Within months McCann was on the verge of bankruptcy and he blamed Martin Alvarez for his problems. When the FBI cut a deal with Lester Dobbs for his testimony, no one was shocked when he named Paul McCann as the man who'd hired him to help kidnap Patty Alvarez.

As Flynn was getting ready to leave the courtroom, Paul's wife, Joan, an anorexic woman with pale skin and jet-black hair, approached him. Flynn suspected that her physical appearance and high level of anxiety were the direct result of living with his client. She had filed for divorce twice, backing out when Paul promised to be faithful and stop beating her. Joan worked as Gene Arnold's legal secretary and it was her salary and savings that were paying Flynn's retainer.

"Mr. Flynn," she asked nervously, "can I speak to you?"

"Of course, Joan."

"What did you think of Dobbs's testimony?"

"Tough to say," Flynn said, hedging. He had learned that honesty was not the best policy with Joan. She was as fragile as a Fabergé egg. Since her husband's arrest she had bitten her nails to the quick and developed a nervous tic in the corner of her left eye.

"You don't believe him, do you?"

Flynn put a comforting hand on her shoulder. "Paul swears he's innocent, Joan. I'm his lawyer."

The answer seemed to pacify her. If she realized that it completely evaded her question, she didn't call him on it.

"I'll be a witness, won't I?" she asked for the millionth time.

"Of course."

"He was fishing. I saw him leave before dawn. He had all of his fishing gear in the van."

"That will help Paul for sure," Flynn told her in a soothing voice. "And the lab found nothing in Paul's van that showed that Mrs. Alvarez was ever in it."

The ransom money had not been found either. And

the tracks on the logging road were from a stolen car that had been abandoned several days later in another county.

"I'm afraid, Mr. Flynn. I don't know what I'll do if Paul is sent to prison." She looked away. "He's not easy to live with. You know he's hit me and he's cheated on me. You know that."

"I know, Joan."

"But he can be so loving."

The way she said it made Flynn feel that she was trying to convince herself of the truth of what she was saying as much as she was trying to convince him.

"The night he proposed, he drove me out to Bishop's Point. We were alone. There was a full moon and the stars filled up the sky. He said he wanted to stay there with me forever. I believe he meant that. We would have been okay if we could have just stayed there."

Joan's shoulders shook as she sobbed. Flynn wrapped her up in a hug.

"Now, now," he said before releasing her. He held out a handkerchief so she could dry her eyes. When Joan handed it back, she tried to smile, but her lips just twisted and she choked back another sob. Flynn touched her shoulder again.

"Hang in there, Joan. The case will be over in a day or so."

"I'll try," she said, then smiled bravely and walked away, leaving Aaron Flynn very much relieved.

By the time Flynn arrived at his office it was 5:30 and his secretary was gone. Flynn was taking his trial materials out of his briefcase when Melissa Arnold knocked lightly on the office door, startling him.

"Sorry to frighten you, Mr. Flynn," Melissa said in a mocking tone. She leaned her hip against the door-jamb. "I believe you wanted to discuss the preparation of a daily transcript of Lester Dobbs's testimony."

"Yes, I did, Mrs. Arnold," Flynn answered nervously. He found it impossible to maintain his composure when he was alone with Gene Arnold's wife. "Why don't you shut the door and come in."

"Preparing a daily transcript is hard," Melissa said as she crossed the room. "I'll have to work late and it's such lonely work."

"Maybe I can help you solve that problem," Flynn said.

Melissa pressed against him and silenced him with her lips. Flynn grabbed the hem of her skirt and hiked it up until he had his hands on her silk panties. Moments later they were on the couch ripping at each other's clothes.

7

In closing arguments, Aaron Flynn played up the deal Dobbs had cut with the district attorney. The man was basically walking away, Flynn told the jurors. He was even out of jail pending sentencing on the attempted kidnapping count, which was the only charge the state was going to bring against him. But even though the jury knew Dobbs had a motive to lie, he seemed to be telling the truth and Paul McCann had no alibi for the time of the kidnapping. Two hours after they retired to deliberate, the jury was back with a verdict of guilty on all charges, including the charge of murder.

McCann didn't take the verdict well. He broke down. He screamed and cried. He swore he was innocent and that Dobbs was lying. Flynn promised to fight his case all the way to the United States Supreme Court if necessary. The appeal he promised would begin as soon as Melissa Arnold, the court reporter, prepared the transcript of the case.

But that never happened. One week after Paul McCann's trial ended, Melissa Arnold disappeared.

Someone was knocking on Martin Alvarez's bedroom door. He sat up groggily and stared at the clock on his end table. It was 2:30 A.M.

"Señor Alvarez," a man called out. Alvarez recognized the voice of one of his guards.

"Come in."

A barrel-chested young man entered the bedroom.

"What is it?"

"Señor Arnold is here."

"What does he want?"

"He wouldn't tell me, but he's very upset."

"All right. Take him to my office, and see if he wants something to drink. I'll be right down."

The day after his arrest, Lester Dobbs had led the police to Patty Alvarez's grave in the desert. Martin was home when he got the news that Patty was really dead. He had identified the body, returned to his hacienda, and remained there, leaving only to attend

Patty's funeral and Paul McCann's trial. Several friends had tried to pay condolence calls, but Martin had turned them away. This was different. Gene Arnold was more than Martin's lawyer. He had worked for Martin for peanuts when Martin was nobody. He had always been there for him when times were hard.

Alvarez dressed quickly. When he walked into his office he found his friend and lawyer pacing back and forth, his cheeks tear-streaked and his hair uncombed.

"She's gone," Gene said.

"Who's gone?"

Gene slumped on a chair and buried his head in his hands.

"Melissa," he moaned.

Gene Arnold was five eight, balding, and had the start of a paunch. He was not much to look at, in other words, which made his marriage to Melissa Arnold so surprising. He had met her during a deposition in Los Angeles, where she was working as a freelance court reporter. According to Gene, she had just left a terrible marriage. He had been pulverized by her looks and had proposed after one date. They married at a wedding chapel in Las Vegas and honeymooned at Caesars Palace.

Almost from the day he came back to Desert Grove with his bride, the gossips said Melissa had married Gene for his money. Martin and Patty Alvarez saw a lot of the couple and it had been Patty's opinion that Melissa was never in love with her husband—he was someone safe and comfortable who would worship her and never betray her.

Alvarez poured Arnold a tall Scotch and forced him to take a drink. When Gene was calm enough to speak coherently, he told Martin what had happened that day.

"Melissa left for work this morning. I went to the office. Around nine-thirty, Marge called from Mel's chambers to ask if Melissa was sick." Gene looked up, his face the very picture of despair. "She never made it to work, Martin."

Martin's first thought was that she had run out on Gene and the tedium of Desert Grove. He knew Melissa had grown tired of Gene and the town fairly quickly. Martin based his conclusion on the fact that she'd come on to him at his Fourth of July barbecue. Martin had rebuffed her gently and had never told anyone about the pass, but he watched her closely after that and noticed her flirting with more than one man.

"Marge said no one had seen Melissa at the court-house. I called home, thinking she was sick and had gone back to the house. There was no answer, so I drove home in case she was sleeping or had fainted or . . ."

"And she wasn't there?"

Gene shook his head. It was still hard for him to talk.

"But all her clothes were there. So were the suit-cases. There wasn't any note. She hasn't run off, Martin."

A feeling of dread began to grow in Martin's stomach.

"Did you call the sheriff?"

"No. What would I have said? I mean, she was

only gone for a few hours. I was worried, but after I called the hospital and they said she wasn't there, I kept thinking that she would call and explain what happened. The sheriff wasn't going to do anything, anyway, until there was proof that something had happened to her."

"And now there is?" Martin asked fearfully.

"There . . . there was a call." Gene stopped and caught his breath. "The voice was disguised. It was so low that I couldn't understand it at first."

Gene started to cry again. Finally, he choked out what he had to say.

"They have her. It's the people who took Patty."

Martin felt sick.

"It's the same people," Gene sobbed. "The caller said so. They'll kill her if I call the police. What should I do? I love her. I've got to save her."

Gene looked at Alvarez for an answer, but Martin couldn't think straight.

"Did they let you talk to Melissa?"

"No. I asked, but they refused."

"What do they want?"

"Seventy-five thousand dollars or they're going to kill her."

"Can you get your hands on that much money?"

"Just. I've got a retirement account. The money means nothing to me. It's Melissa. If they kill her . . ."

"What are you supposed to do?"

"The kidnappers are going to contact me around five tonight at my house. They said they're watching me and they'll know if I go to the cops or have a tap put on my phone."

"What do you want me to do, Gene?"

Arnold raised his eyes to Alvarez's face. It was a block of stone.

"I can't risk going to the police or the FBI. Look at the mess they made in your case."

Martin nodded. Gene leaned forward, his hands clasped like a supplicant before a king.

"Can you bring them the money, Martin?" Arnold looked down. "I . . . I'm not brave. Look at me. What could I do to save her? But you're tough. If there was a chance, you could fight them . . ."

His voice trailed off. The plea was pathetic and desperate.

"That makes no sense at all, Gene. I'm no Rambo, and these guys won't fight fair. This isn't like one of those kung fu movies where the villain throws down his weapons and fights the hero hand to hand. They'll have guns and they'll shoot me in the back if it suits them. They shot it out with the FBI."

"I'm sorry. You're right, I don't know what I was thinking." Gene sounded thoroughly defeated. "I have to take the chance that Melissa is alive and that they'll return her to me if I pay them."

Alvarez looked at the clock on his desk. It was a little after three. His mind was racing. He doubted that Melissa Arnold was still alive, but that didn't mean that he would let his friend deal with her killers. They were the people who murdered his Patty and this was a chance for revenge.

"Let me take you home," Alvarez said calmly, giving none of his feelings away. "I'll stay with you. Let's see what they say. Then we'll decide what to do."

8

By the time the call came, the money was waiting inside a gym bag and Martin had reached a decision. Gene had the receiver pressed to his ear before the second ring. Martin heard him say, "I understand" and "Yes," then, "Is my wife—" and knew by the way Gene's features crumbled that they had hung up on him without letting him talk to Melissa or assuring him that she was all right.

"Gene?" Martin asked softly.

Arnold stared at the phone.

"What did they say?"

"There's a side road off the highway." He sounded dazed. "It's near the bridge that crosses the McPherson River where they have the picnic grounds."

"I know it."

The McPherson River was twenty miles from Desert Grove in a deep canyon. The Park Service had developed a picturesque area near it. Rafters set out from a small park with a picnic area. Last summer, Martin and Patty had rafted that river with Gene and Melissa.

"Tonight, as soon as it gets dark, I'm supposed to drive up the road for a mile and park the car near the trail to the river. They want me to walk down to the river and follow the trail until it curves around the cliff side. I'm supposed to leave the money there and drive home."

"What then?"

"They didn't say."

It was a strange plan. The trail from the road to the

picnic area was the only way in or out. On the other hand, at night, the location was pretty isolated and the kidnapper would see anyone who tried to follow Gene.

"I'm going to take them the money," Martin said.

Gene looked startled. "Forget that. I was crazy to ask you before."

"Someone has to wait here in case Melissa comes home."

"I can't ask you to do this for me."

"You're a good friend, Gene. And I'm not asking for your permission."

Gene started to argue, but the determination he saw on Martin's face stopped him.

"Thank you," he whispered. "I'll never forget this."

It was cold in the desert that night, and Martin was wearing jeans and a windbreaker to fight the chill. The bag of money bumped against his legs as he descended toward the river. Tucked in his waistband was a licensed .45-caliber automatic. A hunting knife hung from his belt in a scabbard. Martin had a simple plan. He would kneecap the person who came for the money, then torture him until he told Martin where to find Melissa Arnold and named everyone involved in the kidnappings.

In sunlight, this was a beautiful spot—high red cliffs, carefully cultivated greenery at the jump-off spot, and the always soothing shush of the rapidly flowing water. At night, with the possibility of a killer lurking in the dark, the spot lost a lot of its glamour.

There was no light except the stars and a half-moon, so Martin moved slowly. It was about a quarter mile until the cliff jutted out where the river turned. The first rapids, a gentle class two, was a short distance past the bend. The trail narrowed where the river curved. A little ways on it dwindled to a footpath. Martin walked past the curve of the rock and looked around. There was scrub brush and not much else except for the high cliff wall. If someone was lurking behind one of the many outcroppings of rock, he wouldn't be able to see them. Martin left the money then walked back along the path and hid in the shadows.

Nothing happened for forty minutes. Then Martin heard a muffled footfall. Clouds suddenly moved across the moon and Martin could barely make out the person bent over the gym bag. He tried for a better look and dislodged a rock. In the stillness the tumbling stone sounded like a stack of bottles shattering in a supermarket aisle. The kidnapper turned and Martin went for his gun. While he was leveling the .45 he heard the crack of a gunshot and felt searing pain in his left shoulder. Martin staggered a few paces, then fell. His head struck the ground. Struggling to stay conscious, Martin fired a shot to discourage the kidnapper from coming over to finish him off.

Two more shots rang out and Martin crawled for cover. Something splashed in the water. Martin peered around the rock. Two muzzle flashes lit up a small raft as it floated rapidly downriver. Martin came up shooting, but the raft was around the bend in the river and out of sight. His shoulder felt like it was on fire. He became nauseated and his legs gave way. Adding to his misery was the knowledge that his incompetence may have cost Melissa Arnold her life.

Martin stumbled up the trail, which seemed impossibly steep and long. After what seemed like hours, he reached his car. He had to fight to stay conscious during the drive to Gene Arnold's house and he let himself collapse on the car horn as soon as he came to a stop in the front yard. Gene was at his side in moments, blanching at the extent of Martin's bleeding as he pulled his friend from the car. With a grunt, he slung Martin's good arm across his shoulder and supported him as they crossed the yard. When they were inside, Gene called the hospital. Then he called the sheriff.

9

"Feel up to talking, Martin?" Detective Norm Chisholm of the Laurel County Sheriff's Office asked as soon as he walked into Martin's hospital room.

"Sit down. I've been expecting you. Any word yet on Melissa?"

Norm shook his head.

"How's Gene doing?"

"Not good. You two weren't acting very smart."

"Don't make me feel any worse than I do already. Gene wouldn't let me call the police. He was terrified that the kidnapper would kill Melissa." Martin's features clouded and his voice caught. "The way the FBI handled Patty's stakeout really spooked him."

Chisholm had no comeback for that, so he asked Martin to tell him what had happened by the river. When Alvarez was through, Chisholm brought Martin up to date.

"We sent a forensic crew to the take-out point downriver from where you were shot. That's where the kidnapper left the river, but we don't have a clue to who he is."

"Nothing?"

Norm shook his head. "Martin, what kind of couple are they?"

"Melissa and Gene?"

The detective nodded.

"Gene worships her."

"And Melissa? She seem happy?"

"Desert Grove is a change from the big city, and there is the age difference," he answered after a pause. "Why do you ask?"

"Gene never said anything to you about marital problems?"

"No, he didn't, Norm. Where is this going?"

He shrugged. "Probably nowhere. I'm just ruminating."

When Norm left, Martin called Gene Arnold, who seemed inconsolable. The pain pills the doctor had given Martin dulled his senses, but not enough to banish the guilt he felt for failing his friend.

10

When Norm Chisholm walked into Ramon Quiroz's office two days later he looked excited. The detective sat across from the DA and handed him an affidavit signed by Aaron Flynn.

"I want you to write up an affidavit for a search warrant for Gene Arnold's house, his cabin near the Meander River, his car, and Melissa Arnold's car. You can use Aaron's affidavit to establish probable cause."

Quiroz looked puzzled. "What's going on?"

"You know that court reporters type a kind of shorthand onto a strip of paper in a stenograph machine while court is in session."

Quiroz nodded.

"Well, there's a computer disk in the machine that acts as a backup. When a lawyer needs a transcript, the court reporter puts the disk in her computer and uses a software program that translates the stenographic notes into English. Flynn needs to get started on Paul McCann's appeal. He called up Judge Schrieber to find out who's going to prepare the transcript of McCann's trial now that Melissa Arnold is missing. A couple of other lawyers had the same question about their cases because Melissa was their court reporter. The judge told Flynn that he'd arranged for another court reporter to prepare the transcripts, but she can't do it because they can't find the disks or Melissa Arnold's notes. They've checked her office at the courthouse and they called Gene. He says they're not in his house. The judge thinks they could be in

Melissa's car, but the car is still missing. The notes are essential, right?"

"Sure. When you appeal a conviction the appeals court looks through the record to see if the judge made a mistake during the trial that could have affected the verdict. Without the record, there can't be an appeal."

"Okay. I want to search Gene's house and that little cabin he keeps by the Meander River for Melissa's notes. That will make the search legal because they're government property."

"Why don't you just ask Gene to let you look around?"

"I don't want to alert him. Gene's become a suspect."

"You're not serious."

"There's nothing concrete yet. The neighbors say that Gene and Melissa have been arguing pretty heavily recently. She may have been thinking of leaving him."

"You think he killed her and faked everything?" Quiroz asked incredulously. "Martin was there when he talked to the kidnappers on the phone."

"He was there when a call came in, but he didn't hear the other side of the conversation. Gene could have arranged for someone to call him, then he could have gone upriver to Angel Ford and rafted downriver to the drop."

Quiroz shook his head. "What if Martin had gone back to Gene's immediately, instead of waiting? Gene wouldn't have been there. It would have given the whole plot away."

"No. He'd just tell Martin that the kidnappers

called, told him where to find Melissa, he drove there, and his wife wasn't where they said she would be, or something like that."

"So do you think that Gene was involved in the Alvarez kidnapping?"

Chisholm thought for a moment before shaking his head.

"No, that was Paul McCann, all the way. But Dobbs got everyone thinking that there was a third conspirator out there, and maybe that gave Gene the idea for his fake kidnapping."

"I don't buy it. I know Gene. He couldn't kill someone, and he worshiped Melissa."

"Ramon, you've been in this business long enough to know that anyone can kill under the right circumstances. Anyway, I'm not saying that Gene's guilty, but he is a suspect. Maybe this is a wild-goose chase, but I wouldn't bet on it."

11

Two days later, at nine in the evening, Martin Alvarez's phone rang. It was Gene. He sounded on the verge of hysteria.

"I'm in jail. They're saying I killed Melissa."

"Try to calm down, Gene. Is anyone with you who can hear what you're saying?"

"Ramon, Norm Chisholm. I know these guys. I can't believe they're doing this."

"I'm coming down now to see you. Be strong and

do not say anything. If they try to talk to you ask for the Miranda rights. Do you understand?"

"Yes. Thank you, Martin."

"Put Ramon on."

A moment later the DA was on the phone.

"What the fuck are you doing, Ramon?"

"This is hard for me, too, Martin, but we've got evidence."

"That Gene murdered his wife?"

"Yes."

"Bullshit. Gene's the gentlest person I know. You fucked up."

"We searched Gene's cabin, the Meander River place. The clothes Melissa was wearing on the day she disappeared were stuffed into a dresser drawer. They were covered with blood. We haven't done a DNA test yet, but the lab's done some preliminary tests. It's Melissa's blood type. We also found her car parked behind the cabin."

"Then someone planted the stuff. Gene's not stupid. If he killed her he'd never leave incriminating evidence around."

"I'm not going to get into this with you, Martin. I'm the elected DA in this county and I've got to do my job."

Martin held his tongue. Ramon was right. It would just get Quiroz's back up if he tried to throw his weight around.

"Can I visit Gene?"

"Yeah, but you'll become a witness if he talks to you about the case."

"I'll keep that in mind. What about you? Are you going to grill him?"

"No. Gene's so messed up right now that a judge would toss out anything he said. If he killed Melissa I'll nail him, but I want to do this right."

They were keeping Gene away from the other prisoners at the end of the cell block. The sheriff had put a suicide watch on him and a guard was sitting outside his cell. Arnold was lying on a metal cot, staring at the ceiling. The guard let Martin into the cell door and he sat on the edge of the cot.

"I didn't kill her."

Martin put his hand on his friend's shoulder. "I know that, Gene."

"She was everything to me." His eyes watered. "My life's . . . I mean, Jesus, Martin . . ."

Gene sobbed so hard that his body shook. He drew up his knees and rolled into a fetal position facing the concrete wall.

"She was going to leave me. She said she was bored, that I bored her. I told her I'd go anywhere, just to be with her."

"Ah, Gene."

Martin reached for Gene's shoulder and gave it a reassuring squeeze. Gradually, Gene's breathing steadied and he wiped his eyes, but he still wouldn't look at Martin.

"I don't care what they do to me."

"You've got to care. You didn't kill her. If you don't fight, the real killer will get away."

"It doesn't matter. They showed me her clothes. They were drenched with blood. She's dead. Finding who killed her won't bring her back."

"Listen to me, Gene. Nobody knows how you feel better than I do. Nobody. But you can't give up. You've got to fight."

Gene didn't answer.

"Do you have any idea what happened, why the clothes and her car were found at the cabin?"

Gene shook his head.

"The cabin is almost two hours away. If the kidnapper was some stranger he wouldn't know about the cabin."

That got Gene's attention.

"There . . . there was someone else. She had a lover."

"Do you know who?"

"She wouldn't say." Gene leaned his head against the wall and shut his eyes. "She could be cruel, Martin. There was a side to her that you didn't know."

Gene's head bowed.

"I'm not much in bed. She was so young, so vigorous. I couldn't please her. She taunted me. Made fun of me. And she said there was this man, someone who . . . who made her feel . . ."

"People say things they don't mean," Martin managed. "Stupid things." Gene opened his eyes and looked directly at Martin.

"I don't think she ever loved me. I think she was escaping from something and used me to get away. As soon as she had the time to really look at me, she realized the mistake she'd made."

"Don't run yourself down like this. You've been through so much you're not thinking straight. I've seen Melissa and you together. She did care," Martin lied. "She couldn't fake that."

Gene turned away. To Martin he seemed the very image of hopelessness.

Martin made it home from the jail at midnight. His wound ached, but his heart ached more, and his mind was racing. After twenty minutes of tossing and turning in bed, he gave up.

It was a hot night, but there was usually a cool breeze on the veranda. Martin filled a glass with Scotch and ice and sat down by the pool. The stars were bright and there were few clouds. If he had never known Patty, it might have been a perfect moment, but Patty was dead, Gene Arnold was locked up in the Laurel County jail, and someone was laughing at everyone. But who?

Lester Dobbs had testified that Paul McCann called someone on his cell phone after he murdered Patty. Whom did he call? Suddenly Martin sat up straight. Did McCann call anyone? The only reason everyone believed that a third man was involved in Patty's kidnapping was because Lester Dobbs claimed to have overheard Paul's phone conversation in the desert.

Alvarez took a sip of Scotch and let his mind wander. What if Dobbs had made up the story about the third man? Dobbs had been out of jail when Melissa was kidnapped. Did anyone know where he'd been at the crucial times? There was definitely another person with Dobbs at the Alvarez drop site, but maybe there were only two people—not three—involved in the plot to kidnap Patty Alvarez.

It was time to talk to Lester Dobbs.

Dobbs had been living in a trailer park on the outskirts of town; a privilege he'd earned when he agreed to turn state's evidence. His trailer was at the far end of the last row; beyond it were wide-open spaces. Martin neared the trailer door. Somewhere in the hills a coyote howled. The sound unnerved him. He collected himself before knocking on the metal door.

No one answered the knock. Martin strained to hear movement inside the trailer. A stiff wind rattled the metal siding.

"Dobbs! Open up!"

The coyote howled again and an eerie wailing answered his call. The coyotes were hunting. So was he.

Martin took out his .45 and opened the door. He paused for a moment, listening. Then he stepped inside praying that Dobbs was not waiting for him in the dark. Another step. Nothing. Martin touched a switch on the wall. Light filled the narrow confines of the trailer. Martin turned slowly and saw a sink filled with unwashed pots and dishes and a countertop littered with empty beer cans. Dobbs's clothes were scattered along the floor leading to his bed. Then he noticed a shape under the covers on the bed, and the hair stood up on the nape of his neck.

"Lester," he called, but he knew that Dobbs was not going to answer.

Martin pulled back the thin green blanket and the sheet, then stepped back and stared. A deep, jagged gash started on one side of Dobbs's throat and ended at the other. The sheets were coated with dried blood. If Dobbs knew anything about the identity of Melissa's kidnapper, he had taken the information to the grave.

"He's been dead for two days," Norm Chisholm told Martin. They were sitting in a police car. It was seven in the morning. Alvarez was cradling a cup of steaming-hot coffee. It tasted like battery acid but helped him keep his eyes open.

"Did anything in Dobbs's trailer connect him to Melissa?"

"Nothing so far, and the forensic guys have been over every inch of the place. But I didn't expect to find anything. We questioned Dobbs as soon as Gene reported the kidnapping. He had an alibi."

"Then why kill him?" Martin asked. "It doesn't make any sense."

"Dobbs must have known something that threatened the kidnapper. Maybe he lied when he testified that he didn't know the person McCann called after he killed Patty."

"Does this let Gene off the hook?" Martin asked hopefully.

"Afraid not. Dobbs was killed the night before we

arrested Gene. Gene was alone all evening. He has no alibi."

12

A week after Dobbs's murder, Paul Mc-Cann's wife was waiting for Aaron Flynn by the door to Judge Schrieber's courtroom.

"Will you get him out?" Joan asked, anxiously twisting the strap of her purse. Her blue eyes were sunk in their sockets and there were dark shadows around them.

"I think so, Joan, but there are no guarantees in this business." Flynn patted her on the shoulder and smiled. "We'll have our answer soon."

Joan started to say something, but she stopped when she saw Martin Alvarez bearing down on her husband's attorney.

"Ramon told me what you're trying to do, Flynn."

"I'm trying to do my job, Martin. This isn't personal."

"It's personal to me," Alvarez said in a chilling tone. "Your client is safer in jail, safer on death row, than he'll be if he walks out of this courthouse."

"Martin, this is not the way," Flynn said in a conciliatory tone.

"McCann killed my wife. If the law doesn't punish him I won't wait to find out if God will. Let him know that."

● ● ●

"You're asking for a new trial, Mr. Flynn?" Judge Schrieber said. He had read Flynn's motion and the memorandum of law in support of it and he looked very troubled.

"Yes, Your Honor. My memo sets out the relevant cases and statutes. Read together, they hold that you must order a new trial if an appeal can't be prosecuted because the reporter's notes have been lost or destroyed through no fault of the defendant, every reasonable effort has been made to find a substitute for the missing record, and the defendant has made a prima facie showing of error or unfairness in the trial.

"I've submitted a list of potential trial errors that I would have asserted as bases for reversal on appeal. There is no substitute for the missing record of Mr. McCann's trial. The police have made every reasonable effort to recover it and the record is missing through no fault of Mr. McCann."

"What do you say to Mr. Flynn's argument, Mr. Quiroz?" the judge asked.

Ramon rose slowly, as if trying to delay the inevitable.

"I agree that Mr. Flynn has raised several issues that could lead to reversal, though I don't think they actually would."

"But that's not the test, is it?" Judge Schrieber asked. "He doesn't have to prove he would win. You aren't asserting that?"

"No. I agree that Mr. McCann has met the test of making his prima facie case on the possibility of error in the trial. I don't agree on much else, though. For instance, the police have searched pretty thoroughly, but they're not through looking. I think the court should give them more time."

"Where are they going to look, Your Honor?" Flynn asked. "They searched both of Mr. Arnold's residences, Mrs. Arnold's car, her office, his office. This appeal has to be prosecuted quickly. We can't wait indefinitely in the hopes that years from now the transcription tapes may show up."

"Mr. Quiroz," the judge asked, "do you have anything more than wishful thinking that leads you to believe that the lost record in this case will soon be recovered?"

Ramon shook his head. "No, Your Honor, I don't. I just feel that it's too soon to give up."

"Is there a substitute for the missing record?"

"No, Your Honor. None that I know of. It seems that the notes and backup disks for every case that Mrs. Arnold had on appeal were with her when she was abducted and there are no copies."

"If that's so, and you have no real hope of finding the originals, and the defendant had made a prima facie case for the possibility of reversal, what choice do I have except to grant this motion for a new trial?"

"We would argue that Mr. McCann is at fault here. How do we know that he wasn't involved in the kidnapping of Mrs. Arnold?"

"Your Honor," Flynn retorted, "this is an argument that grows out of sheer desperation. Mr. Quiroz prepared the warrant that led to the arrest of Gene Arnold for his wife's murder. There has never been a hint of a suggestion that Mr. McCann, who was in jail at all times relevant to the Arnold case, had anything to do with the second kidnapping."

"Mr. Quiroz?" the judge asked.

Ramon knew when he was whipped and he simply shook his head.

"Mr. Flynn, if I could find any legal reason to deny your motion I would do so," the judge said. "But there isn't any and I am sworn to follow the law, even when I don't want to." He paused. "I am going to order a new trial for Mr. McCann."

"Your Honor, I have a further motion," Flynn said quickly. "I move for an order dismissing the charges against Mr. McCann. If this case were retried today it would have to result in a judgment of acquittal as soon as the state rested. Mr. McCann has always maintained his complete innocence and we have always contended that Lester Dobbs accused Mr. McCann in order to escape his just punishment for Mrs. Alvarez's murder. Without the testimony of Lester Dobbs there is no evidence connecting Mr. McCann to the kidnapping of Patty Alvarez."

"Mr. Quiroz, is there an official copy of Mr. Dobbs's trial testimony?" Judge Schrieber asked.

"No, sir."

"Did Mr. Dobbs testify in the grand jury?"

"Yes, but there's no transcript."

"Even if there was," Flynn interjected, "it wouldn't be admissible against Mr. McCann because I had no opportunity to cross-examine Mr. Dobbs."

"I believe Mr. Flynn is correct," the judge said.

"Mr. Quiroz, is there any legally permissible way to present the testimony of Lester Dobbs to a jury in a second trial?"

"Not that I can think of at this moment."

Judge Schrieber was lost in thought. He tapped his pen against the dais. When he spoke he looked very unhappy.

"Mr. Flynn, I am not going to dismiss the charges against Mr. McCann today. New evidence may be discovered. However, I am very reluctant to keep Mr. McCann in jail under the current circumstances.

"Mr. Quiroz, I am going to give you one week to convince me that there is a legal basis for keeping Mr. McCann in jail. If you can't, I'm going to be forced to set him free."

When Ramon Quiroz returned to the district attorney's office he found a furious Martin Alvarez waiting for him.

"What are you going to do about this?"

"There's nothing I can do, Martin. Unless we find new evidence, McCann is going to walk."

"That's insane."

Quiroz shook his head. "That's the law."

"There's got to be something you can do."

"Martin, I've been dreading this since I learned that Melissa's notes disappeared. I once went through something just like it with Gene Arnold and I knew what could happen. I was hoping that Flynn wasn't sharp enough to figure out what to do."

"What do you mean you went through something like this with Gene?"

"Remember when Bob Champion and Gene were partners?"

Martin nodded.

"Bob represented some young kid charged with auto theft. They picked the jury and the state put on some witnesses. There was a three-day weekend because of a national holiday. When the trial started again no one could find the kid. He just took off. Judge Milbrandt decided that the defendant's failure to appear was willful and ordered the lawyers to go on with the trial in his absence. The jury found the defendant guilty. The judge couldn't sentence him unless he was present, so he issued an arrest warrant.

"Three years ago they caught the kid in Canada. He was sent back for sentencing. Bob had retired by this time and Gene filed a notice of appeal, but the court reporter couldn't find her notes. They were in a box of old transcription tapes that she'd destroyed. Gene couldn't appeal because there wasn't any way to prepare the transcript without the notes, but he found that statute Flynn cited and the court had to order a new trial."

Martin left the DA's office. As he drove home he remembered that Joan McCann was Gene Arnold's legal secretary. If she knew about the auto theft case, she would also know that Judge Schrieber would have to order a new trial for Paul if Melissa's notes were lost. Did Joan love her husband enough to kill Melissa Arnold and Lester Dobbs? Was the ransom

demand merely a smoke screen that had hidden a plot
to free Paul McCann from prison? Was she capable of
committing a double murder?

Martin tried to remember everything he knew
about Joan McCann. She had exhibited signs of
tremendous stress lately. Martin had assumed that she
was worrying about her husband's fate, but what if
her gnawed nails and weight loss had been physical
manifestations of unbearable guilt.

13

A week passed. There were no new clues in
the murder of Lester Dobbs, Melissa Arnold's body
and the tapes were still missing, and Ramon Quiroz
had not been able to come up with a legal theory that
would keep Paul McCann in jail. Early Friday morning, Quiroz and Aaron Flynn slipped in the back door
of the courthouse and stole down the corridor to
Judge Schrieber's chambers. It was 7:00 A.M. and no
one else was around. Ramon had phoned the judge
the previous evening and convinced him that meeting
in secrecy was necessary because of the threat that
Martin Alvarez had made to Flynn.

"Good morning, Ramon, Aaron," Judge Schrieber
said. He did not look happy as he signed the paper
that sat in front of him. "I'm dismissing the case
against Paul McCann and signing this release order.
Everything has been done over at the jail to assure
that McCann can walk out the door the minute you

present this. I've arranged for you to go in and leave by the back door. I also instructed the jail personnel that anyone who leaks McCann's release is headed to prison for contempt. That should ensure your client's safety, at least for today."

Flynn drove his car behind the iail and knocked on the rear door. Sheriff Cobb was waiting with McCann, who was dressed in the clothes in which he had been arrested. The sheriff read the release order and told Paul he could go. Cobb looked as happy about this state of affairs as the judge.

As soon as they were in the car Flynn's client closed his eyes, put his head back, and said, "Hallelujah. I am so fucking grateful to be out of that hellhole that I might actually go to church."

"If I were you, the church would be in some city on the other side of the planet. I don't think Martin Alvarez is going to let this rest."

"Well, fuck him," Paul answered angrily. "Alvarez doesn't scare me."

"What are your plans?" Flynn asked.

"A hot shower, an edible meal, a good fuck, and a decent night's sleep."

"And after that?"

"I don't know. I'm thinking of moving. This trial showed me how many friends I have in Desert Grove. Besides, Sunnyvale is dead and your fees about wiped me out."

Flynn pulled the car as close as he could to Paul's front door and prayed that Martin Alvarez wasn't out in the desert with a sniper scope. As soon as the car stopped Joan rushed out of the house. Her arms were around Paul's neck before he was standing. He let her kiss him, but Flynn didn't see much fire on his part. Then Joan walked around to Flynn's window and placed her hand over his.

"I'll never forget you for this, Mr. Flynn. God bless you."

14

The call from Joan McCann came at eleven o'clock. To Martin, she sounded like a woman on the brink of hysteria.

"I'm calling from my car. I'm following Paul. You've got to help me."

"How can you be following Paul? He's in jail."

"The judge dismissed his case, this morning. They sneaked him out of jail because they were afraid of you. Then . . . then he beat me up. He said things to me . . ."

She started to cry. Martin did not understand half of what she said, but he understood that Paul McCann was leaving town without his wife.

"He killed Patty. I can prove it."

Now Martin was completely focused.

"How do you know that?"

"Mr. Flynn came back an hour ago. He was very upset. He took Paul into the den, but I listened at the door. Someone called Aaron at home and said he had Melissa's notes and the disks. He wanted two hundred thousand dollars for them. Aaron told him it wasn't a scam. When Patty was murdered, she was wearing a topaz ring you'd given her for your anniversary, right?"

Martin's heart lurched. He remembered Patty's exclamation of joy when she saw the present and recalled the kiss she'd given him.

"Yes, she was wearing the ring. The police held back that information. How did you know?"

"Aaron told Paul that the caller described it."

"What did Paul say to Flynn?"

"He was angry. He claimed he didn't have two hundred thousand dollars. He said he thought the caller was a con artist. They argued for a while. Then Mr. Flynn left. As soon as he was gone, Paul started packing. I asked him what he was doing and he told me to shut up. He . . . he said I made him sick, that he was leaving me for good."

Joan burst into sobs again and Martin waited for her to calm down.

"What do you want from me?"

"I want you to stop him. Before he gets the money and escapes."

"What money?"

"The ransom money."

"How do you know he has it?"

"He's going to Laurel Canyon State Park, to the caves. He must have hidden it there. Why else would he go to the park in the middle of the night? If he has the ransom money, Mr. Alvarez, he killed Patty."

"Why are you calling me? Why aren't you calling the police?"

"I don't want him arrested. I want him dead."

• • •

Laurel Canyon State Park was a twisting, turning maze of dry riverbeds and towering cliffs that was known to rock climbers all over the world. At the base of some of these cliffs were caves. There was a parking area near the entrance and Martin found Joan McCann parked at the far end of the lot where she'd told him she'd be. McCann's car was at the head of a trail that led down to the caves.

"He has a fifteen-minute head start. You'd better hurry. He's on the Bishop's Point trail. It's where he proposed to me," Joan added bitterly.

Martin had been to the park many times and knew the trails by heart. He put his gun in the waistband of his pants and grabbed a flashlight before starting on a path that led up to Bishop's Point, a lookout spot with an awesome view, and wound down to the desert floor, where there were several caves.

It took twenty minutes to reach the base of the cliff along the narrow footpath. Martin switched on the flashlight for a few seconds and played it over the rock-strewn floor at the foot of the cliff face. Then he walked toward the mouth of the nearest cave. There were large boulders on both sides of the entrance. Martin edged around one rock formation and peered into the cave hoping to see the beam of Paul's flashlight, but there was only stygian darkness.

"You son of a bitch," McCann screamed, just before he cracked Martin's cheekbone with his pistol. Martin staggered backward and swung the flashlight. It caught McCann on a raised forearm but didn't stop him. McCann aimed a punch at Martin's wound. The pain was blinding. A kick to the knee knocked Martin's legs out from under him and sent him to the ground. He tried to get up, but McCann kicked him in the ribs, then stomped on his head. Just when Martin thought he would pass out the beating stopped.

McCann collected Martin's automatic from the ground, where he'd dropped it after the first, surprise blow. Martin was certain that there were broken bones in his face. His ribs stung, but he didn't think they were broken. He struggled into a sitting position.

"Did Joan tell you I was coming here?" McCann asked in a hate-filled voice.

Martin held his tongue. McCann glared at him.

"It doesn't matter. You're not here because of that bitch. You're here for the money. Well, you'll see the money, all right. You're going to dig for it. Then you and I are both going to disappear. Now get up."

He gestured with the pistol and Martin made it to his feet with only one minor stumble. McCann pointed the flashlight beam into the cave and Martin preceded him inside. It was cold, but Martin was in too much pain to notice. The cave was deep and the roof, which was about nine feet high at the entrance, quickly dropped, so that they were soon moving forward in a half crouch. After they had walked for fifteen minutes the roof rose dramatically and they found themselves in a high-ceilinged chamber. McCann told Alvarez to stop in front of a large pile of rocks that looked as if they had been undisturbed for centuries.

"Start digging. The bag is at the bottom of that

mess. It took me almost two hours to put it there."

McCann propped the flashlight on a mound of rocks on the other side of the cave so that it pointed at the pile that concealed the money. Martin started throwing rocks from the top of the pile off to one side. Every movement hurt, but digging in the rock pile was keeping him alive and giving him time to think.

After a while McCann eased himself into a sitting position against the far wall. His gun was aimed at Martin, who was certain it would soon grow heavy. As he dug he kept an eye out for a few heavy rocks. Every time he spotted one, he moved it to a spot where he could grab it quickly.

Martin's chance came after he had been working for half an hour. The barrel of the handgun wobbled then sagged downward. Then McCann leaned his head back and closed his eyes for a second. Martin was moving before he opened them. The first rock hit McCann in the forehead. He screamed and fired, but he wasn't aiming. Martin was on him before he could focus, smashing down with a second rock that sent McCann's head ricocheting off the wall, stunning him. A moment later Martin had the gun.

"Look around you, Paul," Alvarez said when he was certain that McCann was fully conscious of his situation. "This cave is where your body is going to rot."

McCann paled.

"You should be happy. I'm going to bury you with your blood money. You'll have an eternity to spend it in hell."

Anger suffused Martin's features as he aimed the gun.

"Goddamn you for killing Patty," he said, but he never pulled the trigger. Another gun fired from behind Martin. The explosion reverberated in the cave. Martin pitched forward, unconscious.

Part V

Deep Cover

30

"I don't know how much time passed before I regained consciousness," Alvarez said. "When I came to I wished I hadn't."

He paused for a moment, reliving the agony of those moments.

"How did you get out of the cave?" Kate asked.

"Joan McCann brought the police. She was attacked while she was waiting for me."

"Who . . . ?"

"She doesn't know. The person was wearing a mask. He put a gun to her head and forced her to tell where I'd gone, then she was knocked out. When she came to I hadn't returned, so she called the police. I was barely alive when the search party found me and Paul."

"McCann was still there?"

"He was dead, shot between the eyes. The ransom money was gone."

"Did Aaron Flynn have an alibi?"

"He was never a suspect. Six months later he quietly left town. I had no idea where he'd moved until today."

"Did anyone else connected with the case move away?"

"Joan. She left within three months. She visited me several times at the hospital while I was recuperating. The last time, she told me that she couldn't stay in Desert Grove any longer."

"Was there a theory about the identity of Paul McCann's killer?"

"No. I'm certain that McCann and Lester Dobbs killed Patty, and that the same person murdered McCann and Dobbs. In the end, the most widely accepted theory was that an outsider was behind the plot."

"Do you believe that?"

"Absolutely not," Alvarez said, his voice as hard as granite.

"What happened to Gene Arnold?"

"I hired the best criminal lawyer in Arizona to represent Gene. He convinced Ramon that there wasn't enough evidence to hold him. It was obvious to everyone that Melissa's clothing and the car had been planted at the cabin. The crime lab was all over the place and couldn't find any evidence that Melissa or Gene had been there recently. Melissa's body was never recovered, so there was no forensic evidence connecting Gene to the murder. All they had were the arguments and Ramon wasn't going to prosecute Gene on the basis of a few domestic spats."

"Were there any new developments after you were shot?"

"Not until now."

"Can you think of anything else that might help, Mr. Alvarez?"

After a moment Martin shook his head. "You realize, of course, that Gene's death may have nothing to do with what happened here. It was a long time ago."

"That's true, but Aaron Flynn . . . The coincidence bothers me."

"Life is full of coincidences."

Kate stood and extended her hand. "Thanks for seeing me."

Alvarez took her hand and held it for a moment before releasing it. Kate handed him her card.

"If you think of anything else, please call me."

Martin nodded just as his assistant appeared on the patio.

"Anna will see you to your car. Good luck."

Martin Alvarez watched Kate Ross cross the terrace. Though she looked nothing like Patty, the investigator reminded him of her. They both had the same purposeful stride, and Patty had always shown a core of strength that he sensed in Kate Ross. Alvarez closed his good eye and rubbed his temples. There were times when he imagined that his wife was still with him, taking her morning ride, just out of sight and soon to return. Thoughts like that were calming, like a belief that he and Patty would be reunited in a life after death.

There were other times when memories of Patty stoked an impotent rage. It was that rage that was building as Martin entered the hacienda and went to his office. As soon as he closed his door he picked up the phone. A man answered in Spanish.

"You know who this is?" Alvarez asked.

"Yes."

"I have work for you. Come on the evening plane."

31

Saturday morning, Daniel bolted out of sleep thinking that he was still in his cell. When he realized that he was safe in Kate's guest room he fell back on the bed. Daniel was normally an early riser, but he had slept past nine. Just being in a place where the lights were not on twenty-four hours a day and screams and moans did not jerk him awake at all hours had been a luxury greater than silk sheets.

There was a note from Kate on the kitchen table. She had taken an early flight to Arizona and hadn't wanted to wake him. He wished she had. He remembered how happy he had been to see her waiting for him at the jail and he missed her already.

Daniel reread Kate's note. He liked holding something that she had touched and reading something that she had written just for him. Kate was very kind and very thoughtful. There hadn't been many people like that in Daniel's life. In truth, Kate was the single positive note in the sorry mess that had become his life. Despite their barely knowing each other, Kate had made sure that a top defense attorney represented him, she was paying some of his legal fees, and she was letting him stay with her—knowing that he was charged with murder. Her support conveyed her complete confidence in his innocence. He couldn't imagine getting through his ordeal without her.

After breakfast, Daniel wandered aimlessly around the house, flipped channels on the television, and quickly lost interest in a science-fiction novel he found in Kate's bookcase. Its plot wasn't nearly as surreal as his life. What had happened to him? A little more than a week ago he'd been living a dream he had never dared imagine as a child. Now someone had stolen that dream. Daniel wanted his life back.

One of the worst things about jail was being forced to stay inside. Daniel realized that he needed to get out in the world. He called Joe Molinari.

"How's the convict?" Molinari joked.

"I'm cooped up at Kate Ross's house and I'm going nuts."

"Ross, huh? That'll make juicy office gossip."

"There's nothing to gossip about. I'm hiding from reporters and Kate was kind enough to put me up."

"Of course."

"You're a pig, Molinari."

"I assume you didn't call just to insult me."

"True. Do you want to go for a run? I've got to get some exercise."

"Sounds good."

"Can you drive me over to my apartment so I can get my car and my running gear?"

"No problem. See you soon."

• • •

A fire-engine-red Porsche pulled up in front of Kate's house. Joe honked the horn and waved.

"Jesus, Molinari, I'm trying to be inconspicuous."

"Don't worry," Joe said as he peeled out, "you're too ugly to attract attention. Everyone will be looking at me."

Daniel relaxed and enjoyed the ride. It was cool, but the sun brought everyone out and the streets of northwest Portland were crowded with strolling couples.

"Go around the block once," Daniel instructed when they were a few streets from his apartment building. "I want to make certain that there aren't any reporters waiting for me."

"This celebrity thing is going to your head. Who do you think you are, O. J.?"

"Hey, I'm feeling a lot of empathy for O. J. at the moment."

As the Porsche cruised by Daniel's apartment house, a large man in jeans, a black windbreaker, and a baseball cap came out of the front door and crossed the street to a black pickup truck. He looked familiar, but Daniel was certain he had never seen him in the building. When they came around the block the next time, the pickup was gone.

Molinari parked in the street and Daniel ran up the stairs. Kate had been right about the chaos inside. The cops had obviously never heard that neatness counts. Daniel didn't feel like dealing with the mess right away. He grabbed his workout gear and changed in the bathroom, then he stuffed some extra clothes in a duffel bag and ran down to the small lot at the side of the building where his car was parked.

With Molinari following behind, Daniel drove past the zoo and the Forestry Center and parked up the road from the Vietnam Memorial. The two men stretched before taking off through the woods along one of the trails that wound through Washington Park. It took a while for Daniel to get his rhythm, and it didn't help that the first half mile was uphill.

"Feel like telling me what's going on?" Molinari asked.

"You shouldn't get involved."

"From what I can see, you don't have too many people on your side. I'd like to be one of them."

Daniel knew that he probably shouldn't talk about his case with Molinari, but Joe was one of the few people at the firm who'd stood by him. And he was smart. Maybe Joe would see something that he had missed. It would also be a relief to be able to talk about everything he'd kept bottled inside.

Daniel started with the night that Susan conned him into reviewing the discovery and ended with his arrest. The only part of the story he omitted was the call from Arthur Briggs and his presence at the cottage. The prosecutor couldn't prove he'd been at the scene of Briggs's murder and Daniel didn't want to make Joe Molinari a state's witness.

"Any brilliant insights you'd care to share?" Daniel asked when he was through.

"Not really, but it's sure a funny coincidence that

Flynn got lucky again so soon after finding the Kaidanov letter."

"What do you mean?"

"Jaffe demolished Fairweather under oath. After Oregon Mutual sees a transcript of her testimony they'll be begging Reed, Briggs to settle and Flynn will collect a nice fat attorney's fee."

As they ran up a small rise Daniel suddenly remembered that Flynn had sent one of his associates to sit in on his hearing. An odd thought occurred to him. Did Flynn know what was going to happen when Fairweather took the stand? Was Flynn the guardian angel who sent Amanda the videotape of Fairweather's speech?

"You know, I just got a crazy idea," Molinari said as they started downhill. "Do you think it's possible that Aaron Flynn has a mole at Reed, Briggs?"

"Like in the spy novels?"

"Seriously, think about it. How did Kaidanov's letter get into the box of discovery? How did a tape from Arthur Briggs's office find its way to Amanda Jaffe?"

The trail narrowed and the men ran single file in silence until it widened giving Daniel time to think. He liked Flynn. He remembered how natural he'd been with Patrick Cummings. Daniel knew that Flynn was flamboyant and aggressive. He didn't want to think that he was dishonest.

"Someone at Geller could have included Kaidanov's letter by mistake when they compiled the discovery," Daniel said.

"You told me that everyone at Geller swears that

they've never seen that letter or the Kaidanov report," Molinari countered.

"They would if they're lying."

"But how would someone at Geller know about Fairweather's case?" Joe insisted. "It has nothing to do with Geller Pharmaceuticals. If someone at Reed, Briggs sent Amanda that tape to help Flynn they could also have slipped the Kaidanov letter into the discovery."

"Okay, suppose you're right. Who's the mole?"

"Oregon Mutual was Briggs's client, so, technically, the suit against Fairweather was Briggs's case, but Brock Newbauer and Susan Webster were doing most of the work on it. They'd know about the videotape."

"Brock and Susan are also on the Insufort team," Daniel said.

"Something happened after you left that fits into my theory," Joe told Daniel. "Briggs called a meeting on the day he was killed to discuss what to do in the Insufort litigation. Brock Newbauer was complaining that he wanted Geller to settle, but Briggs wouldn't listen to him."

"Is Brock running the Geller defense now?"

"Technically, but I'm guessing that Susan is calling the shots."

"Why do you say that?"

"Brock only made partner because his family owns Newbauer Construction, one of our biggest clients. He's a joke around the firm. Haven't you noticed how long he takes for lunch, and have you ever smelled his breath when he gets back? He could never get a handle on a case as complex as the Insufort litigation. The science would be beyond him. Briggs represented the Newbauer account, which brings in mucho dinero. He had to baby-sit Brock to keep the client happy."

"And you said that Brock wanted Geller to settle?"

Molinari nodded.

"If Flynn does have a mole at Reed, Briggs that's exactly what he would want."

32

The next morning, the sun was hiding behind a lead sky and there was a threat of rain in the chill air. Daniel was sore from his run and he limped out of bed. After breakfast, he watched the first half of a Seattle Seahawks' game on TV, but Kate's house was beginning to feel claustrophobic. He remembered the mess in his apartment and drove over at halftime.

The apartment didn't look any better than it had the day before. Daniel turned on the football game and watched while he straightened up. Everything was in decent shape by the time the game ended. Daniel was wondering when his life would be put back together when the phone rang. His hand hovered over the receiver as he debated whether to take the call. He had no desire to talk to a reporter, but it could be a friend and it would be nice to talk to someone who cared enough to call.

"Hello?"

"Daniel Ames?" a man asked. He had an accent—Slavic, Russian perhaps.

"Who is this?"

"We have to meet."

The man sounded desperate.

"About what?" Daniel asked cautiously.

"I witnessed Arthur Briggs's murder." The answer was rushed. "I know you didn't kill him. That's why you're the only one I can trust."

The hair stood up on the back of Daniel's neck. "Dr. Kaidanov?"

"Will you meet with me?"

"Will you go to the police and tell them I'm innocent?" Daniel asked excitedly.

"We must talk first."

"Fine, where are you? I'll come right away."

"No, not in daylight. You might be followed. Tonight at ten come alone to Rest of Angels Cemetery. I'll meet you near Simon Prescott's mausoleum."

"You're joking?"

"I lost my sense of humor when those bastards tried to kill me at the lab."

"But a cemetery, after dark?"

"Rest of Angels is where my mother is buried. Are you going to be there?"

"Yeah, don't get excited."

"I've earned the right to be excited. I've been running for my life for almost a month. You should be able to relate to that."

As soon as Kaidanov told Daniel how to find the mausoleum, he hung up and Daniel dialed Kate's house, hoping that she was back from Arizona, but all he got was her answering machine.

33

Daniel left for Rest of Angels at 9:30 without having heard from Kate. The main gate closed at sundown. Kaidanov had instructed him to park in a housing development that was separated from the cemetery by a shallow ravine and a quarter acre of forest. Daniel put up the hood from his windbreaker. Heavy rain had turned the walls of the ravine to mire. He slid down one side then scrambled up the other. By the time he was out of the depression, he was shivering and covered with mud.

Rest of Angels sprawled across a hundred and twenty-five hilly and wooded acres overlooking the Columbia River and was surrounded by another hundred and seventy-five acres of forest. On summer days the cemetery was a serene and picturesque shelter for the dead. When Daniel broke out of the forest, the rain-slashed graveyard looked like a set from *Dracula*.

A cemetery after dark would never have been his

first choice of a place to meet, especially with a murderer running loose. The mausoleums and monuments provided excellent cover for a killer. Daniel ran
between the graves to the Prescott mausoleum, then
ducked behind the crypt. The rain and the biting wind
were making him miserable and he pulled the strings
of his hood tighter to protect his face, all the while
looking around for Kaidanov. His senses were
strained to the limit, but the downpour made it hard
to hear and his hood limited his peripheral vision.

"Ames."

Daniel spun around, fist cocked. He held his punch
when he recognized Kaidanov. The scientist looked as
miserable as Daniel felt. Water ran down his face and
beaded a mustache and beard that Daniel had not noticed in the picture on the liquor cabinet in Kaidanov's
living room.

"You scared the shit out of me," Daniel said as he
sagged against the tomb.

"We don't have much time," the Russian answered. He was shivering and his voice trembled from
the cold. "I want you to tell Geller Pharmaceuticals
that I'll testify that my study is a hoax."

"The results aren't real?" Daniel asked, stunned by
Kaidanov's revelation.

"Of course not."

"And Insufort is safe?"

"I don't have time for this," Kaidanov said impa-
tiently. "You tell Geller's people that I want money
and protection. I'm not meeting anyone until I've
been paid and all of the safety precautions have been
arranged to my satisfaction."

"Why me?"

"Because I don't know who to trust at Reed, Briggs or Geller. I want one million dollars. That's cheap considering how much I'll save them. I also want a safe house and bodyguards." Kaidanov looked around nervously. "They tried to kill me at the lab. Then they tried again when they murdered Briggs."

"Who tried to kill you?"

"I don't know. I never met anyone. I received my instructions by phone or in the mail or at a drop. They paid me to transform that building into a lab and to phony up the study. They told me the results they wanted."

"Why did you do it?"

Kaidanov shrugged. "Gambling debts. They promised me enough to pay them and more. I was stupid. I believed them."

"Do you know who killed Arthur Briggs?"

"I'm sure it was the same person who tried to kill me at the lab, but I didn't see his face. Everything happened too fast. Arthur warned me and I got away. I was lucky at the lab, too." Kaidanov laughed. "That fucking monkey. It saved my life."

"The monkey that was shot?"

"I was seconds away from being set on fire when the little beast came out of nowhere. It was amazing. Its coat was solid flame and it still had the strength to attack." The Russian shook his head in awe. "The last thing I saw was its teeth sinking into the killer's shoulder."

Kaidanov shuddered. Blood, skin, and brains spattered Daniel's face. He stepped back instinctively, making a strangled sound as he stared in shock at the remains of Kaidanov's face. The scientist lurched forward and clutched Daniel's jacket. His back absorbed the next bullet. The explosion acted like a slap. Daniel shoved the body away and jumped behind the mausoleum, barely avoiding a bullet that nicked the edge of the crypt and sprayed him with rock chips.

Daniel sprinted between the graves toward another mausoleum. Someone was running parallel to him, several rows over. The killer pulled up and assumed a shooting stance. Daniel dove behind a stone angel just as the angel's head exploded.

Daniel scrambled forward, crablike, but he held out little hope of escape. It wouldn't take long for the killer to figure out that he was unarmed and helpless. He took a quick look around. The mausoleum was two rows away. The killer would expect him to head for it because it provided the best shelter, so he started circling back toward Kaidanov's body, hoping that the heavy clouds and rain would cloak his movements.

Daniel risked a look over his shoulder and saw a figure racing toward the mausoleum. As soon as it disappeared he leaped up and raced away. A gun fired and Daniel felt the wind track of a bullet speeding by his cheek. He shifted gears and ran all out, dodging behind the tallest monuments and widest headstones. Another bullet ripped the fabric of his hood and creased the side of his head, sending him sprawling headfirst into a granite slab. Fighting for consciousness, Daniel gritted his teeth and struggled to one knee, then tumbled back down. Footsteps pounded the ground, drawing closer. A shot. Daniel braced for the impact, but none came. Two more shots, but from opposite directions, then another and another. Daniel looked around. A figure was firing toward his assailant, who turned and fled.

"Stay down," Kate Ross yelled. Daniel crawled behind a large headstone. His head was throbbing. When he touched the skin above his left ear, blood dampened his palm and pain flared in his temple.

Kate crouched beside him, a gun in her hand.

"Get up. We've got to go, *now!*"

Daniel braced himself on the headstone and levered himself to his feet, before doubling over from nausea. Kate gripped his arm.

"Suck it up and move."

Daniel stumbled forward like a drunk with Kate following, gun in hand. Gradually, his head cleared enough for him to get his bearings.

"Where's your car?"

"Over there," Daniel said, pointing toward the ravine where he'd come in. Kate worried that the shooter was waiting in the woods, but she angled toward the trees. Daniel had all he could do to keep his feet moving. At some point Kate took his arm, steadying him. Kate breathed a sigh of relief when they entered the woods without incident.

When they found Daniel's car, Kate took his keys and helped him into the passenger's seat, then went around to the driver's side. The dome light went on. Kate got a good look at Daniel's face and gasped. Daniel stared in the rearview mirror. His blood drenched the left side of his head and Kaidanov's blood and brains speckled his face and the front of his windbreaker.

"Oh, Jesus," he said as a wave of nausea rolled through his stomach. He pushed open the door and threw up on the macadam. Kate put a hand on his back.

"How badly are you hurt?" she asked.

Daniel ran the back of his hand across his mouth and squeezed his eyes tight.

"It's not all my blood," he managed. "Kaidanov . . ."

Another wave of nausea hit him and he gritted his teeth.

"The scientist you came to meet?" Kate asked.

Daniel nodded. "His body is back there by the mausoleum."

Kate made a decision. She punched in a number on her cell phone and Daniel looked at her.

"I'm getting you an ambulance."

"No," Daniel gasped. "They'll send me back to jail."

Kate gave their location to 911, then dialed another number.

"You're hurt and there's been a murder," she answered as she waited for the party on the other end to pick up.

Daniel was too weak to talk and almost too dizzy to think, but he shook his head. Kate grabbed his shoulder and squeezed.

"Do you trust me?" she asked.

Daniel used most of his energy to muster a nod.

"Then stick with me." A voice on the other end of the phone distracted her.

"Hello," she said. "It's Kate Ross, Amanda. I'm with Daniel Ames. We need you."

34

When Billie Brewster and Zeke Forbus drove up, the medics were treating Daniel's head wound in the back of an ambulance. An officer was stationed at the rear of the ambulance, guarding Daniel. The detectives conferred with him for a few minutes. Then the officer pointed to Kate's car, where Kate Ross and Amanda Jaffe had taken shelter from the rain. Billie ran over and knocked on Kate's window. Kate got out of the car just as Forbus joined his partner.

"Why couldn't your boyfriend commit murder on a sunny afternoon?" he grumbled.

"Daniel didn't kill anyone," Kate snapped, too exhausted to be polite.

Forbus barked out a sour laugh and threw a thumb over his shoulder toward the uniform. "Harris told me the bullshit story you gave him about a mysterious stranger and your heroic rescue. Sounds a little like *Lethal Weapon Nine.*"

"Listen, you fat—"

"Hey!" Billie shouted, stepping between them.

"We're all tired and we're all wet. Let's try to act civilized, okay? I do not want to play referee to you two."

Forbus smirked as Amanda Jaffe joined the trio. Kate glared at Forbus.

"Tell us what happened!" Billie said.

"I already gave a statement," Kate answered belligerently, still pissed.

"Then repeat it to me," Billie asked calmly. "Please."

Kate looked at Amanda and the lawyer nodded.

"I was out of town on business. When I got home there was a message from Daniel on my answering machine. He said that Sergey Kaidanov had called him."

"The missing scientist?" Billie interjected.

Kate nodded. "Kaidanov wanted Daniel to meet him at Rest of Angels. He was going to testify that his study was a hoax, but he wanted to be paid. He wanted Daniel to negotiate with Geller Pharmaceuticals."

"Why Ames?" Forbus asked.

"Kaidanov was at the cottage when Arthur Briggs was killed. He knew Daniel didn't kill Briggs, so he trusted him."

"This is what Ames told you?" Forbus asked skeptically.

Kate nodded.

"I don't suppose he has a witness to back him up?"

"Let her tell the story," Billie told her partner.

"By the time I got here Kaidanov was dead. I saw Daniel go down. The killer was trying to finish him off. I started shooting and scared him away."

"Where's your gun?" Forbus asked.

"I turned it over to the first cop who showed up. It's already bagged."

"What were you using?" Billie asked.

"A nine-millimeter Glock. You should find a lot of spent shells out there. I was spraying shots."

"Sounds familiar," Forbus muttered.

Billie's head snapped around and she glared at Forbus. He shrugged and held up his hands, but Kate caught his cruel smile.

"Where's the body?" Billie asked Kate.

"In the cemetery. There should be someone out there already. They called for forensics."

Billie was about to ask another question when a car pulled up. Mike Greene opened an umbrella and ran over.

"I should have stayed in L.A.," he swore. "Hi, Amanda, ladies and gentlemen. What have I missed?"

Billie quickly repeated what Kate had told her.

"Where's Ames?" Greene asked when she was finished.

"In the back of the ambulance," Amanda answered.

Greene thought for a moment. Then he looked at Daniel's lawyer.

"Let's get out of this rain and talk. There's a Denny's down the road."

"We've got to get over to the cemetery to scope out the crime scene," Billie said. Greene nodded and Amanda followed him to his car.

Kate turned to Billie. "What are you going to do about Daniel?"

"He's a suspect, Kate."

"Damn it, Billie, I told you what I saw. Daniel was supposed to die, too. He's been shot. Take a look at his wound. He'd be dead if I got here a few minutes later."

"This is the second crime scene Ames has been caught at."

"You didn't catch him. I called 911 with his consent. We could have been long gone if he gave the word. You'd never have connected him to the killing if he didn't wait here."

"You've got a point."

"The person who killed Briggs and Kaidanov is a cold-blooded psychopath. Daniel's nothing like that."

"Is this your heart or your head talking?" Billie asked, watching her friend carefully.

"How many times do I have to say it? I saw someone shoot Daniel."

"Who?"

"It was dark. Everything happened very fast."

Billie was quiet for a moment. When she spoke she looked uneasy.

"I'm gonna be blunt, Kate. Right now I've got a murder victim and a guy who's charged with another, connected murder. What Ames has is a witness who came on the scene after the victim was killed, and that witness is a friend of the suspect—maybe a very good friend."

"You think I'm lying?" Kate asked, aghast at the accusation.

Billie broke eye contact for a moment. When she reestablished it she looked embarrassed.

"What happens to Ames isn't my call. Mike Greene and Amanda Jaffe will work out the details. Right now all I want to do is get my work done and go home to a hot drink and a very hot bath. You should get out of the rain."

35

When Mike Greene and Amanda Jaffe returned, the ambulance was gone and Daniel was under guard in the back of a patrol car. In view of Kate's account of the shoot-out and Daniel's wound, Greene decided that there was too much uncertainty to arrest Daniel.

The shock of being seconds from death, the discomfort from his wound, and the discovery that Kaidanov's study was a hoax gave Daniel a lot to think about during the ride to Kate's house. As soon as they were in the door Kate led him into the bathroom. His clothes were still covered with gore.

"Give me those," Kate said while she filled up the bathtub. "I'll put them in the wash to get this . . . stuff off."

Daniel stripped and settled into the scalding water. The painkillers he'd been given by the EMTs had kicked in. He closed his eyes and drifted off, but a recurring vision of Kaidanov's head exploding kept him from falling asleep, as did the sudden understanding that the only person who could tell the police that he did not murder Arthur Briggs was dead.

The water cooled off and Daniel hoisted himself out of the tub. Every movement hurt. After he dressed in clothes that Kate had left for him, he limped into the living room. She was sitting on the couch clutching a glass of Scotch. The bottle stood in front of her on the coffee table. Kate's eyes were closed and her head was back. She looked exhausted. Daniel felt guilty that he had only been thinking about himself.

"Are you okay?" he asked anxiously. "Can I do anything?"

Kate opened her eyes and shook her head.

"What's wrong?"

"I was in a shoot-out once before. I never thought I'd have to go through that again."

Daniel sat next to Kate on the couch. "I saw how you looked at the lab when Forbus called you Annie Oakley. Was that because of the shooting?"

Kate nodded.

"What happened?"

Kate closed her eyes and pressed the glass to her forehead.

"There wasn't enough action in solving computer crimes, so I asked for a transfer to narcotics," Kate said in an exhausted monotone. "About six months after I went undercover I busted Clarence Marcel, an enforcer for Abdullah Hassim, a major dealer.

"While Clarence was out on bail, he and Abdullah had a falling-out over three missing kilos of cocaine. Clarence decided to rat out Abdullah in exchange for witness protection. I'm the one he called to set up the

deal. The DA had an orgasm when I told him. He'd
been trying to catch Abdullah for years. Only problem was Clarence insisted on turning himself over at
the Lloyd Center mall at high noon. I told the DA that
Clarence's plan was insane—too many people could
get hurt if Abdullah tried to take out Clarence—but
the DA was so desperate to turn him that he went
along with it."

Kate took a stiff drink. "I remember every second
of that afternoon," she said, a faraway look in her
eyes. "It was Christmas. Carols were being piped
through the loudspeakers, kids were skating at the ice
rink, and the mall was packed. We were supposed to
meet Clarence in front of a camera store. There were
shoppers all over the place: a pregnant woman with
her child, a Hispanic family, a cute, blond kid about
twelve in a baggy Spider-Man sweatshirt.

"Clarence appeared out of nowhere and our guys
moved to surround him. Watching from the doorway
of a record store across the way were two black
teenagers in Oakland Raiders gear. I was window-
shopping, next door. As soon as they spotted Clarence
they pulled out automatic weapons."

Kate shook her head slowly.

"I shot the first one in the chest. He fell sideways
into the guy on his right, who had his finger on the
trigger of an Uzi. I shot the second guy. He stumbled
forward, spraying bullets into the crowd. A mother
and daughter went down, one of our men was hit.
There was complete panic and everybody started diving for cover.

"The crowd had separated Clarence from our guys

and he took off for the nearest exit. I went after him. Running hard on his heels was the little white kid in the Spider-Man sweatshirt. Just as they reached the exit the kid said something and Clarence stopped and turned. I had almost caught up with him when this hole appeared in Clarence's forehead."

Kate touched a spot above her right eye.

"Who shot him?"

"It was the fucking kid. He was working with the brothers in the Oakland Raiders togs. Later on we found out that the hit wasn't his first." Kate shook her head as if she still couldn't believe it. "He was twelve years old and he did it for two Baggies."

She paused, drained her glass, then refilled it.

"I thought someone behind me had killed Clarence. It never dawned on me that it was the kid until he shot me, too. I was so shocked that I froze. Then he shot me again and I started squeezing the trigger. When the other cops got there every pane of glass in the exit door had been blown out, the kid was lying in a pool of blood with his chest torn apart, and I was standing over him jerking that trigger even though there wasn't a bullet left in my gun."

"How could you still be standing?" Daniel asked, awed by Kate's story.

"On TV, people fly through the air when they're shot or they fall down and die. That's not the way it happens in the real world. I've heard of shoot-outs where robbers took shot after shot and kept coming. Even a person who's shot in the heart could have as much as a minute to act before he bleeds out and goes unconscious. I didn't even know I'd been hit until I saw the blood. That's when I collapsed."

"Jesus, that's amazing."

"The DA didn't think so," Kate concluded bitterly. "Neither did the press. They called the shoot-out 'The Holiday Massacre.'" She looked at Daniel. "They needed a scapegoat, so they chose me. I'd lost Clarence and I killed a little kid. It didn't matter to the press that the kid was a hired assassin. I was expendable. I could have fought it, but I'd had enough, so I resigned."

"It sounds to me like you have nothing to feel bad about."

Kate smiled without humor. "I don't feel bad. I never did. After the shooting I had to visit a shrink. It was department policy. He told me it was common to experience feelings of guilt even when a shooting was righteous, but I never felt guilty and that really bothered me."

"What about tonight?"

Kate looked directly at Daniel. "Truth?"

"Of course."

"I was pumped. My motor was going every second I was trading shots."

"That's adrenaline."

Kate shook her head. "I know what adrenaline feels like. This was something different. This was a high like no other. So, what does that say about me?"

"It says that you're too hard on yourself. Are you forgetting that you saved my life? You're my hero, Kate."

Kate's laugh was sharp and biting.

"I mean it," he insisted. "I'd be dead if it wasn't for you. What you did was very brave."

Kate touched his cheek. "You're sweet."

Daniel reached up and took Kate's hand. It was light as a feather. He turned her palm and kissed it. She hesitated for only a second. Then she pulled Daniel to her and kissed him. Daniel winced. Kate sat back.

"Are you okay?" she asked, alarmed.

"Never felt better," Daniel answered, grimacing.

Kate laughed.

"I hate to say this," Daniel said, managing to smile, "but I'm in no condition to play Don Juan tonight."

Kate squeezed his hand. "Do I get a rain check?"

"Most definitely." He grinned. "I've got to thank you properly for riding to my rescue."

She laughed. "I did arrive in the nick of time, didn't I?"

"Just like the cavalry"—Daniel smiled—"but please feel free to rescue me sooner in the future."

36

The slender, dark-skinned man was waiting patiently for Claude Bernier when the photographer reached the landing of his third-floor walk-up. Bernier hesitated even though his visitor was dressed in a conservative suit and carrying a briefcase. He had been robbed at gunpoint recently and the man looked sinister enough to make him uneasy,

"Mr. Bernier?" the man asked in a heavy Spanish accent.

"Yes?" Bernier answered warily.

"My name is Juan Fulano and I am here to do business with you."

Photographers—even those with Claude's talent— had to scramble to make a living, and the mention of business erased the last of his doubts. He unlocked his door and invited Fulano inside. The apartment was small but clean. The walls were decorated with Bernier's photographs and the works of friends. Claude put down the bag of groceries he was carrying on the table in his narrow kitchen.

"I don't have much in the fridge," he apologized, "but I could make us some coffee."

"Not necessary."

Bernier led Fulano into the living room and offered him the most comfortable chair. Fulano sat down and carefully crossed his left leg over his right.

"How can I help you?" Bernier asked.

"I am interested in buying a copy of a photograph that was originally purchased from the Pitzer-Kraft Gallery in late February by a lawyer named Gene Arnold."

"Are you with the police?"

"No, Mr. Bernier. Why do you ask?"

"The police in Portland, Oregon, called me about that photograph. Do you know that Arnold was murdered?"

Bernier's visitor nodded. "Why did the Oregon authorities contact you?"

"They want a copy of the photograph, too."

"Have you sent it to them?"

"No. I just found the negative. It was misplaced. I'm mailing a print to Portland tomorrow."

Fulano smiled. "I wonder if I could induce you to sell me a copy of the photograph as well."

"Sure. I can make another copy."

"How much do you require?"

Bernier did a quick calculation based on the quality of Fulano's clothes.

"Fifteen hundred dollars," he said.

"A reasonable price, but the photograph would be worth five thousand to me if you would do me a small favor."

Bernier managed to conceal his surprise and excitement. He had never sold a photograph for that much money.

"What would you want me to do?"

"Do the authorities in Oregon know that you've located the negative of the photograph?"

"No. I just found it this morning."

"The five thousand is yours if you wait to send the photograph until I tell you to do so."

"I don't know," Bernier answered, suddenly worried. "It's a murder investigation. The detective I spoke with thought the people in the picture might be involved in Mr. Arnold's death."

"I, too, am interested in discovering the identity of Mr. Arnold's killer. I have no desire to obstruct a police investigation."

"Then why do you want me to wait to send the photograph to the police?"

Bernier's visitor leaned back and steepled his fingers. "Is five thousand dollars a fair price for your photograph?"

"Yes."

"Is it more than fair?"

Bernier hesitated, certain that the man knew he had inflated the price.

"It's very generous."

"Then I would hope that you would permit me to simply say that your assistance is important to me."

Bernier considered the proposition for a moment more before accepting.

"Do you think you could have the photograph for

me by this evening?" Fulano asked. "I have an early flight?"

"That shouldn't be a problem. Come by at eight."

Bernier's visitor opened his briefcase and handed him a stack of currency.

"A down payment," he said. "I hope you don't mind cash."

37

The aroma of coffee lured Daniel out of a fitful sleep the next morning. When he limped into the kitchen Kate was finishing her breakfast. She looked up from the paper and smiled.

"How are you feeling?" she asked.

"I'm okay," Daniel answered unconvincingly. He poured himself a cup of coffee.

"I forgot to ask, last night. Did anything happen in Arizona?"

She nodded as Daniel put two slices of bread in the toaster.

"I'm pretty certain I know why Gene Arnold came to Portland."

Daniel carried his coffee to the table and Kate told him about the kidnappings in Desert Grove and her discovery that Aaron Flynn had been Paul McCann's attorney.

"So you think Gene Arnold recognized Flynn in the photograph?"

"I can't think of any other reason for him to come here."

"But why—" Daniel stopped in mid-sentence. "The guy!"

"What?"

"Saturday, Joe Molinari took me to my apartment to get my running gear. When we pulled up I saw a man leave my apartment house and get into a black pickup. I was certain I'd seen him someplace before. I just remembered where. The day I dropped off the discovery Flynn and this guy came into the reception area together. I got the impression he worked for Flynn."

"Describe him to me."

"He looked like a weight lifter, a big neck, thick shoulders. I'd guess he was in his forties."

"Burt Randall. He's Flynn's investigator."

"Why would he be at my place?"

Kate was quiet for a moment. "Did you tell anyone other than me that you were going to meet Kaidanov at the cemetery?"

"No."

"Then how did the killer know?"

"Maybe someone followed Kaidanov."

"That doesn't work," Kate said. "If the people who wanted him dead knew where he was, they would have killed Kaidanov before he could tell you that the study was a hoax."

"Maybe I was the one who was tailed."

"But they'd have to know you were meeting Kaidanov. Kaidanov called you at your apartment, right?"

Daniel nodded.

"Randall knows all about electronic surveillance. You may have a tap on your phone."

"Is there any way you can tell?"

"I know someone who can sweep your apartment."

"Shit. The only person who could clear me is dead and my apartment might be bugged. This is getting worse and worse."

38

Paul Durban, a chubby, bespectacled man in a white shirt, gray slacks, and a gray sweater vest, finished his sweep of Daniel's apartment as Kate and Daniel watched from the couch. Durban concentrated his equipment on an area of molding for a few moments, then he turned to Kate.

"One bug in the phone, one in the bedroom, and one in here."

"Thanks, Paul. You know where to send the bill."

"Anytime," he said as he gathered up his equipment and left.

Durban had placed each listening device in its own evidence bag and left them on the coffee table. Daniel picked up one of the plastic bags and examined the bug.

"I've been doing a lot of thinking," he said. "Until Kaidanov told me that his study was a hoax, I was sure that Geller was trying to cover up Kaidanov's results. Now that I've learned about Aaron Flynn's con-

nection to Gene Arnold, I've been looking at everything that's happened in a different light."

Daniel put the bug down.

"When I dropped off the discovery I had a talk
with Flynn. He told me that he'd hired more than
twenty people to deal with the Insufort case and had
leased another floor in his building to house them.
That had to cost him. Now add in the expense of hiring experts at three hundred to six hundred dollars an
hour and the other assorted expenses of litigation and
you're looking at hundreds of thousands of dollars in
costs.

"Flynn made a lot of money from his other cases,
but I bet he's plowed a lot of that dough back into the
Insufort case. That's a good investment if he wins. In
some of the Insufort cases, the plaintiffs are perma-
nently injured babies. You're talking about a lifetime
of damages. There's lost earning capacity, medical
costs, lifetime care. The life expectancy of a male is
around seventy-two years and a female's life expectancy is a little under eighty years. What kind of
care does a severely handicapped child need? There's
nursing care, doctors' visits, psychiatric counseling
for the parents. We're talking a hundred thousand
dollars a year, easy. Now multiply that by seventy or
eighty years and multiply that by the number of plaintiffs. Potentially that's millions in attorney fees. When
the first few plaintiffs showed up, Flynn must have
thought that his ship had come in. I bet he started
spending money like crazy, figuring he'd make a fortune when the cases were over."

"But the studies failed to show a causal connection between Insufort and the birth defects," Kate said.

"Exactly. And Flynn figured out that it was only a coincidence that the plaintiffs were taking Insufort and their children had birth defects. That's when he decided that he had to manufacture evidence."

"I see a problem," Kate said. "Flynn would have to put on admissible evidence to prove Insufort causes birth defects. If the study is phony it would be torn apart by Geller's experts at trial."

"The operative words here are 'at trial,'" Daniel said. "That's where evidence is put to the test and a fraud can be exposed. But what happened when Kaidanov's lab was destroyed? The media jumped to the conclusion that Geller was covering up problems with Insufort. That's what we believed, and it's what a jury might believe. Now someone has murdered Kaidanov and Geller Pharmaceuticals has the obvious motive. With Kaidanov dead and the lab destroyed, Geller can't refute his study results. They can claim they're phony, but they can't prove it. There's going to be tremendous pressure on Geller to settle rather than run the risk of a catastrophic jury verdict."

"You're right," Kate said. "If the case settles, no one gets to show whether or not Insufort is safe."

"And Aaron Flynn wins a huge attorney fee instead of losing millions of dollars in costs."

Kate hesitated. "If Flynn is behind Kaidanov's hoax, why did he try to hide the results of the study by erasing it from the hard drive on Kaidanov's computer? Wouldn't Flynn want us to find the study?"

The question stumped Daniel for a moment. Then he brightened.

"When I broke into Kaidanov's house it looked like a hurricane had swept through it, but there was one thing in that house that was untouched and sitting exactly where it was supposed to be."

"The computer!"

"Whoever trashed Kaidanov's house left his computer alone so I couldn't help but notice it in the wreckage. He couldn't have done more to draw my attention to it if he painted it red and stuck sequins on it."

"You're right. They wanted us to think that there had been an unsuccessful attempt by Geller's people to erase the file, but a pro would have left no trace on the hard drive. It was a snap for me to recover the study."

"There's something else, Kate. Think about this. Flynn finding Kaidanov's letter in the documents Geller produced was like buying a winning lottery ticket. But that's not the only time that Flynn's gotten lucky. The eyewitness in my murder case just happens to be April Fairweather, the defendant in another one of his cases. Then a guardian angel sends my lawyer a videotape that enables her to destroy Fairweather so badly that the insurance company Flynn is suing will have to settle. Bingo, Flynn collects another big attorney fee."

"That is quite a string of good luck," Kate mused.

"What if Flynn is making his own luck? I talked with Joe Molinari about my case when we ran. He wondered if Flynn's got a mole at Reed, Briggs who stole the tape and put the Kaidanov letter into the discovery."

"Did he say who he thought it was?"

"Brock Newbauer or Susan Webster. Both of them are involved with the Insufort and the Fairweather cases."

Kate was quiet for a moment. When she spoke Daniel could tell that she was upset.

"You might be onto something. About a year ago Brock Newbauer settled a lawsuit because Aaron Flynn found a witness no one outside our office was supposed to know about. The way I remember it, aside from the lawyers, only our client was supposed to know that this guy existed. A lot of people in the firm were upset when they received Flynn's witness list. There were rumors that someone at Reed, Briggs tipped off Flynn, but they never came to anything. The next time you talk to Joe Molinari ask him about the Romanoff case. He was working on it with Newbauer. It was shortly after you started at the firm."

Kate thought for a moment before making a decision.

"I think our best chance of clearing you is to help the police find the person who killed Briggs and Kaidanov. I'm going to show Billie the bugs. We can tell her about Burt Randall. She'll question him and find out who told him to install them. I'll tell Billie about Flynn's connection to Gene Arnold. We'll nail him."

39

When Kate walked into the Taco Bell, Billie Brewster was working on a burrito in a back booth. Kate bought a cup of black coffee and slid in across from her.

"What, no password? I thought this was a top-secret meeting."

Kate smiled. "I'm here to talk about Kaidanov's murder."

"And I thought you wanted some fashion tips." Billie took a bite of her burrito. "I assume there's going to be a little quid pro quo here."

Kate nodded.

"A neighbor who lives near that ravine heard the shots and looked out her window. She saw someone run out of the woods a little before you and Daniel came out, but it was too dark for her to give any kind of ID. She also saw a car drive off without lights, but can't tell us the make or color. That's all we've got."

"I think you should take a hard look at Aaron Flynn and Burt Randall, Flynn's investigator."

"This on the up-and-up?"

Kate nodded.

"Aaron Flynn has lots of important friends," Billie said.

Kate leaned across the table. Her voice and her stare were intense.

"Kaidanov phoned Daniel's apartment to set up the meeting at the graveyard. Daniel didn't tell anyone except me that he was meeting Kaidanov there at ten, but the killer knew. The day before the call, Daniel saw Burt Randall leaving his building. I had Dan's apartment swept for bugs and my technician found these."

Kate placed the evidence bags containing the bugs on the table. Billie whistled softly.

"Randall must have planted them and whoever listened to Daniel's calls knew that Kaidanov would be at Rest of Angels at ten o'clock."

The detective picked up evidence bags and studied the listening devices.

"Okay, you've got me thinking about Randall," she said. "Why Flynn?"

Kate told Billie everything she had learned in Arizona about the Alvarez and Arnold kidnappings.

"I'm certain that Gene Arnold was killed because Flynn was afraid that he would expose his connection to the Arizona kidnappings."

"Was Flynn ever a suspect in the Alvarez or Arnold murders?"

"Not that I know. But I called your friend at the Benson Hotel. He went over Arnold's phone records.

Gene Arnold called Aaron Flynn's office from his room."

"Why would a hotshot lawyer like Aaron Flynn be killing people and setting monkeys on fire?" Brewster asked.

Kate told the homicide detective how much money Flynn would make if he won the Insufort litigation and how much it would cost him if he lost it.

"You think Flynn or Randall killed Arthur Briggs?" Billie asked.

"I'm certain of it. Kaidanov was going to tell Briggs that the study was a hoax. The study was all Flynn had going for him. He had to kill Kaidanov and anyone he talked to."

Billie took a bite of her burrito and mulled over all she'd just learned.

"I think I'll pay a visit to Mr. Flynn," she said.

40

Zeke Forbus was at his desk in the Justice Center writing a report when his intercom buzzed.

"I've got a caller on line two for a detective who's working on the Ames investigation," the receptionist said.

"Though he works from sun to sun, a detective's work is never done." Forbus sighed. The receptionist laughed. "I'll take it, Millie."

"Detectives," Forbus said as soon as he punched line two.

"Ask Arthur Briggs's secretary what Daniel Ames said when he called her the afternoon her boss was murdered," a muffled voice said. Then the line went dead.

Zeke Forbus flashed his badge and told the receptionist at Reed, Briggs that he wanted to talk to Renee Gilchrist. Then he took a seat and leafed through a magazine while he waited for Renee to appear. As soon as she walked into the reception area, Forbus remembered her. She was tall and sleek and easily distracted him from the article he had been reading.

"Ms. Gilchrist?" Forbus said.

When she nodded Forbus showed Renee his identification. Renee looked nervous.

"I'm one of the detectives investigating the murder of Arthur Briggs. We spoke right after your boss was killed."

"Oh, yes. I remember."

"Is there someplace quiet where we can talk now?"

"There's a room down the hall that's not being used."

"That'll do."

"What's this about?"

Forbus smiled. "Why don't we get settled first."

As soon as they were inside, Forbus shut the door and motioned Renee into a seat. The room was small and the air close. Forbus moved slowly to the table and took his seat, staring at Renee the whole time and not saying a word. The detective enjoyed using his size to advantage in a situation like this and he felt a surge of pleasure when Renee lowered her eyes. He had intentionally scooted his chair close to her so their knees were almost touching.

"After we talked the first time I wrote a report."

Forbus pulled three folded sheets of paper out of his inside jacket pocket and pushed them across the table. Renee looked at the report nervously but did not reach for it.

"Read it," Forbus ordered.

Renee hesitated, then started turning the pages. When she finished she looked at the detective expectantly.

"Anything missing?" he asked.

"Missing?"

"Yeah. Is there anything that you should have told me that's not in there?"

Renee looked confused. "What do you mean?"

"I got a call from someone who thinks you're concealing information in this investigation."

Renee's shoulders hunched a little and she looked down at the table.

"Ms. Gilchrist, how did you and Daniel Ames get along?"

"Okay. Fine."

"Care to elaborate."

"He . . . We worked together."

"Do you like him?"

The question seemed to startle Renee. "Like him?" she repeated. "Well, I mean, he's a nice guy, sure."

"That's not what I'm talking about, Ms. Gilchrist. You two ever date?"

"No! He did a lot of work with Mr. Briggs. I just saw him in the office."

"So you'd have no reason to cover for him, to conceal evidence that would prove he killed your boss?"

"Certainly not," she answered, but there was a tremor in her voice.

Forbus smiled. He leaned back and studied Renee. She shifted on her chair.

"Then I suppose you have a good reason for not telling me about the phone call you got from Ames on the day your boss was killed?"

Renee hesitated.

"Did he call you, Renee?" Forbus demanded, putting emphasis on the secretary's first name. "Do you understand that it's a felony to obstruct a police investigation?"

Renee's eyes dropped and she fidgeted in her seat.

"I'm gonna ask you once more: Did you get a call from Daniel Ames on the day Arthur Briggs was killed?"

"Yes," Renee answered, her voice barely above a whisper.

"Good, Renee. You just took the first step toward staying out of jail. Step two is to tell me what Ames said."

41

When Billie Brewster entered Aaron Flynn's suite of offices, she was as impressed by the lobby as Daniel had been, but Brewster had no trouble separating her admiration for the things someone owned from her opinion of the person who owned them. Flynn's office was as impressive as the lobby. It was paneled in mahogany and decorated with fine art and tributes to Flynn's courtroom triumphs. When Flynn's secretary brought the detective to meet him, he rounded his polished oak desk and crossed the Persian rug that covered his hardwood floors.

"Sit down, Detective Brewster," he said, flashing a warm smile and giving Billie's hand a firm shake. "Can I get you anything to drink?"

"I'm okay, thanks," Billie answered as she settled onto a comfortable couch that sat against one wall. Flynn sat opposite her, completely at ease.

"How can I help you?" he asked.

"Have you heard about the shooting at Rest of Angels Cemetery last night?"

The lawyer's smile disappeared. "It was in the morning paper." Flynn shook his head sadly. "Dr. Kaidanov's death was a tragic loss."

"You knew him?"

"No, but I was hoping that he would be the key witness for several clients of mine who have given birth to babies with defects we believe were caused by Insufort, a Geller Pharmaceutical product. Dr. Kaidanov authored a study that showed that the product was harmful. He disappeared before I could question him about his work."

"Did you try to find Dr. Kaidanov?"

"I've had my investigators trying to locate him since I learned about the study."

"Is Burt Randall one of the people you were using?"

"Yes. Why?"

"Did you instruct Mr. Randall to put a tap on Daniel Ames's phone?"

"A tap! Of course not."

"Mr. Flynn, I've received information that your investigator did exactly that, which we both know is quite illegal."

"Of course I know that. That's why I would never do such a thing." Flynn paused. "Ames. Isn't he the young man charged with killing Arthur Briggs?"

Billie nodded.

"I'm completely lost, Detective. What makes you think that Burt would do something like that? If you're going to make serious accusations against one of my employees, I have a right to know the basis for them."

"I'm sorry, but this comes from a confidential source. You understand confidentiality, being a lawyer and all," Brewster said, feigning a friendly smile.

"Well, I don't know what to say. This is very unsettling."

"Is Mr. Randall here? I'd like to speak to him."

"I don't believe he came in today."

"Can you give me his home address and phone number?"

"I'd have to ask Mr. Randall for his permission, first. Why don't I arrange to have you meet him here, tomorrow?"

"I appreciate the offer, but I need to see him today."

"Then I can't help you."

"Or won't," Brewster answered, her smile gone. "Mr. Flynn, does the name Gene Arnold mean anything to you?"

The question seemed to take Flynn by surprise. "I knew a lawyer named Gene Arnold years ago when I was practicing in Arizona."

"That's the Gene Arnold I'm interested in. He was stabbed, then set on fire at the primate lab where the Kaidanov study was conducted."

Billie watched Flynn's reaction carefully.

Flynn seemed confused. "Gene was the dead man at that lab?"

She nodded.

"My God. What was he doing there?"

"I thought you might be able to tell me."

"I have no idea. I haven't seen Gene in years."

"What was your relationship to Mr. Arnold when you did know him?"

Flynn shrugged. " 'Relationship' would be too strong a word. We were acquaintances. Both of us practiced law in Desert Grove, which is a fairly small town. There weren't many attorneys in Desert Grove, so we socialized at Bar Association meetings, things of that sort. We were adversaries on occasion, legally speaking, though this was some years ago. I don't remember any specific cases offhand."

"Do you know of any connection between Mr. Arnold and the Insufort litigation?"

"None."

"So he didn't mention the lab or the Insufort case when he called you?"

"Why would he call me?"

"I don't know, but the phone records from the Benson Hotel show a call from Mr. Arnold's room to your office that lasted fifteen minutes."

"I never spoke to him. I told you, I haven't seen him or spoken to him since I left Desert Grove."

"If you didn't talk to him when he called, who did?"

Flynn spread his hands and shrugged his shoulders. "I have no idea, Detective."

Billie told Flynn the date and time of the call.

"Were you in the office when he phoned?" she asked.

"I can't say for certain."

"Fifteen minutes is a long time, Mr. Flynn. Mr. Arnold must have been talking to somebody."

"Maybe I was on another line and he held for a while, then hung up. I frequently have phone conferences that last an hour or more. I'm involved in cases all over the country. I'm even representing some of the families from that air crash in India."

"Would your staff be able to help? Maybe they remember the call."

"I'll ask, but I'm assuming this would have been several weeks ago, right?"

"Your billing records would show what you were doing when Mr. Arnold called, wouldn't they?"

"They might."

"Will you ask your secretary to make a copy of them for me?"

"I'm afraid I can't do that. It would violate client confidentiality." Flynn smiled. "There's that word again."

Brewster studied Flynn. He seemed to be getting a second wind.

"Can you think of any reason why Gene Arnold would be in Portland?"

"No."

"You represented Paul McCann, didn't you, the man accused of killing Patty Alvarez?"

"Yes."

"And you know about the murder of Mr. Arnold's wife."

"I wasn't involved in that case," Flynn answered, shifting uneasily in his chair.

"Could Mr. Arnold's visit have had anything to do with the death of his wife and Martin Alvarez's wife?" Billie asked.

Flynn looked very uncomfortable. "I can't think of how it could."

Billie waited a moment, watching Flynn closely.

"Well," she said as she stood up, "I guess that does it. Thank you for your time."

Flynn stood, too. "If there's anything I can do . . ."

Billie handed Flynn her card. "The time sheets for the day Mr. Arnold called. Why don't you think about letting me see them."

As soon as the door closed behind Billie Brewster, Aaron Flynn told his secretary to hold his calls. Then he dialed a number he knew almost as well as his own. A moment later the call went through.

"We got a serious problem," Flynn said, speaking urgently into the phone. "A very serious problem."

42

One wall of Geller Pharmaceuticals' conference room was glass and provided a view of the atrium with its indoor waterfall, but no one in the room was looking at the view. Their attention was focused on J. B. Reed, who had just entered with Brock Newbauer and Susan Webster in tow. At six five and almost three hundred pounds, Reed, Briggs's most powerful partner was used to being the center of attention.

Isaac Geller crossed the conference room and grasped Reed's hand.

"Thank you for coming, John," Geller said. "How are you holding up?"

"It's been hard, Isaac," Reed answered, shaking his head sadly. "Art and I were more than law partners."

"I know."

"We go back to high school. We founded the firm."

"We're all still in shock," Geller said.

Reed's features hardened into a look of rocklike determination.

"I'm stepping in, Isaac. That's why I'm here, to let

you know that I'm making these lawsuits my number-one priority."

"And none too soon, either," interjected Byron McFall, Geller's president, as the lawyers took their seats at the conference table. "Kaidanov's murder couldn't have happened at a worse time."

McFall's callousness made Geller flinch, but no one noticed. Their eyes were on Reed.

"How is this going to affect our position?" McFall asked.

"I've been briefed about the case by Brock and Susan," Reed replied, "but I don't have enough of a handle on the facts yet to give you an intelligent answer. Susan?"

All eyes turned toward Susan Webster, the elegant associate who had taken the seat next to Reed.

"Sergey Kaidanov's murder is a public relations nightmare, Mr. McFall. I pulled up several stories on the Kaidanov killing on the Internet. It's front-page news all over the country. The press is hinting that Geller Pharmaceuticals is behind the destruction of the lab and Kaidanov's death because the company wants to cover up his study. There's pressure on the district attorney to start an investigation. Not surprisingly, Aaron Flynn is talking to every reporter he can find. If he brings this case to trial we'll never find twelve jurors who haven't heard the rumors."

Isaac Geller closed his eyes and shook his head. He looked exhausted.

"What do you suggest we do?"

Susan looked at Reed. "Maybe I should wait for

Mr. Reed to get up to speed on the case before offering any advice."

"That's okay," Reed prompted. "I want to hear where you think we are in the case."

"I'd start discussing a settlement, Mr. Geller," Susan said reluctantly. "It could be a bloodbath if we go to trial."

"Goddamn it!" Byron McFall said bitterly. "We had nothing to do with that lab or the study or Kaidanov's murder."

"That may be irrelevant if everyone believes that we did," Susan said evenly. "We should approach Mr. Flynn with a reasonable offer. There are good arguments for admissibility and exclusion of the evidence of the murders, the study, and the destruction of the lab. Right now neither side knows what Judge Norris will let in at trial. This is the best time to feel out Flynn. If Norris rules in his favor he'll want to try every case, and once he wins one of them we won't be able to hold back the flood."

Geller's in-house counsel made a comment just as Susan's cell phone rang. Newbauer, who was seated to Susan's left, watched her answer it and noted her surprise. She walked to the far end of the conference room, away from the others, and continued her conversation in a voice too low to hear. She seemed concerned when she returned to the conference table.

"Anything wrong?" Newbauer asked.

"No," Webster answered unconvincingly.

●   ●   ●

Kate Ross split her attention between *The New York Times* crossword puzzle and the exit to Aaron Flynn's garage. An hour after she'd seen Billie Brewster leave Flynn's building, Flynn's car appeared. Kate put down the paper and followed him across town to the Sunset Highway entrance. It was almost 6:30 and the traffic had thinned out. Kate stayed several car lengths back as Flynn headed toward the coast. After half an hour, the lawyer left the highway and took a route that wound through farm country. Ten minutes later he pulled into the dirt parking lot of the Midway Café, a run-down roadhouse with a neon sign that advertised beer and fried chicken. It was the type of place where truckers and farmers stopped for coffee and pie, and high-priced lawyers rarely entered.

Kate drove by the restaurant then made a U-turn and parked at the far end of the lot just as Flynn was walking inside. Moments later another car pulled into a parking space near the door and Susan Webster got out.

"Bingo," Kate said to herself. She thought about following Susan inside, but the restaurant was too small. Kate leaned over her seat. When she surfaced, she was holding an expensive camera with a telephoto lens.

Thirty minutes later the door to the restaurant opened and Susan Webster and Aaron Flynn walked out. Kate snapped off several shots.

Juan Fulano had been surprised to see another car following Aaron Flynn from his office building to the roadside café. He had been careful to stay far enough back of both cars so he would not be seen. When Kate parked in the lot Fulano drove down the road, made a U-turn, and pulled to the side of the road, where he waited until Aaron Flynn and Susan Webster came out of the restaurant. His only worry was that Flynn's tail would follow him after he left the diner, but she did not.

As soon as Flynn drove away Fulano turned on his headlights and followed. Flynn stayed on the highway until he was back within the Portland city limits. When he turned off the highway, Fulano followed at a discreet distance. Once he was certain that Flynn was going home, Fulano fell farther back to give Flynn time to park. Then he found a spot on Flynn's block where he stayed, watching Flynn's house. When the lights went out near midnight, Fulano drove back to his hotel and phoned in his report to Martin Alvarez.

43

Billie ran a check on Burt Randall after visiting Aaron Flynn's law office. Besides getting his address, she had discovered that Randall was an ex-marine with combat experience and former LAPD. Deciding that discretion was the better part of valor, the detective had a patrol car follow her to Randall's house. Brewster drove along Northwest Twenty-third until she reached Thurman, then turned left into the hills. Randall's modern A-frame was set back from an unpaved street on the outskirts of Forest Park. A black pickup truck stood in the driveway.

"Let's you and me go to the front door," Billie told Ronnie Blanchard, a uniformed officer who had played linebacker at Portland State. "Radison can cover the rear of the house."

"Sounds like a plan," Tom Radison, Blanchard's partner, said. He headed toward the back of the house.

"You know this guy's background," Billie said. "Let's not take chances."

The house was dark. Billie rang the bell. There was no answer. She tried again while Blanchard tried the door. It was unlocked. The officer looked at Billie and she nodded. He edged the door inward.

"Mr. Randall," Billie called out. Silence. "I'm Billie Brewster, a police detective. Are you home, sir?"

The living room had a vaulted ceiling. The dying rays of the sun cast a pale light through ceiling-high picture windows. Billie pointed to a dark hallway. Blanchard edged down it while Billie cautiously climbed the stairs to a sleeping loft that overlooked the entryway and the living room. The moment Billie's head cleared the landing she knew something was wrong. She gripped her weapon a little tighter before climbing the rest of the stairs in a crouch. The blinds were closed and all Billie could tell was that there was someone sprawled across the bed.

"Mr. Randall?" she said loudly.

There was no answer.

"I do not fucking like this," Billie mumbled to herself as she stepped onto the landing. As soon as her vision adjusted Billie made out Burt Randall in a T-shirt and boxer shorts. There were two bloodstained holes in the T-shirt and a third in the center of Randall's forehead.

44

Daniel was fixing dinner in Kate's kitchen when he heard her car pull up. She was holding a roll of film when she walked in the door.

"What's that?"

"Photos of a secret meeting between Aaron Flynn and Susan Webster. Tomorrow morning, I'm going to have a talk with that little bitch. If she'll admit she's been working with Flynn to fix Insufort, we may be able to nail him."

"That's terrific," Daniel said.

The phone rang and Kate answered it. She listened intently for a moment, then swore.

"What's wrong?" Daniel asked.

"It's Billie," Kate told him. "Randall is dead, murdered."

Kate listened while Brewster described the crime scene.

"No sign of a struggle?" Kate asked.

"None," Billie told her.

"When was Randall killed?"

"Medical examiner's rough guess puts the death around the time Kaidanov got it, give or take an hour either way."

"It sounds like someone is tying up loose ends," Kate said. "Did you talk to Flynn?"

"Yeah, but I didn't get a thing. He was very nervous when I asked him about the call from the Benson. He denied talking to Arnold, even though the call lasted fifteen minutes. And he refused to let me see his time sheets so I could find out who was with him when the call came in. I'm sure he's hiding something."

"With Randall dead, we won't be able to prove that Flynn ordered him to bug Daniel's apartment."

"With Randall dead, we can't prove a thing against Flynn." Billie sighed. "I phoned Claude Bernier. He's still having trouble finding the negative. If we ever get a print of the photograph, and Flynn's in it, I might be able to get a search warrant for Flynn's time sheets."

"Go get some sleep," Kate said. "You sound all in."

"Good advice."

Kate hung up. "That was Billie Brewster. Burt Randall's been murdered."

"Then we're fucked. The cops are not going to go after someone like Aaron Flynn without proof."

"Maybe I can crack Susan with the photos when I—"

Kate froze. Then she smiled.

"What?" Daniel asked.

She started toward the door to her basement workshop.

"Come on. We're going to take a trip in cyber-space."

Daniel followed Kate downstairs. She flipped on the light and headed to one of her computers.

"One of the reasons Reed, Briggs hired me was to advise them on computer security. If you want to know how to protect files, you have to know how to invade them. I'm going to hack into Flynn's computer."

Kate checked her watch. "Flynn's employees should be home by now, so we're good to go."

"What are you looking for?" Daniel asked as Kate started pounding her keyboard.

"If he operates like most lawyers, Flynn posts his time sheets to his law office server," she answered while focusing her attention on her monitor. "They stay there until his secretary uploads them to her workstation when she does his billing. I should be able to access the time sheet for the fifteen minutes when Gene Arnold called Flynn's office. If someone was with Flynn when Arnold's call came in, we'll soon know."

"How are you going to get in?"

"That's simple. I'll access the files at Reed, Briggs and get Flynn's E-mail address. That'll give me his Internet Protocol address. Once I log onto Flynn's server, I'll use the software that found Kaidanov's password to get the password for Flynn's law office server. When I'm in, I can go to any file in the server and download any information in the file to my computer."

"It can't be that easy. What if Flynn has security?"

"He might have installed a firewall to block unauthorized intruders, but I doubt it's one I can't circumvent. The best defensive software has weaknesses.

Even Microsoft has been hacked. I doubt Flynn put a lot of money into his security system. Most law firms don't."

"Can this be traced back to you?"

Kate laughed. "I'm going to give Flynn's server a frontal lobotomy when I'm through. I'll erase the transaction. It'll look like someone randomly logged on by mistake and was kicked off."

"You're sure about this?"

"Relax. This is what I do. In three to four hours we'll know the name of the person Flynn was with when Gene Arnold called."

45

Alice Cummings lived in a cheap garden apartment behind a strip mall and a car wash a few blocks from Portland's worst commercial avenue. Daniel remembered how tired she had looked wheeling Patrick's stroller into Aaron Flynn's lobby on the day he delivered the boxes containing the discovery documents. She looked worse today.

When Cummings visited Flynn she'd been wearing makeup and a dress. When she opened the door, she was in soiled jeans and a stained sweatshirt and there was no mascara or pancake makeup to hide the lines that the pressure of raising a handicapped baby had etched in her face.

"Hi," Daniel said, flashing a pleasant smile. "You probably don't remember me, but Aaron Flynn introduced us about a month ago."

Alice examined Daniel's face. Her eyes lingered on the bandage that covered his head wound, but only for a moment. He hoped that she did not recognize him from one of the television news programs that had filmed him at the courthouse.

"We met in the lobby of Mr. Flynn's office. I was just leaving as you came in for your appointment."

Alice brightened. "Oh, yes. Now I remember. Did Mr. Flynn send you?"

"Can I come in?" Daniel answered, finessing the question.

Alice stepped aside and let Daniel into a small front room.

"How's Patrick?" he asked.

"He had a bad night, but he's sleeping now."

Daniel heard the resignation and exhaustion in Cummings's voice. Kate had looked up Alice in the records at the courthouse. Daniel knew that her husband had filed for divorce soon after Patrick's birth, which meant that she was raising her son alone.

"When he has a bad night yours must be rough, too," he said.

"My nights are never as bad as my baby's. Sometimes I wonder how he goes on, but he's never known anything else."

Alice rubbed her hands on her jeans and surveyed her front room. There was laundry on the sofa. She took a toy off an armchair and motioned Daniel toward it.

"Please, sit down. Can I get you some coffee?"

"I'm fine," Daniel said, waiting for Alice to push some of the laundry aside and take a seat before he sat down.

"Has Mr. Flynn heard anything?" she asked anxiously. "We're really counting on him."

"I'm not here about your case." Alice looked confused and Daniel felt horrible about deceiving her. "It's something Mr. Flynn wanted me to ask you about. Do you remember visiting his office in early March?"

She nodded. "That was my first time. I . . . I read about the Moffitts. I wanted to see if he could help me, too."

"So you remember the consultation?"

"Of course."

"Because a matter came up in another case I need your help with. It has to do with a phone call that Mr. Flynn insists that he received while you were with him. Another lawyer is claiming that the call never took place. Mr. Flynn's time sheets indicate that he was meeting with you when the call came in. Do you remember a call interrupting your meeting? Or the receptionist talking to Mr. Flynn over the intercom while you were with him?"

Alice thought about it for a moment. "Yes, I do. There was a call. Mr. Flynn apologized when his receptionist interrupted the meeting. And . . . Of course! Now I remember. Mr. Flynn was upset when his secretary buzzed him. He told her that he didn't want our meeting interrupted. She was speaking on an intercom and I heard her. She said the man was calling about a murder and was very insistent. That's one of the reasons I remember the call. I don't hear people discussing a murder very often."

"That's the call I need to know about," Daniel said, trying to sound businesslike. "Do you happen to remember the caller's name? That would be very helpful."

"His last name was Arnold," she said with a laugh. "My father's first name is Arnold, so I remember it perfectly."

Daniel laughed, too, even more enthusiastically than Mrs. Cummings.

"Wow," he said, "that was easy. Thanks."

"I'm glad I could help. Mr. Flynn has been so good to Patrick and me. I don't know what we'd do without him. He's going to get us the money for Patrick's operations. I don't have health insurance and my husband walked out when Patrick was born." She looked down. "He couldn't take it. He couldn't even look at Patrick," she said softly. "If Mr. Flynn wasn't fighting this case for us . . ."

Daniel felt sick inside, both for her plight and for deceiving her. He couldn't imagine how she would feel when Flynn was arrested and she learned that her suit against Insufort was baseless. Daniel said goodbye, feeling like the worst kind of traitor. Partway down the block he looked back. Alice Cummings smiled and waved hopefully from her front door. Daniel couldn't bring himself to wave back.

46

Susan Webster looked up when Kate Ross walked into her office and closed the door behind her.

"Yes?" Susan said.

Kate sat down without being asked and laid the envelope she was carrying on Webster's desk.

"It's Kate, right?" Webster asked after a moment of silence, annoyed when Kate continued to sit and stare.

"That's right."

"Why are you here?" Susan demanded.

"Show-and-tell," Kate said, opening the envelope and handing Susan a picture of her and Aaron Flynn standing outside the Midway Café.

Susan flushed, then glared at Kate. "How dare you follow me."

"If you don't like it, why don't we both go up to J. B. Reed's office? You can complain that I'm harassing you and I'll tell J. B. about your clandestine meeting with Aaron Flynn."

Susan gave herself time to calm down by looking at the photograph again.

"Why are you showing me this?" she asked.

"I want you to know that I'm onto your arrangement with Flynn."

"Aaron and I don't have an arrangement."

Kate smiled. "Beer and fried chicken never struck me as your cuisine of choice. I always pictured you as more the Pinot Noir and coq au vin type."

"Cute," Susan answered sarcastically, "but I didn't pick the restaurant. Aaron wanted to meet where no one would see us. He chose the Midway Café. As you said, I don't usually do business over fried chicken and beer. Neither does anyone else at Reed, Briggs, so we knew we'd be alone when we discussed settling the Geller case."

"Why would Flynn discuss a settlement with you? Brock Newbauer is the lead attorney."

Susan laughed. "Brock is clueless in a case of this complexity. Flynn knows I'm running the show. And he didn't want Brock around when he tried to bribe me." Kate's eyebrows went up. "Aaron offered me a job at his firm at significantly more than I'm making if I convince Geller to settle."

"Which I assume you're trying to do."

"Of course, but not because I plan to leave Reed, Briggs. The Insufort case is a sure loser in court. We have to settle to save the company."

"Was Arthur Briggs murdered so you could control the Insufort litigation?"

"What!"

"You can stop the act, Susan. I know you're helping Flynn fix the Insufort and Fairweather cases."

"What are you talking about?"

"Before Kaidanov died, he told Daniel that his study is a hoax. Flynn's plan is going to fail and you're going down with him."

"You better think twice before you threaten me, Ross."

"I don't make threats," Kate said. "Either you go to the police and confess or I'll make sure that J. B. and the DA learn about your deal with Flynn."

Susan shot to her feet. "Listen, you bitch. If you say one word of this to anyone, I'll sue you for slander and see that you're fired. Joe Molinari can't keep a secret. Everyone knows that Ames is staying with you. Why don't you tell J. B. your ridiculous theory and see if he believes you? But don't forget to tell him you're fucking the man who killed his best friend."

Kate colored, but she held her temper.

"I'll give you until the end of the day to decide what to do. After that, you're on your own."

Kate walked out and Susan slammed her hand on the desk. Was Ross bluffing, or would she really go to J. B. Reed? Then she suddenly realized that Kate had said that Daniel Ames could testify that Sergey Kaidanov's study was a hoax. She sat down heavily. Before he died did Kaidanov give Ames hard evidence to back up his claim?

Susan tried to calm down so she could think more clearly. After a moment she dialed Aaron Flynn's office.

47

There was an urgent message from Amanda Jaffe for Daniel on the answering machine when Daniel returned to the house. He called her office immediately.

"We have a problem," Amanda told him as soon as they were connected. "Mike Greene wants to reopen your bail hearing."

"How can he do that? The judge already ruled I could stay out."

"Mike has a witness who can corroborate April Fairweather's testimony."

"Who?" Daniel asked, alarmed.

"Did you call Renee Gilchrist after you heard Arthur Briggs's message on your answering machine?"

Daniel's face fell. "Oh, shit."

"I take it that's a yes?" Amanda said sharply. Daniel could tell that she was upset and disappointed in him. "It would have been nice if you'd let me know that there was a land mine right in front of us."

"I knew they'd interviewed Renee once. I didn't figure they would talk to her again."

"Well, they did. Someone dropped a dime on you."

"What's that mean?"

"An anonymous caller told Zeke Forbus to ask Gilchrist about a call you made to her on the day Briggs was shot. She told Forbus that you said Briggs wanted to meet that evening at the cottage where he was killed to talk about the Insufort case."

Daniel felt sick. "Greene let me go at the cemetery. He saw my head wound. I thought he was convinced that I'm innocent."

"No. He just had some reservations about last night's shooting, and Forbus is still certain that you killed Arthur Briggs. He's the one who's pushing Mike. Now tell me what happened with Renee Gilchrist."

"I couldn't figure out why Briggs wanted to see me," Daniel said, "so I called to talk to him. Only he'd left. So I asked Renee if she knew about a new development in the Insufort case that involved me. When she asked why I wanted to know, I told her about Briggs's call."

"You know what you said to her is admissible as an exception to the hearsay rule because you're the defendant," Amanda said. "The judge can consider your statements as proof that you intended to meet with Briggs."

"Do you think that's enough to change Judge Opton's decision on bail?"

"Come on, Daniel, be smart about this. Bail could end up being the least of our problems."

• • •

When Kate walked into her house, Daniel was sitting on the couch in the dark. One look told her that something was wrong.

"What happened?" she asked.

Daniel told her about Amanda Jaffe's call.

"I don't think Renee's testimony will be enough to convince the judge to deny bail," Kate said. "They still can't prove that you killed Briggs. The best they can do is place you at the crime scene."

"Renee can also corroborate Fairweather's testimony about my argument with Briggs after he fired me."

"How did things go with Cummings?" Kate asked to change the subject.

"I can prove that Flynn got a call from Gene Arnold," Daniel answered without looking at her. "Alice Cummings was in Flynn's office when Arnold called. She even remembers Arnold's name."

"That's great!"

"Yeah."

Daniel should have been thrilled, but he sounded depressed.

"What's going on, Dan?" Kate asked with concern.

"When we bring down Flynn, we'll also be destroying his suit against Geller."

"So? The suit shouldn't have been brought in the first place."

"But Flynn convinced Alice Cummings that it should. She lives in this tiny apartment. She has nothing. Her son, Patrick, desperately needs medical attention, and he's not going to get it because of us."

Kate sat on the couch next to Daniel.

"Remember, I told you that my sister went through this with her baby? She's a good person and no one knows why her baby was born the way it was. And remember what you told me about life being unfair, about bad things happening to people for no reason? It's true. We have to accept that, even when it's hard, even when we need something to rail against. Insufort is not responsible for Patrick's birth defect, and the courts aren't always the right place to go for help."

"I still feel like I robbed that poor woman. I used her to get at Flynn. The end result is that I'll be killing her dreams and Patrick's future."

"You have to bring down Flynn. He's a murderer."

"That doesn't make me feel any better."

Kate put her arms around Daniel. "Don't get down on yourself, Daniel. You're a good man. I can see how hard this is for you, but we're so close. Don't fold when we're almost there."

Daniel sighed. "I'm okay. I just wish—"

Kate put a fingertip to his lips. "Don't," she said. Then she kissed him—once quickly, her lips lingering the second time. They looked at each other for a moment, then Daniel let himself go, losing himself in the contradictory softness of her breast and hard muscles of her back. After a moment they broke their kiss. Daniel closed his eyes and rested his cheek against her hair. It smelled sweet and felt so soft. Kate was a haven from all the bad things that had happened to him.

Daniel felt Kate move and he opened his eyes. She stood up and took his hand. "Come on," she said softly, pulling him slowly to his feet and toward the bedroom.

48

The call from Susan Webster had confirmed Aaron Flynn's worst fears. Before he died, Kaidanov had told Daniel Ames that his study was a fraud. But Flynn didn't know if Ames could prove the study was a hoax. Without proof, all Geller would have was the hearsay testimony of a man charged with murder and Flynn was certain he could still force a settlement.

"Alice Cummings is on line two," Aaron Flynn's receptionist announced.

Flynn debated not taking the call for a moment, but little Patrick was worth a bundle if everything worked out.

"Good afternoon, Alice," Flynn said in his heartiest voice. "How's my boy?"

"He had a rough night."

"I'm so sorry. What can I do for you?"

"I hope I'm not interrupting, but it's been bothering me since your associate left. He never said if you needed me to sign anything about the phone call. I can come down anytime."

"The phone call?"

"From Mr. Arnold." Flynn's eyes shut reflexively and a sick feeling spread through his gut. "Your associate said a lawyer is claiming that you never talked with him, but I remember it very clearly. Did you want me to sign an affidavit?"

"What was this associate's name, Alice?"

"You know, I can't remember. I'm not certain he even told me. But you introduced us. It was several weeks ago. I wheeled Patrick into the lobby in his stroller and you brought him over to meet us."

Flynn felt a flash of fear.

"Ah, yes," he said. "Well, I appreciate your call, but I won't need you to sign anything. The matter has been resolved. Thank you for calling, though. Give Patrick a kiss for me," Flynn said as he hung up.

"Everything is falling apart," Aaron Flynn said as soon as he was through the front door. A look of panic was etched on his face. "Ames found the client who was with me when Gene called."

"How did he do that?"

"How the fuck should I know? He just did and she remembers Gene's call. She just phoned me. She wanted to know if I needed her to sign an affidavit that could be used as evidence. Jesus Christ!"

"You've got to calm down so we can think this out."

"There's nothing to think about. If that homicide detective, Brewster, finds out I lied about Gene's call, we're dead."

"Who is the client?"

"Alice Cummings, the mother of one of the Insufort brats."

"Where does she live?"

"I don't know offhand."

"But it's in your file?"

"I can get it."

"We have to kill her."

"What?"

"We have to kill her and Ames and Ross."

"You're insane."

Flynn felt a hand snake through his hair. Then warm lips brushed his and a hand stroked his crotch. It took all of his willpower, but he broke away and headed for the couch. Flynn heard a cruel laugh behind him.

"You didn't mind when I took care of Briggs, Kaidanov, and Randall. Why are you so squeamish now?"

"Alice is . . . She's just this woman."

"No, Aaron, she's not just some woman. The bitch is a witness who can put both of us on death row, not to mention rob us of millions we have worked very hard to earn." A hand strayed to his zipper. "I'll kill them to protect you—to protect us—so we can be together."

A finger brushed the tip of his penis, emphasizing the point.

"You can't do this again," Flynn protested weakly.

"We can do anything."

Flynn was having trouble thinking. There were warm lips on his, fingers stroking his nipples, and a hand as soft as silk inside his fly.

"If it bothers you, I'll take care of Cummings while you take care of Ames and Ross."

Flynn's eyes went wide. "I can't. I've never killed anyone before."

"It's easy, baby," he heard as his body moved against its will to the rhythm set by the fingertips, tongue, and lips that were everywhere at once. "I'll tell you how to do it. Besides, we don't have a choice. The cops don't know about Cummings yet. If they did, she wouldn't have called you. That means that Ross and Ames haven't told them yet. We've got a window of opportunity here, but we've got to move, and I can't be in two places at once."

Flynn wanted to protest, but he was having trouble thinking. One part of his brain knew that someone who killed so easily could kill him, too, but the part of Flynn's brain that craved sex whispered that he was safe because only he could collect the millions from the Insufort settlement. And his partner had sworn they would be together after he'd banked his attorney's fee, living on a beach in an exotic country with servants and hot sex whenever he wanted it. That's what he'd been told and he wanted to believe—had to believe to rationalize the things that had been done and would be done for the millions they craved.

● ● ●

Juan Fulano smiled as he pulled down the binoculars. He'd gotten a very good look at the person Flynn was meeting before the front door closed. Martin would be pleased. Fulano took out his phone and made a long-distance call to Desert Grove, Arizona.

49

Kate's doorbell rang at two in the morning. After the third ring, she staggered out of bed in a T-shirt and sweatpants. Daniel pulled on a sweatshirt and followed her to the front door. Kate looked through the peephole and was surprised to see Aaron Flynn looking wild-eyed and agitated.

"It's two in the morning, Flynn. What's going on?" she asked.

"I'm desperate. We have to talk. I need help. I'm afraid."

Daniel and Kate looked at each other.

"Let him in," Daniel said. "This could be our break."

Kate opened the front door. Flynn had barely stepped inside when he turned and struck her viciously in the head with a gun butt, sending her into the wall. Daniel started forward as Kate slid to the floor, but Flynn extended a .22 pistol in his direction.

"Get inside," he ordered as he bolted the door.

Daniel hesitated.

"Do it," Flynn screamed, pointing the gun at Kate. His hand was shaking badly.

Kate was dazed. Blood trickled from a gash on her cheek. Daniel helped Kate to her feet and stepped backward into the living room.

"Why couldn't you stay out of this?" Flynn shouted. "Why did you have to go to Alice Cummings?"

Flynn was sweating and his eyes were wild. Daniel knew that he had to keep him talking.

"You framed me for murder," he said. "Now you're angry because I'm trying to clear my name?"

"You stupid bastard. You're going to die, your girlfriend is going to die, and Cummings is going to die, too, and it's your fault."

Daniel was stunned. "You don't have to kill Alice."

"You put her in this position."

Kate sat on the arm of the couch and put a hand to her head. Daniel took a step forward.

"Stop! I *will* kill you," Flynn said as if to reassure himself that he could do it.

Out of the corner of his eye, Daniel saw Kate pull herself together. She was taking in the situation, focusing on Flynn.

"I know you've got someone at Reed, Briggs who's helping you," Daniel said to Flynn. "Tell the cops who it is. We can help you cut a deal."

Kate stood up.

"Goddamn it, stop," Flynn shouted as he moved the gun between Daniel's body and Kate's. He'd been told to kill them quickly and get out, but he was having trouble pulling the trigger.

Daniel lunged. Flynn fired into his torso. Daniel grunted with pain as he hit Flynn with every ounce of his strength. Flynn staggered into the door and fired again, shocked that Daniel hadn't fallen. The second shot stunned Daniel, but he still had enough strength to drive his thumb into Flynn's eye. Flynn screamed. Daniel's knees gave way. Flynn lashed out, using the gun as a club, and knocked Daniel to the floor. As he fell Kate made a spearhead with her rigid fingers and struck Flynn in the larynx. His hands flew to his throat and the gun dropped to the floor.

Flynn had trouble seeing and breathing, but he lashed out with a wild punch that caught Kate in the temple, dazing her. Flynn grabbed Kate by the throat. She tried to break the hold, but he kneed her in the stomach and she sagged. A blow to Flynn's crotch went wide and glanced off his thigh. Kate couldn't breathe. Her sight dimmed and she lashed out ineffectively in a panic. Flynn smashed her head into the wall and her body grew limp. Then there was an explosion. Blood bathed the side of Flynn's head and the grip on her throat relaxed.

Kate staggered away from Flynn and gasped for air. Flynn fell to the ground. Daniel was on one knee holding Flynn's gun. Then he toppled over on his back and clutched his stomach, now saturated with blood.

Kate dropped beside him. "Oh, God! Daniel!"

A wave of nausea swept through him. Daniel's vision blurred, but he forced himself to speak.

"Nine-one-one," he croaked. "Save Alice Cummings."

"Don't talk," Kate said as she pulled up his shirt so she could see the bullet wounds. Daniel tried to give Kate Alice Cummings's address but he felt like he was lost in a patch of fog. He knew that Kate was talking to him because he could see her lips move, but he couldn't hear her words. Those lips were the last thing he saw before he slipped away.

50

Aaron Flynn's partner pulled on a ski mask and cut across a yard that backed on the ground-floor garden apartment where Alice Cummings lived. A door at the back of the house opened onto the postage-stamp-size patch of lawn, which was enclosed by a low wood fence. The screen door was unlocked and the lock would not be much of a challenge. The plan was to jimmy the lock and cut the bitch's throat. To kill or not to kill the kid, that was the question. If he was as fucked up as Flynn said, the brat was probably better off dead.

The door only took a few minutes to open. Flynn's partner pulled a hunting knife from a sheath and took a step into the apartment.

Alice Cummings sat up in bed. Her clock read 2:13. The house was quiet, but she was certain that a noise had awakened her. Maybe Patrick was having a dream and made the noise in his sleep, because he was quiet now.

Alice lay down and closed her eyes. It was always a blessing when Patrick slept. She'd put him down at ten and crashed immediately. Five hours was good.

Alice's eyes opened wide again. She was certain that she'd just heard something. She slipped out of bed and walked to the bedroom door, which she always kept open so she could hear Patrick, and peered into the front room. Nothing seemed out of place.

The only part of the apartment she couldn't see was the kitchen, which was at the back. She edged along the wall. As soon as she turned the corner Alice saw that the back door was open.

The moment Flynn's partner took a step into Alice Cummings's apartment, a sixth sense warned her of danger. She was half turned when a damp ether-soaked cloth pressed across her mouth and nose and a muscular arm circled her chest, pinning her arms to her side. She tried to kick free as she was hoisted off her feet. She knew she only had moments before she passed out. In desperation she raised her heel and jammed it down on her attacker's instep. He swore, but his grip did not weaken. As she was dragged back across the lawn she saw the stars swirling above her, twisting in faster circles.

Alice froze at the entrance to the kitchen. Was someone in her house? Was Patrick safe? She switched on a light as she rushed to his room. His door was open. She stopped at the railing to his crib. He was curled on his side, breathing fitfully but sound asleep.

Relieved, Alice checked the rest of the small apartment. When she returned to the kitchen a cold wind swept through the door. She shivered as she pushed it shut. Then she turned the lights off so she could see outside, pressing her nose to the kitchen window to see every inch of the yard and beyond. She saw nothing strange. But someone had definitely tried to get in. Why had they left? Who had they been?

51

Kate tried to keep her face neutral when the police guard showed her into Daniel's hospital room. There were bruises on her face and the gash on her cheek had required stitches. But Daniel's injuries had been far more severe.

"You look awful," she said.

"Gee thanks," he said, his voice subdued by painkillers. "You look pretty ugly yourself."

Kate smiled, relieved that he could joke. "That picked my spirits up." She sat down next to Daniel's bed. "Now I'm going to pick up yours. Amanda and I had a long talk with Mike Greene. I think we convinced him that Flynn framed you. Amanda is pretty certain your case will be dismissed by the time you're discharged. Also, Alice Cummings is okay. When the police got to her house she told them that someone tried to break in. Her back door was wide open. But nothing happened."

Suddenly Daniel grimaced. Kate took his hand. "Are you okay?"

"Yeah. My meds must be wearing off. But I'll be fine. The bullets went through my small bowel. I only had to have minor surgery. I should be out of here in a few days."

"Charging Flynn's gun was very brave. You saved my life."

Daniel smiled. "Turnabout is fair play. Besides, I wasn't worried. I remembered what you said."

Kate looked confused. "About what?"

"You know, about how being shot in real life is different from TV. Flynn's gun was a twenty-two. I knew it wouldn't pack the wallop of a larger-caliber gun, and I knew you knew all that judo stuff." Daniel shrugged. "I figured I'd get in a few good punches to soften him up and you'd finish him off and call the medics."

Kate looked horrified. "You idiot. That only works if you're shot in the body. You'd be dead if Flynn had shot you in the head."

Daniel's eyes widened in mock horror. "You never told me that," he said. Then he laughed.

Kate shook her head. "You really are hopeless. I'm going to have to stick around to baby-sit you."

Billie Brewster knocked on the door.

"Thought I'd drop by and see how you're doing," she said.

"What happened with Webster?" Kate asked. Then she turned back to Daniel. "Billie questioned her today."

"Either she's innocent or she's got ice water for blood," Billie said.

"Did you hit her with the photographs?"

"She's sticking with the story she told you. She denies having anything to do with fixing cases for Flynn and she's got an answer for everything."

Billie suddenly remembered the envelope she was carrying. "By the way, I got this in the mail. It's Bernier's photograph. Flynn is in it, but Webster isn't. I thought you might be able to tell me who the woman is."

Kate took out the photograph. Daniel leaned over to see it.

"Oh, shit," Kate said, and she suddenly knew why Gene Arnold had almost fainted when he saw Claude Bernier's photograph.

52

Anna Cordova escorted Kate Ross and Billie Brewster across the terrace to the poolside table where Martin Alvarez was waiting. Alvarez stood as Kate introduced the detective.

"Claude Bernier finally sent us a copy of the photograph that Gene Arnold bought in New York. Flynn is in it, and we've identified the woman he's with."

"Really. Who is she?"

"Renee Gilchrist, a secretary at Reed, Briggs," Kate said. "Flynn represented the plaintiffs in a number of lawsuits that my firm was defending. We think that Gilchrist was working with Flynn to fix those cases."

"What does she say about that?" Alvarez asked.

"We haven't been able to ask her," Billie answered. "She disappeared the same day that Flynn was killed."

"That would certainly indicate guilt, wouldn't it?" Alvarez said.

"It's definitely suspicious."

"Do you think this woman was involved in Gene's murder?"

"Yes, we do," Billie said. "That's why we're here. Kate has a theory about why Mr. Arnold was killed and she thinks you can help us find out if it's correct."

Alvarez spread his hands. "Anything I can do . . ."

Kate took Bernier's photograph out of the envelope she was holding and set it on the table. Alvarez showed no emotion as he studied the photograph.

"Is that Melissa Arnold, Gene's wife?" Kate asked. "The woman who was supposed to have been kidnapped and murdered seven years ago?"

Alvarez nodded slowly. His eyes never left the photograph.

"Here's what Billie and I think happened," Kate said. "When the FBI botched the arrest at the drop site, McCann got away with the ransom money, but Lester Dobbs was arrested. Dobbs cut a deal and named McCann, the only other person in the plot that he could identify. McCann was arrested quickly, but not before he hid the ransom money.

"I'm guessing that McCann refused to tell Melissa where the money was unless she got him out of jail. There was also the threat that he would cut a deal to save himself. That's when Melissa conceived the brilliant idea of faking her kidnapping.

"Looking back, Melissa had to have been involved. When she faked her own kidnapping, she only asked for seventy-five thousand dollars, instead of the million dollars she asked from you. Seventy-five grand was an amount that Gene Arnold could cover from his retirement account. Melissa would have known Arnold's financial situation."

"Of course," Billie interjected, "Melissa's kidnapping was only a smoke screen to cover up the real reason for her plan: the destruction of her court reporter notes, which would force the judge to order a new trial. After she murdered Lester Dobbs, the court had to let McCann out of jail and she was able to kill the only witness who could identify her and get away with the money. No one thought Flynn was involved, so he was home free. Even McCann might not have known. And no one was looking for Melissa, because everyone thought that she had suffered the same fate as your wife.

"Then Mr. Arnold saw Melissa and Flynn in Bernier's photograph and flew to Portland. He phoned Flynn from his hotel the day he landed. Flynn or Melissa killed him and burned the body in the lab."

Alvarez shook his head. "I can't believe it, but it must be true."

Kate studied him carefully. She was certain that her news had not come as a surprise.

"It's too bad we can't find Melissa," Brewster said. "Whoever burned down the lab was bitten by a rhesus monkey. The medical examiner has a swab with material she found on the monkey's teeth. If we had Melissa we could run a DNA test that would prove she was at the lab. We also have an impression of the monkey's teeth that we could match to any bite marks she has on her shoulder."

"Do you have any leads?" Alvarez asked.

"Actually, we do," Billie answered. "It's another reason we came to see you. Claude Bernier called me, yesterday. His conscience was bothering him. It seems that a Hispanic gentleman visited him the day after Kate told you about Mr. Bernier's photograph. He called himself Juan Fulano. I'm told, by a Hispanic friend, that Juan Fulano is the Spanish equivalent of 'John Smith.' Is he right, Mr. Alvarez?"

"Yes."

"Fulano wanted to purchase a copy of Bernier's photograph, but he paid Mr. Bernier to do something else. Can you guess what that was?"

"I have no idea," Alvarez answered coolly.

"Mr. Fulano asked Bernier to hold off sending us the photograph until he gave the okay. Paid extra for the favor. Then, the day after Melissa Arnold disappeared, Fulano gave the okay to send the photo to Portland. Interesting, no?"

"I'm afraid I don't follow you."

"Don't you, Mr. Alvarez?" Billie asked. "You know, I made some inquiries about you to police acquaintances in Mexico and Arizona. They say you're straight now—have been for a while. But they say you ran with a very rough crowd early on. The type of people who would think nothing of abduction or murder."

Alvarez did not act offended by the accusation. "Your information is correct. I was very wild in my youth. But those days are behind me."

Billie stared hard at Alvarez. He returned the stare without blinking.

"If I asked you to predict the future would you hazard a guess for me?" the homicide detective asked.

"I have no psychic powers, Detective."

"I give you my promise that your answer will stay with the three of us."

Alvarez considered Billie's request for a moment. "Ask your question."

"My department has limited funds. I'd rather spend them on crime fighting than on a wild-goose chase. What would you guess my chances are of finding Melissa Arnold alive?"

As Alvarez thought about the question he looked at the two women. They stared back impassively. Alvarez made a decision.

"Melissa is a very clever woman, as you have discovered. My guess would be that someone so clever would be able to disappear without a trace. Whether she is alive or dead is not for me to say, but I would guess that she will never be found."

Then Alvarez shrugged and his features softened. "But the police have all sorts of modern devices I know nothing about. Really, crime detection is not my area of expertise."

Billie stood and Kate rose with her. "Thank you for your time, Mr. Alvarez," the detective said. "Kate has told me how deeply you loved your wife. I'm sorry if we uncovered old wounds."

Kate picked up the photograph and replaced it in the envelope. Alvarez did not glance at it.

As soon as the women were out of sight, he entered his office and closed the door. Then he took a copy of

Claude Bernier's photograph from a wall safe concealed behind a small painting. He studied it one last time, then set it on fire. As Melissa Arnold's image burned, Alvarez turned toward the photograph of Patty Alvarez that stood in a prominent place on his desk. A tear appeared at the edge of Alvarez's good eye. He made no effort to wipe it away. He dropped the burning photograph in a wastepaper basket and watched it turn to ash.

"It's over, Patty," he whispered. "It's over."

53

"Come in, Joe," J. B. Reed said as his secretary showed Joe Molinari into his corner office. Reed was puzzled by Molinari's visit since he was not working on any of Reed's cases. To be honest, he only remembered Molinari's name because his secretary had told it to him when she buzzed him to say that one of the associates wanted to talk to him.

"What can I do for you?" Reed asked as Molinari sat down. He noticed that Molinari did not seem nervous or deferential the way most of the new associates were in his presence.

"Something is going on that you need to know about."

"Oh?"

"Just before he died, Mr. Briggs fired Daniel Ames." Reed's features clouded when Molinari mentioned his friend's murder and accused murderer. "That was wrong."

"I don't see how any of this is your business, Mr. Molinari," Reed snapped.

Molinari met Reed's fierce gaze and returned one of his own.

"It's my business," Joe said forcefully, "because Dan is a friend of mine and someone has to tell you what he's done for this firm and Geller Pharmaceuticals."

Daniel was engrossed in a thriller when J. B. Reed and Isaac Geller walked into his hospital room. Daniel paused in mid-sentence and stared, as surprised by their appearance as he would have been if Mark McGwire and President Bush had strolled into his room.

"How are you feeling?" J. B. Reed asked.

"Okay," Daniel answered tersely.

"I've come to apologize for agreeing to have you fired," Reed said.

Daniel waited for Reed to go on. The senior partner saw how tense Daniel looked and he smiled.

"I don't blame you for being very angry with our firm, but we didn't have the whole picture until Joe Molinari explained everything to me."

"Joe?"

Reed nodded. "You have some very loyal friends at Reed, Briggs. I've also spoken to Kate Ross. Molinari came to my office two days ago and read me the riot act. Said the firm owed you an apology. When he finished explaining what you'd risked for our client, I called Isaac immediately."

"I don't believe I'm exaggerating when I say that your actions may have saved my company, Mr.

Ames," Geller told him. "If Flynn's scheme had worked we would have had to take Insufort off the market and I can't begin to imagine how much the company would have lost paying off legal judgments."

"I know there is no way to repay you for what you've gone through," Reed said. "The disgrace of being fired, the time you spent in jail, not to mention being shot . . . It's terrible, and I sincerely regret any part Reed, Briggs had in your ordeal, but Mr. Geller and I want to try to make it up to you. I want you back at the firm and we're prepared to give you a hefty raise."

"And Geller Pharmaceuticals wants to reward you with a substantial bonus," Isaac Geller added.

Daniel was stunned and did not answer right away.

Reed smiled broadly, fully expecting Daniel to leap at his peace offering. After all, what young lawyer in his right mind would reject a chance to work at Reed, Briggs?

"I know this must come as a shock, so there's no reason to rush your decision," Reed said. "Concentrate on getting well and call me at your convenience."

"I am overwhelmed by your generosity," Daniel said, thanking both men, "but I don't need any time to think. Actually, I've had plenty of time to think while I was in jail and while I've been recuperating. I appreciate the offer to come back to Reed, Briggs, but I don't really fit in at the firm. I respect the work you do, but I would be more comfortable working at a smaller firm, one that represents the type of person I grew up with, people who don't have anyone else to look out for them."

"Surely you must see how much good a company like Geller can do," Reed said, amazed at Daniel's rejection of his generous offer.

"I do, and I know how sleazy and dishonest a lawyer like Flynn can be, but you'll always be able to find top-notch lawyers to represent your clients, Mr. Reed. You pay for the best and you get the best." Daniel smiled. "I don't know where I fit in, but I'd like to try and level the playing field a little."

"Well, if that's what you want, you must do what you think is best. But the offer is open if you change your mind."

"Thank you. I appreciate that."

Reed started to leave.

"You know, there is one thing you two can do for me, if you're still feeling generous."

"What's that?" Isaac Geller asked.

54

Daniel woke up slowly to the sound of the surf. When he opened his eyes he could see sunlight through the thin curtains that covered the picture window in the bedroom of the beach house. He stretched and smiled. The first thing Amanda had said when Judge Opton dismissed all the charges against him was, "I bet you've never had a job interview like this before." Then she offered Daniel the use of her beach house so he could get away from Portland and the press. His interview with the rest of the partners at Jaffe, Katz, Lehane and Brindisi was set for next Wednesday.

Daniel hoped that he would get the job with Amanda's firm, but he had no regrets about turning down J. B. Reed. Amanda Jaffe had let him see first-hand that there was another, better, way to use his law degree. Still, Daniel had not walked away from his meeting with J. B. Reed and Isaac Geller empty-handed. Alice Cummings would not have to worry about Patrick's medical expenses anymore. Daniel had sold Isaac Geller on the public relations benefits that Geller Pharmaceuticals would reap by agreeing to help Alice's son. Daniel didn't want any credit for the good deed. Knowing that Patrick would have a chance at a normal life was payment enough.

Daniel rolled onto his side and noticed that Kate was not in bed. In the past few days he had learned that she was an early riser. Daniel smiled at the thought of her.

Amanda's house stood on a bluff overlooking the Pacific, which was calm today. Last night, Kate and Daniel had sipped hot buttered rum and let the heat from the bedroom fireplace warm them while they watched a brutal storm assault the beach. This morning, the sand was littered with driftwood.

Daniel washed up and found Kate on the phone in the kitchen. She smiled when he walked in. He poured a glass of orange juice and sat down at the kitchen table while Kate finished her call.

"That was Billie," she said as soon as she hung up. "She found out some more information about Gilchrist. Her name was originally Melissa Haynes. Her father was a colonel in the army. He was away a lot and she grew up wild. Billie says she had a string of juvenile arrests, some involving violence, but her father used his influence to get her out of most of her scrapes.

"When she turned eighteen Melissa left home and moved to California. She married an actor wannabe, but the marriage lasted less than a year. She went to secretarial school, then learned how to be a court reporter. Gene Arnold met her during a deposition in L.A."

"Is Billie certain that Renee was Flynn's partner?"

"She'll probably never be able to prove it, but everything makes sense if Renee was the mole at Reed, Briggs. She was in a perfect position to slip the Kaidanov letter into the discovery and send Amanda the videotape. If Kaidanov called Briggs at his office to arrange the meeting at the cottage, Renee would have answered the phone and could have eavesdropped on their conversation. But there's something else that convinces me that Renee is guilty.

"We were never able to figure out why Arthur Briggs wanted April Fairweather to meet him at the cottage on the night he was killed."

"Right. It made no sense, since her case and the Insufort case were totally unrelated."

"I'm certain that Briggs never wanted Fairweather at the cottage. Renee was in the waiting area when Fairweather saw you blow up at Briggs. I bet she heard Briggs leave the message on your answering machine asking you to meet him at the cottage. I think Renee told Fairweather to go to the cottage so she would see you leaving after Briggs was murdered. With you as the main suspect, no one would look at anyone else. But better still, Renee knew that your lawyer would use the videotape to thoroughly discredit Fairweather when she was under oath, assuring another hefty attorney fee for Flynn that she would share."

"Renee probably made the anonymous call that tipped off Zeke Forbus about my call to her."

"That's my guess. But I don't think we'll ever know for certain."

Daniel stood up and took Kate in his arms. "I don't want to talk about the case anymore. We're out here to forget about it."

"If you don't want to talk about the case, what do you want to do?" Kate asked mischievously.

"I'd like to kiss you, but I'm afraid you'll use your self-defense moves on me."

"I might if there was a bed nearby."

"I guess ugly women need judo to get a handsome guy like me in the sack."

The next thing Daniel knew, Kate was behind him and had him in a hammerlock. The idea of resisting never entered his mind.

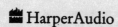